THE STRENGTH OF BONE

The Strength of Bone

Lucie Wilk

A JOHN METCALF BOOK

BIBLIOASIS
WINDSOR, ONTARIO

FIRST EDITION

Library and Archives Canada Cataloguing in Publication

Wilk, Lucie, 1972-
The strength of bone / Lucie Wilk.

Issued also in electronic format.
ISBN 978-1-927428-39-9

I. Title.

PS8645.I434S77 2013 C813'.6 C2013-902003-9

Edited by John Metcalf
Typeset by Chris Andrechek
Cover Designed by Kate Hargreaves
Cover Photograph by Ben Tullis

Canada Council for the Arts
Conseil des Arts du Canada

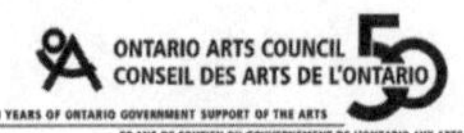

Canadian Heritage
Patrimoine canadien

Biblioasis acknowledges the ongoing financial support of the Government of Canada through the Canada Council for the Arts, Canadian Heritage, the Canada Book Fund; and the Government of Ontario through the Ontario Arts Council.

PRINTED AND BOUND IN CANADA

For

Eric,
Amber &
Aidan

The way of love is not
a subtle argument.
The door there is devastation.
Birds make great sky-circles
of their freedom.
How do they learn it?
They fall, and falling,
they're given wings.

Rumi

The sky was milky blue. It seemed wet and somehow stained. Beneath it the ground was dry and untended. Nothing moved. It was winter.

Inside, a young girl lay on a bed in the dark in a room that was filled with the sound of her breath. In and out. In and out. The air was saturated with her breath just as her lungs were sopped in fluid, semi-submerged. Her chest lifted and fell. In. Out.

The visitors who came tried not to share the air. They breathed short and shallow. They tried to be as unaware of their own breath as they were before they entered the room. Because noticing it somehow created lack and just for a moment, they knew suffocation. That is why after a short while they left.

The girl once held her breath. Maybe a year ago she did this. Just an inch under the bath water, her small body still, muscles relaxed, face serene. After what became too long, her mother reached under the water, grabbed her under her arms and pulled her up and when the girl emerged into the air she was triumphant with her discovery. That she could control these sorts of things. She could stop breath like this. On a whim.

Her right arm was folded across her stomach and exaggerated the lift of her chest—a barometer of breath. Her legs were askew, scissor-like. Her skin was sallow but warm. The angle where her neck met her jaw fluttered twice with each pause of her heart. Her lips were dry. Her eyes were closed. Because she was sleeping.

Night or day, the room was kept dark. Because letting the sun in might have been too hopeful. Because hope at this stage was irresponsible.

Around her and inside the room were objects still animated by her presence. A doll, a hairbrush with six brown hairs entwined, a box of colouring pencils of different lengths, two parents, one hunched forward, the other leaning back. Their meaning existed because she did, because the girl who held them or hugged them or regarded them with a precise, thoughtful intention still lay sleeping nearby.

She slept because she was tired. She was tired because she was ill. She was ill because—and this was where the chain broke. There was no because. There was no reasonable answer. There was no reason.

May 12, 1995

He waited in Lilongwe airport for an hour. He sat on a chair in the near empty single room, contemplated buying something from the little stand where food was on offer. This consisted mainly of fresh fruit—bananas and tangerines. Hard-boiled eggs. Clawed chicken feet, deep-fried and glistening with nails still intact. Sleep deprivation and strange airplane air clogged his thoughts. He struggled to sort it all out. He was here. He wouldn't be there (Toronto) for months, maybe years. Who knew? And this—that he didn't know, exactly, what his plan was. There were two more steps on the bulleted list folded up in his dossier next to his passport (- find apartment, - go to hospital) and then the plan that had seemed so detailed, so well-laid from his apartment in Toronto was complete. The details, he now understood, were in the preparations—what to bring, what to put into storage, when to shut off his phone line, his utilities, immunizations, flight times. But what came after was unplanned, undetermined, a white space beneath the printed list. Sitting in that airport he was hard-pressed to believe this was what he really wanted. There was a rising sense that what propelled him onto the plane and out of Toronto was something as unreal as what faced him here. It could follow him.

He sat there looking at the food and at the vendor who ignored him pointedly for countless minutes. Then he somehow knew (did someone tell him, was there an announcement) that he needed to get up and join the short queue for another plane, a twin-prop that crouched on the runway while passengers climbed into the cavern of it. The plane doors were pulled closed and they were taxiing along the red earth.

Red. Burnt, ferrous red of old blood. This was the colour of the place. Along with the yellow of tall grasses. Yellow-brown thatch of village roofs from the air. And as they approached Blantyre there were corrugated metal roofs that sent sunlight upwards in sharp sudden flashes.

They touched down in Blantyre, his second and final stop in Malawi. The wings fought the wind and the plane gradually slowed, its wheels bumping tentatively then more certainly along the ground. Red earth tumbled up and blew past his window. It obscured his view. When he climbed out of the plane the ground was still agitated, dust swirling up as he clambered down. He rubbed his eyes. It settled on his travel-weary clothes and skin as a fine grit.

In the Blantyre airport he found a man who would drive him (possibly a taxi driver, probably not), fumbled for the address somewhere in his pocket, found his assigned apartment on a hillside, met the sullen man who would be guarding against intruders, found his bedroom and his bed with a dirty tangle of netting above it, and fell asleep.

When he wakes it is dark and the flickering bulb dangling from the ceiling casts a sepia glow on his quarters, shows him that they are as he recalled in his dreams. His watch indicates that it is 5 AM, local time. He washes in a bathroom still damp with someone else's (the last doctor's?) shower. A lone gecko up on a wall near the ceiling doesn't budge its splayed round toes. He dresses and sits at the table in the kitchen in the rising grey light. When it matches then exceeds the lamplight, he goes outside where he finds the sullen guard having a smoke. He asks him where the hospital is and the man points down the road and up the hill.

In his room his backpack still leans against the wall where he dropped it uncounted hours ago. He opens it and finds his stethoscope coiled between T-shirts. He pulls it out and feels more certain. It reminds him of something. A remote urge. A quiet desire. The sense of something being possible. It reminds him of hope.

Part I

Out beyond ideas of wrongdoing and rightdoing

Chapter 1

Dust returns to the land in the mornings. It settles in a thick layer and smothers the early light so that the colour is soft, a blush on the horizon. The effect is calming, far different from the experience of living with the dust itself. When he first arrived in Malawi, Henry would swing at the dust, cough it up, rub it out of his eyes, find pale grains in his tears. The dust, combined with the heat and the diesel exhaust, made the air feel thick and stifling. He choked on every breath.

He walks across the land with less resistance now, with less fight in him. He is willing to accept certain things about the place, things he cannot change, like the dust, or the heat, or the geckos that scurry across the walls. But there are things he is still unwilling to accept, and he senses that the land, this place, feels the same way about him. There are things that it just won't compromise on. And so, to him, it remains round and hard like a bone, blanched and chafed from centuries of sun and drifting dust. He sees the convexity of the surface on which he walks, how it arches and bends away from him. Always, no matter where he is, he can see the curve to the horizon—out there where the baobab trees show their root-like branches to the amber sky.

He climbs the hill, keeps a steady pace. Henry can see the hospital now. At home in Toronto the hospitals are neat white boxes, packaged like takeout containers, compartmentalized and sterile. The stink of illness is swept clean and the suffering is tucked into bed with the curtains drawn. Here in Blantyre, bodies are wet with the sweat of prolonged struggle and the air is thick with the sour odour of a losing battle. For the first few weeks it seemed to Henry that most people went there to die.

Henry reaches the hospital and pulls open the heavy door with effort. He feels himself move like an old man, as if he has already lived a full lifetime. But he is only thirty-five, and just two months older than he was when he arrived here, in the spring of 1995, brimming with piss and vinegar and idealism—the particular blend unique to a doctor who has been Canadian-trained, and who has travelled through life with pale skin, and red hair, and blue eyes. He has never been more aware of these unchangeable aspects of himself since arriving here, where he is reminded of the immense significance of his appearance constantly, wherever he goes, to whomever he speaks. The gaze is just as prolonged and considered no matter who it is considering him.

He steps into the dim foyer and moves down one of the hallways. Sunlight from open windows struggles through the interior shadows, brightening no more than a few feet. He walks past the windows and sucks in the outdoor air —dusty, but odourless. Blankets hang from clotheslines outside, in the hospital courtyard. Blankets, sheets, and hundreds of gloves—ghostly wisps of hands waving from the line. Even sterile gloves are recycled.

Henry enters an office off the main medical ward and slips on his lab coat. He nods to the nurse seated at the desk.

Sister Iris Mwachilale regards him briefly with hooded eyes, and then returns to her charting. Henry takes his stethoscope out of the pocket of his lab coat and hangs it around his neck. He pauses as Sister Iris flips another page, head down. It is too early in the morning to contend with one of her moods, but he proceeds anyway.

"Any action on the wards last night?"

Iris lifts her eyes and looks at his nose. "One of the TB patients," she says, "respiratory failure."

"No bed in the ICU?"

Iris shrugs.

"You should have called me," he says, "I could have tried. To intubate, or resuscitate."

Iris lifts her head, meeting him more squarely. Her eyes tighten a little. Her jaw juts sideways. More effort has been put into this last non-verbal exchange. The tumult of possible meaning kaleidoscopes in front of him. *It would have been futile.* Or, perhaps, *it is invasive, a cruel intervention from the Western tradition.* Or even, *he's more my brother than yours.* And finally: *it is not your right.*

But it is! Henry feels like yelling, although she has said nothing to him at all. *I have knowledge. I have skill. I have the desire.* To do what? He wonders this, stuck for a moment in the quagmire of wants, needs and frustrations that slop about messily in his mind.

Instead, he mutters, "I'll start on rounds." And exits the room, leaving Sister Iris to flip another page and watch his departure in the same viscous silence.

Henry enters the general medical ward, feels its damp breath on his skin and wonders why it is always so dark in this place. Despite the bulbs hanging from the ceiling, the long wall of open windows, why is the light so meagre? Beds are lined up, a foot or two apart, in row upon row. There are bundles of blanket and cloth under and between the beds and angular limbs jut out of them—another tier of patients waiting for care. Henry sees Dr. Kumwembe a few rows down, clipboard in hand, interviewing a patient, frowning and looking studious as usual.

Henry moves to one of the beds in the front row. A new patient lies on it with his arm draped across his forehead. Jutting up from the bed, each rib is well-defined and evenly spaced, like struts in a house. Henry rests his hand on his shoulder. "Sir?" he asks and then waits. The patient's mouth spreads into a wide smile. Despite his illness, he savours the rare pleasure of a white doctor calling him sir.

Henry picks up the clipboard hanging off a hook at the end of the bed. The patient's vital signs are scrawled across the top of the page: temp: 39.5. A fever. Ubiquitous here. Blood pressure: 75 over 40. In his boots. Heart rate: 120. Racing to keep up. All in all, likely septic. Probably malaria but there are so many other possibilities. Henry glances at the name on the chart: Juma. And his age: based on the date of birth, he is just 16. A child. Just old enough to have outgrown the paediatric ward. Henry now notices the soft growth of fuzz on Juma's chin.

Henry takes Juma's hand and searches for the radial artery that is strung along the ropes of tendons in his wrist. Juma's pulse is bounding, his arteries wide open, flooding his extremities, making them hot and dry. Septic. Henry reaches for the IV bag to check its contents, expecting one to be there like there always is at home, but there is nothing, not even a pole. He looks around the ward for the recognizable white sail of a nurse's hat drifting somewhere in the sea of bodies but sees only a few scattered visitors, crouching over a bed or squatting beside a prostrate figure on the floor, and Dr. Kumwembe, even farther away now, many rows ahead.

Henry returns his attention to Juma who has reached out to touch his lab coat, fingering it like rare silk. Not knowing how much English the boy understands, Henry explains, "I need to find an IV bag. Some fluids for you. So your heart doesn't have to work so hard."

Juma places his hand over the left side of his chest and Henry sees the vigorous efforts of his heart transmitting through his hand. "My heart works hard all my life." Juma says. "Strong."

Henry smiles. "Yes." He turns and sees Sister Iris a few feet away with a pushcart of medications and supplies. Watching them with an empty face.

"Is there an IV pole around? I need a bag of normal saline." Iris turns and walks away from them and Henry can only hope that she has gone to collect the supplies.

Iris returns within a few minutes and passes the requested plastic bag of intravenous fluid to Henry, pushes the IV pole over to Juma's side. Henry accepts the bag, "Thank you, Sister." As he crouches over Juma's arm and pushes a large-bore IV needle into the largest vein he can find, he feels her behind him, moored to the concrete floor. "Shouldn't you be heading home now?" He asks this as the needle reaches a vein and Juma's blood flashes back, dark purple-red in the tube.

"Sister Josephine is sick today," she replies.

Henry fixes the IV tubing onto Juma's arm with some tape. He stands up and adjusts the drip of the IV so it flows in quickly. Snaps off his gloves. Iris has been working for over 12 hours now; she had just been on night shift, overseeing the ward. Satisfied with the drip, Henry turns to Iris. Her hat is still in place; Henry has never seen her without it. But wiry strands of hair have sprung loose from under it, released from their knot.

"Maybe you should head home," he says, "get some sleep."

Iris shakes her head, tightens her lips and squeezes the pushcart handles, stares at Juma as if expecting him to argue alongside Henry. But Juma is watching his arm where the doctor has thrust the plastic tube, where he can feel the cool fluid enter his body. He looks at it as though he knows that this is where the cure will begin to take effect.

Henry sighs. "We'll need blood cultures and a malaria smear on this one," he says and then steps a few feet past Juma to crouch down to his next patient: a tangle of blanket and limbs on the floor. Iris follows, nudges the pushcart over and quickly smoothes her hair back into place under her hat.

*

Henry observes the top of Dr. Kumwembe's head with its compact spirals of hair as he bends over his plate and eats quickly, his fingers wet with food. The man had apologized once, many meals ago, for leaving his fork at the side of the plate. "When I'm at home, I do what comes most naturally," he'd said with a shrug.

Henry lifts a forkful of rice to his mouth, chews it slowly, swallows it down. Kumwembe wipes his hands and face with a napkin, rolls his tongue over his teeth. His eyes settle on Henry's respiratory mask sitting on the table beside his plate. It is becoming discoloured and worn.

"How many of those did you bring?" Kumwembe inclines his head toward the mask.

"A few."

He had packed a box full of the masks. Upon first entering the TB ward, Henry felt vertiginous with the thought of a room full of millions of TB particles, colliding in the air, spinning toward him in an invisible, chaotic cloud. He moves his hand over to the mask and fingers the green elastic bands. Kumwembe watches him with his moist brown eyes. It is futile, wearing the mask in the TB wards. Unless he is willing to wear the mask all day long and everywhere, he will inevitably be exposed, it is only a matter of time. Despite this, he knows he will go back to his apartment tonight, pull out a fresh mask from the box and bring it to work tomorrow.

"We isolate people. At home." As soon as Henry says this, he knows how it sounds. Of course Kumwembe knows. Kumwembe trained in England, attended medical school in Cambridge on scholarship, then completed residency in Internal Medicine in London. Kumwembe knows about respiratory isolation. He knows about the masks, gowns, goggles and gloves: the uniform for the Western hospital. Kumwembe continues to look at Henry, nodding slowly.

"Yes," is all he says.

*

Henry can see that Iris has spotted him and now her low and sturdy figure wades through the beds and bodies, over to where he stands fiddling with his lab coat, mustering up the energy to begin his rounds.

"Juma."

"Yes? Yes, Sister Iris?"

"Juma is still sick."

Henry studies Iris's face, as implacable as ever. She would be less plain, he thinks, if she did not frown quite so much. The tightness of her mouth further thins her lips. Her eyes, already tucked deep beneath her brow, darken and disappear with these looks she carries around with her and inflicts on them all, doctors and patients alike. But he trusts her. Her mood may be permanently sour but her intelligence shines through her observations and her pointed, perfunctory statements.

And now she is telling him that Juma has not improved. But the malaria smear had been positive. He had seen it himself, the ring-like organisms squatting in Juma's red blood cells, two or three to a cell. The malaria here is not drug-resistant; he should be improving. By now, his symptoms should be resolved. He goes to Juma's bedside and picks up his chart. The fevers are still there, the messy little x's scattered on the graph above the line indicating 38 degrees. He looks down at Juma who lies with his eyes closed. He sucks in and pushes the air through widened nostrils—long, languorous breaths.

"Juma."

Juma opens his eyes to Henry, widens his mouth in his usual broad grin.

"How are you feeling?"

"Better." He shrugs his narrow shoulders. "But not so good." He moves his arm—bones wrapped in papery brown skin. "Here." He points a long finger to his abdomen.

"He still vomits," offers Iris from the side.

Henry palpates Juma's abdomen. He feels the folds of bowel shift under his fingers. He taps over Juma's belly, one finger over another: tap, tap, tap, testing it like a drum. Hollow, except over his liver, which is as expected. Henry moves the blanket around, exposing first one long meatless leg, then the other. His puppy feet, still too large, are stuck awkwardly to the ends of his legs. A few dark, male hairs sprout from the skin of his lower legs and across the tops of Juma's feet, matching those above his lip and over his chin: evidence of his adolescence making way for adulthood. Henry places his hands across the tops of Juma's feet to feel his pulses and then sees the rash. Just a few bumps on the sides of the feet—small, barely there. Round swellings coalescing together with their dimpled centres. *Molluscum contagiosum.* Suggestive of an immuno-compromised host. In these parts, synonymous with HIV.

Christ.

Henry moves his gaze to a point above and beyond Juma's beatific face. Over to the back of the ward, with its green walls and open windows. To the red earth fields beyond it. To the baobab trees beyond those. To the horizon which bends away from him, pulling him with it, taking him away from this place.

He looks at Juma, there on the bed, gazing at him, confidence coming through in the smoothness of his face. So damn young. Although he is not surprised to discover another HIV diagnosis in these beds, he had hoped for Juma. There's where he went wrong.

Henry pats him on the shoulder. "We'll get this sorted out." He feels the chafing scrutiny of Iris to his right as he scribbles orders on the chart: stool for culture, HIV serology. He places the chart back on the hook at the end of Juma's bed and moves away, to someplace else.

*

Ellison claps a hand on Henry's shoulder: firm and warm. Together, they walk down the corridors, traverse the foyer and push out and through the heavy doors. Were there patients lining the corridors they walked? Women wrapped in blankets, boys clinging to IV poles, mothers nursing babies? For the first time, Henry is not sure. He did not look.

Outside, the world is darkening and the streets are emptying. Vendors are packing up, people are receding from the city like a tide. After the frenzied bustle of the hospital, this progressive quiet leaves Henry with a sense of dread. The slow emptying of the future.

But Ellison is too solid and animated, even in silence, for Henry to feel this way for long. They walk to a favourite watering hole of Ellison's. A bar with a single counter and a collection of mostly Carlsberg bottles in the fridge behind it. The place is lit with a single bulb and filled with a few tables and chairs. There are drunks on the inside and hookers on the outside and once they go in and encounter the smell of the place—the yeasty warm smell of beer and people drinking it—Henry feels oddly buoyant. He clasps the cold and sweaty bottle passed to him at the bar and doesn't bother pouring it into a glass, just holds it to his lips and takes a long pull. When he places it down it is three quarters empty. Ellison laughs and claps him once again on the back and says how well he'd fit in in Oz. He is on to his next bottle before they take their seats at a small, round, plastic table that wobbles. Henry folds up his paper napkin and places it under one of the legs. He leans both elbows on the table and pulls his hands through his hair, massages his neck. Ellison regards him with a knowing smile and leans back.

"Looks like this is overdue."

"Yep."

Behind Ellison a television is mounted on a shelf bracketed precariously to the wall behind the bar. Metal girders wrap around the top and bottom of the TV, holding it in place and posing a challenge to any who might consider taking it. The screen bulges heavily from the frame and loud, large-pixel colour images flash across it. The man on the screen is familiar. The US president. He is standing on a patch of green lawn saying something to a group of journalists. Then he stops talking and takes a swing with his nine iron. Everyone but the camera follows the ball down the green. There is a smattering of applause. The President leans on his nine iron and looks back at the journalists with an aw-shucks sort of grin then continues his talk on more serious matters.

A red ribbon of newsfeed scrolls across the bottom of the screen. It alerts in white text of recent troubling events. Iraq has invaded Kuwait. President Bush, that man on the green, plans to send troops. Now the television blasts images of war-torn deserts, of cities devastated by floods and quakes in sharp, sudden bursts. They move and change and Henry who sips beer here in this bar in Blantyre watches. The images, or what they reflect, are too close. The scenes flash before him as if they are projections from his own memory, as if he has just been there, as if this is where he will always be.

He looks back down at his second empty bottle and feels his thirst acutely, as though just outside this bar is the endless blowing sand of a desert. The drops running down the outside of the bottle and pooling on the table tempt him further. He rises and goes to the bar for another.

When he returns, Ellison is eyeing a woman's round backside, a woman dressed in a very short and tight skirt. She stands beside their table and chats with another woman similarly dressed. Her buttocks are amazingly round and full and when Henry takes his seat he is so close to her body he could easily reach over and caress one soft cheek or slip a hand beneath her skirt. He is stunned by the pull, the need to touch a woman. He catches himself trying to smell her and when he comes up from another long swallow of his beer he sees Ellison leering at him.

"Hot."

Henry nods.

"The sex'll blow your mind but you have to be careful."

"Clearly."

"So you wanna say hello?"

"No thanks."

"It'll do you good."

"I'm already good."

"You don't look it."

At this, both men look away. Finally, Ellison speaks again. "So you going to talk about it?"

"What."

"Whatever it is. Whatever drove you here. Whatever's driving you now."

Henry pauses. Taps his finger on the bottle. "I just want to help."

"Bullshit."

Henry feels something strange rising in him. Something like relief.

"If you don't want to be honest with me, at least be honest with yourself." Ellison pauses and gives him some kind of look. Henry can tell, from that look, that Ellison has never lost what he's lost. Maybe because he never got attached in the first place. It all comes so easy to him. "Whatever it is, you're here now. You need to learn some ground rules. Some rules of survival."

Henry raises his eyebrows.

Ellison ticks off fingers. "One. Don't be a perfectionist. It might have gotten you your medical degree but it's no good here. Two. Don't count. Don't count successes and don't count failures. Three. Don't think too much. Your instincts are better than your mind. Four. Don't compare. Here to there, I mean." Ellison inclines his head toward the television, presumably to the first-world country from which the news is being broadcast. "Five. Don't work too hard. A corollary to that is *do* drink too hard, occasionally." He lifts his beer and tips it toward Henry. "And indulge a little. Once in a while. And always use a condom."

He grins. Henry notices, for the first time, the large gap between his front teeth. A thick space that Ellison could probably whistle through. He is probably a good whistler. Probably whistles in the shower. Henry feels his thoughts slipping slowly over to that pleasantly vague place populated with non sequiturs and hyperbole. He watches the television again and when the woman with the gorgeous rear end positions it firmly on his lap he feels himself respond, he feels his body respond, while his mind slips steadily away, over to a place like those scenes still flickering on the television: remote, irrelevant.

*

Shouts and excited chatter have replaced the usual oppressive quiet in the ward, and a small crowd gathers in one corner, most of them standing with their hands in their pockets: the casual posture of curious sidewalk loiterers. Sister Iris's white hat floats among them, dipping down out of sight for a moment, and then rising up, shifting over, tossed in this storm that has blown into the ward. *Chakudya choyikidwa chiphe. Kapena ululu. Ayi!* The chatter is thick around them when Dr. Kumwembe and Henry push their way into the clot of onlookers. Iris glances up at them as she tries to wrap a blood pressure cuff around the arm of a man who thrashes in a gurney. She says nothing as Henry grabs hold of one arm so she can place the cuff. Kumwembe shoos away the group of onlookers and then joins Henry and Iris at the gurney. The man is slick with sweat and Henry has trouble holding him firmly for a blood pressure reading. Henry takes the man's pulse as he holds him down: 140 beats per minute. His blood pressure is likewise elevated. Iris mutters the reading, then rips off the cuff and looks at Kumwembe who is rummaging through the medication cart.

Kumwembe hands Henry an intravenous needle and he removes the cap with his teeth, holding the man's arm with one hand and the needle with the other. He searches for a site—not too difficult—the man's veins bulge with effort. Henry pierces the skin with the needle and the blood flashes back. He slides the IV tubing into place and steps aside, gives Iris some room to fix it into place with tape. Kumwembe moves in with an ampule of medication drawn up in a syringe. He holds the man's arm down against the gurney, pushes the needle into his IV line, and then plunges the liquid through. Within seconds, the man begins to breathe more easily. He closes his eyes.

Kumwembe indicates to Iris where in the ward she should place the man. There are no beds left; he will have a spot on the floor. She starts to wheel the gurney away. The crowd of onlookers has thinned, and they stare at the man, exchange opinions in Chichewa. Henry walks over to Kumwembe and they both watch the man's chest rise and fall with large, hungry breaths.

Kumwembe speaks before Henry can ask.

"OP poisoning."

"OP?"

"Organophosphate. A pesticide used on local crops. A popular way to do people in here. They slip it into a bottle of soda. Odourless and tasteless. We get a few of these a year. Even if they survive, the neurotoxicity can be devastating." He looks over to the floor where the man has been transferred. He lies still, taking deep breaths, looking at the ceiling. Thinking, perhaps, of the perpetrator. Kumwembe continues. "That one will do fine. He was lucky." He gathers up the debris: empty syringe, needle caps, vial of medication. "We keep some atropine on hand for this sort of thing." He walks over to the nearest bin, tosses in the rubbish, and rejoins Henry.

The two of them stand at the front of the ward, their hands on their hips, surveying the room. Dim quiet has returned to the place. Henry can feel how taut he is becoming, strung like a bow, still unprepared for all this. He pulls himself tighter, day by day. Eventually, there will be no more give and then, with the slightest pluck, he will snap and recoil, frayed and twisted ends will be all that is left of him.

Kumwembe does not look at him when he speaks.

"There is a lot of fighting here. That is all we know. If we don't fight disease or poverty or drought, we fight each other."

"I'm not much of a fighter." Henry looks out at the ward. "That's why I'm a doctor."

Kumwembe turns to Henry, his eyes the same calm brown-black liquid. "If you are not able to fight, I'm sorry to say you will suffer, Dr. Bryce. This place is not for the weak of spirit. A strong mind is not enough."

Henry looks away. “There are other ways.”

“The other way is to leave.”

Kumwembe goes to the patient who has been gesturing for him from where he sits on the edge of his cot. The patient shows Kumwembe a tissue containing his sputum: thin lines of blood in the yellow. Kumwembe places one hand on the man’s shoulder and points with his other arm in the direction of the TB ward. The patient looks where Kumwembe points and Henry can see him take a large breath, can see the acceptance in his sigh.

Henry’s mother, a doctor herself, taught him how to be a doctor. She taught him about resolve and she taught him about silence and she taught him about love. All these in no particular order, a cycling and recycling of these teachings in the time he had with her. But right now he isn’t doing it quite right and he knows it. Right now he is applying his resolve to obstinately ploughing through each day, love and silence existing only in the wake he leaves behind himself, all those gathered moments rippling backward and Henry too busy to look, or listen.

Chapter 2

Jakob rises from where he had been sitting, helping to shell peas in a group of his aunties. It is women's work, but he enjoys it. He likes listening to the women talk and sing. He easily moves from groups of men to women, boys to girls, children to adults. His foot buys him entry. If he is honest with himself, he will admit to exaggerating the limp as he approaches a group of girls, he will bask in their sympathetic sounds. With the boys, he hides the limp, walks as smoothly and normally as possible with a foot that is like a clenched fist, on a leg that is too short. He has a foot like a horse, he has been told. But he keeps up, or nearly does. He runs on it, even kicks a football around with it. And the boys respond in as supportive a way as they can: they allow him to stay.

He walks over from the group of aunties to where his mother sits, looking drawn and tired, massaging her lower leg with her thumb. She has positioned herself near the well, and Jakob knows this means she wants him to fetch some water. He nods at the people he passes along the way and receives broad smiles in return.

Jakob's foot may be like a horse but his face resembles something less earthbound. His aunties used to hold him by the chin, turn his face this way and that, try to isolate the angelic ingredient. "It's not that he's handsome, exactly," they would say, "but there's something honest about it. Open and honest. Clear like a lake." And then they would let him go, watch him wend his way through the community, nearly an orphan (God knew his mother was on her way to join Him soon) yet such a part of everyone, and everyone wanting a part of him, somehow.

His mother calls him *aliyense* for this. Everyone. He is everyone to her: son, brother, daughter, sister. He has to be, for he, like no one else he knows, has no siblings and no father. His mother lost her womb after delivering him. She delivered him and then a river of blood that wouldn't stop flowing. Eventually, she had to be taken to the hospital on the hill where they cut the bleeding womb out of her. They stitched her up and sent her home with her newborn, her only child with his strange and twisted foot. Soon after this Jakob's father died from an illness of the blood, though the *sing'anga* had another opinion. And since then Jakob has tried to fill those roles, as many roles as stars in the sky, it sometimes seems.

Now he crouches down over his mother's foot and unwraps the bandage around it. The odour of the wound grows as he uncovers the flesh, the mangy bandage soaked with fluid from the wound and coloured milky yellow, brown, and green. The wounded area has been expanding and the flesh itself is looking more chewed up each time he uncovers it to cleanse it. It looks like a beast has been gnawing on it. And the smell is getting worse. He dabs at it with a wet cloth, wipes off the thick substance collected within it. Underneath there is a clean, pure white spot. He tries not to look at that spot; seeing the skeleton of a person still alive seems a bad omen. He takes a clean cloth and wraps it up again.

Earlier today Jakob saw a man at the market. He was walking along the other side of the road from where Jakob sat with his cousins, selling their carvings. Jakob was kneeling beside some Chief's Chairs, rich mahogany slabs of carved wood that fit together to make a low and impractical seat that tourists love. The crowd shifted between them and for a moment he lost sight of the man across the road. His cousin beside him said: "He's not a tourist. He's one of the new doctors at the hospital." Jakob watched the man as he dodged the crowd, his head tucked down, his neck flushed and damp, his mouth wide and flat.

"Look at his hair," he said.

"Like a tomato."

"Brighter than that. Like some kind of metal. Or fire." How could you describe that hair? Brassy and loud as the marching band he'd seen once celebrating some other people's victory.

"Maybe he has feathers on his head." His cousin laughed and resumed his carving, chipping away chunks of wood with delicate taps on the chisel. "Anyway, there's no point bothering with him. These doctors only buy when they're about to leave."

Jakob watched the doctor make his way down the lane and eventually he and his red hair disappeared from view.

Now, looking at his mother's leg, Jakob thinks of this doctor. This is the type of man who should be looking after his mother. This is the type of man—he is sure of it—who could save her. A man like that.

"We should go to the hospital," he says.

He has said it before and each time she always shook her head and replied: "They will take it. They will take off my foot like they took out my womb." Then she would go to where her money was stored, pull out a few *kwacha*, and instruct him to go to their local *sing'anga*, a secretive and strange man who lives alone and prefers to keep himself and his home in shadows. Also, he has a reputation for being dishonest. Jakob hated handing the money over to him which he took quickly and with dirty fingers, throwing back at Jakob a bundle of herbs. "Boil them in water. Put them on the foot." Then he'd turn away, light up a cigarette, tuck Jakob's mother's money into a pocket of his silty grey trousers.

And now, when his mother does not reply, he says it again. He thinks of the doctor in the market and says it again. If necessary, he will remind her that their savings, gathered *kwacha* by *kwacha* from years of his father's work in the tea fields, are gone. Into the pockets of the *sing'anga*. They have nothing left to spend. But he does not have to remind her because this time his mother nods.

Jakob has seen the hospital from the outside, but has never ventured inside. Except, of course, when he was carried in and out as a newborn. Even the doors are huge, much bigger than they need to be. They force him to stagger to pull them open. Perhaps this is the test: if you haven't enough strength to move the doors, then you shouldn't bother coming in at all. But Jakob manages to get one of them open and holds it open for his mother whose grip on him is weakening. Together, they struggle into the dim entranceway.

A man at a kiosk in the foyer glances up at them and then gestures wordlessly, points to somewhere further into the building. They make their way down the corridor. Having now entered this place, Jakob understands why his mother did not want to come back here. The size of the entrance is bigger than the church, bigger than the entire marketplace near their home. And then there are the people in smart uniforms who bustle past them. And the endless branching corridors and gaping rooms they pass filled with beds. Filled with bodies. Everything here seems important. This place feels bigger, more powerful, and capable of more miracles than the Church of St. Michael and All Angels which they attend every Sunday.

The long journey to get here—almost a full day's walk from the outskirts of town—has taken its toll. His mother struggles to walk now, and leans heavily against him, eyes closed. Her cheekbones seem to have grown sharper just over the day. She breathes quickly through her mouth.

They are waved on to three different kiosks at the ends of three different corridors before a nurse, after looking at them grimly from the other side of her desk, finally rises from her chair, comes round to where they stand and fastens a plastic band on his mother's wrist with something scribbled on it in pen. His mother's name. Jakob recognizes some of the letters, symbols he had learned once, years ago, before he stopped attending school. The nurse is wrapping something around the upper part of his mother's arm. It puffs up and then wheezes out air. She scribbles something on a piece of paper. She tells Jakob to take his mother to the end of the corridor, where there should be a place to sit on the floor. Jakob rouses his mother and they make their way down the corridor, choose the next empty space, sit down and wait.

*

There have been no miracles in the time they've been here at the hospital. Not for Jakob's mother, nor for any of the other men, women and children who line its corridors, fill its beds and floors. Jakob had not expected anything; he does not know what it is to have an expectation, to feel that something good must happen. But he does know hope, and he'd hung a lot of it over the doorway of this place, even before his mother became ill. Maybe because he knew the hospital had saved his mother when he was a baby, thus rescuing him from the responsibility of her death so soon after she gave him life. Maybe it was the influence of the strong and powerful who created this place, who named it after their queen. Perhaps it was the name itself: The Queen Elizabeth Hospital, as if it were guarded by royalty. Over the years as he grew up, every time he passed the building, or glimpsed it through the trees up on the hill, he had felt a stirring of hope, like it safeguarded the chance of a better future within its walls.

But since arriving here, the future has taken on the long, narrow and dark dimensions of the corridors in this place. The doctor—Kumwembe is his name—knelt down and studied his mother's foot the first day. He tsked as he held the heel and ignored her wincing as he turned and lifted it so he could see the wound in the light that came through the window above them. A nurse had then come to tunnel a tube beneath the skin of his mother's arm, and a bag of clear, clean water now hangs above them, slowly emptying into her. When she has to go to the toilet, Jakob takes care to move the pole alongside her and he guards the lengths of tubing to not disturb the flow of the water. But each time the doctor checked her foot he tsked again, shook his head, muttered under his breath that it was not responding, not responding. It was then that they met Dr. Ellison.

The big, white doctor filled the hallway. He bent his head slightly and Jakob could see where the thin yellow hairs sprouted from his shiny red scalp. This is a surgeon. A man who uses knives to cure and Jakob couldn't help feel his mother's fear of his knife, where it might land. After looking at Jakob's mother's foot from his great height, he squatted down and pointed his red, thick finger at her lower leg, above the wound. He traced a line across the leg with his finger. His nail left a white line in her scaly skin. "Right here," he said as he traced. "Okay?"

Jakob watched his mother when the doctor touched her leg, but her eyes were closed. He wondered if she'd understood. When he told her in Chichewa that she would indeed lose her foot, she just nodded, eyes still closed. He'd looked up at Dr. Ellison and nodded. "Yes, okay," he heard himself say.

He hoped his mother hadn't heard him speak.

It wasn't very long after he said those words—yes, okay—that they came to take his mother away. They brought a gurney for her. He helped her up onto it from where she had spent so many days slumped against the wall in the hallway; they had never made it into a ward. But now she would earn a place on a bed and the price of admission was her foot. She lay on the gurney and opened her eyes once to look up at the ceiling before closing them again. His mother had spent most of her hours in the hospital—awake or asleep—with her eyes closed. Jakob squeezed her hand once and whispered, "God willing, you will be safe, Mama," before they wheeled her away.

When Jakob's mother is returned from the surgical suites, he follows her squeaking gurney down the hall to a new room—one of the expansive rooms that she will occupy with a sea of others who have shared a taste of the surgeon's knife. She is groggy. A thin sheet is draped over her and Jakob can see where her right leg ends too soon, lacking the tented rise of a foot beyond it. It looks just like he had feared it would.

His mother finds his face with eyes that are cloudy and confused. "My foot," she says to him.

"Yes, Mama."

"Is it safe?"

He hesitates only briefly. "Yes, Mama."

He wonders if she had asked this of the doctors when she lost her womb. A womb is easier to lie about, hidden as it is inside the body. He squeezes her hand and watches her drift off again.

*

Jakob's mother has TB. It is in the lungs. This was the reason for the cough she'd had for as long as he could remember. It had been living in her foot, too. He is going to be checked for it and they will both need treatment. They will both need to stay here for a long time.

Dr. Kumwembe explains this to them in Chichewa so his mother can understand, too. The only English word he uses is TB. He lifts his arm and points down the long corridor.

"The TB ward is that way," he says. "Down the main corridor, left at the junction, at the end of that corridor. You'll see the sign." He assumes that Jakob can read. This flatters Jakob and he wishes he could show the doctor that his assumption is right. He is determined not to get lost on the way to the TB ward.

As he leads his mother down the hallway to the ward, pushing her in the wheelchair a nurse found for them, Jakob thinks of his aunties and cousins and friends back home. The two of them have been in the hospital for many days, and now they will be here much longer. The treatment requires taking medicine every day for many months. He pushes his mother easily up the slope of the corridor. She is very light and pushing her takes no effort at all.

He nods to a group of orderlies who loiter at one end of the hall. They wave back. There are familiar faces as he moves down the corridor, now. There are smiles, nods, knowing looks. He is not sure if this lightness has always been here, or whether the cloud has only recently lifted. But gradually he is starting to recognize within the wards and halls what he'd felt when he viewed the hospital from the outside: that feeling of something better.

He sees the letters on the sign and knows them right away: TB. So this will be their new home. He pushes his mother's chair into the ward.

Chapter 3

The sky opens up above Henry as he heads down the road, away from the hospital and the trees that surround it. He walks everywhere right now—he doesn't own a vehicle, although he knows he will need one. He will need it for outreach work, and he won't be able to afford the time it will take to get to these places by public transport—days upon days.

Now that his rounds are done, he is not sure if he did them quickly or slowly, whether it is morning or afternoon. Time is beginning to lose relevance, but Henry clings to it nonetheless. All his life, he has treated time as a commodity and over the years it has taken on an exact monetary value. And thus, he has spent time frugally, dispensing each hour carefully, filling it with activities, making the most of it. He abhors waste, time included.

He continues down the hill to the Blantyre downtown market. Trucks and minivans rattle past; passengers hang off the backs and sides of the vehicles, fan out in layers—an odd but somehow graceful spray of human petals. He ignores the people he passes on the path—their long looks and attempts at eye contact—he has grown tired of being a curiosity, of trying to be polite, of answering the searching questions. He turns off the main road and onto a narrow laneway, moving through the throng of people who gather in the marketplace to peruse, shop, steal, socialize, and loiter. It is the loiterers who know him best. The men who lean against buildings, arms and legs crossed, caps pulled down over their eyes. Theirs are the faces which follow him, barely perceptible nods of recognition as he passes by. They know his routine, he knows theirs.

The shopkeepers know him, too. Henry walks over to a stand piled high with fruit: bananas, plantains, tangerines, and overripe, bruised tomatoes adorned with flies. The shopkeeper moves closer to Henry. "Doctor." He points to a pyramid of tangerines. "Good."

Henry is increasingly being addressed this way, although he has never introduced himself outside of the hospital. He nods back, smiles. He picks up two tangerines and hands over a few *kwacha*. He waves back the change and the shopkeeper grins and nods.

Henry pockets the fruit and weaves his way through the narrow rows of wooden stands, walks in the yellowed shade of the corrugated plastic awnings. Here in the market, Henry feels the push of the crowd, feels Blantyre as the second largest city in the country and home to some 700,000 Malawians. Elsewhere the population scatters and disappears into the low-lying buildings that spread out from the small city core. He passes a stand displaying medication. Pills of various shapes, colours and sizes are bagged and organized in some way, unlabelled. Probably knock-offs, created in a basement warehouse somewhere in the anonymity of the city.

The pill culture. Salvation in a bottle. No longer a wing and a prayer, it is a pill and a promise. Just a few generations beyond the travelling salesman touting miracle tonic, he plies pills for a living and is charged with fixing all human ailments armed with a stethoscope and a prescription pad.

There was a time when his position, this ambassadorship, was a source of pride. A badge of honour.

Music plays from a nearby radio, reggae with choppy cuts of static.

A woman with a big-eyed child on her back and three more straggling behind her has approached the stand. The children gape at Henry. Their mother touches her stomach delicately.

"Bilharzia."

The pill vendor reaches for a bag of orange tablets. The woman takes them then rummages in her wrap for a crumpled bill. She hands it over and the vendor whips it away. It disappears into his pocket and he turns back around to the radio, adjusts the long, segmented antennae. The reggae is overcome by static as the woman leaves the stand, her children still trailing behind, all three pairs of eyes fixed on Henry as they stumble forward after their mother then disappear into the crowd.

*

Jakob swallows his TB pills and looks at his mother who is sleeping in her cot. She is thinner. Each time he grasps her wrist there is less of it, more of his hand can wrap around it. Despite all the medicine that has been poured into her by pills or tubes, she is dwindling in size and energy and, worst of all, spirit. Perhaps the *sing'anga*'s treatment had not been as useless as he had thought. Perhaps he should seek him out again, bring back something from his coffers: some foul-smelling bottle or dried up herb paste. Maybe there was less magic in the bottles and more in whatever deals he made with the spirits in the darkness of his hut after he took the money. Perhaps the man had done more than just smoke and spit after all. Jakob sits on the edge of his mother's cot and taps his club foot on the floor. It twists inward and he has to walk on the side of it. The hard floors here make it ache more.

He can't bring anything back from the *sing'anga* until he has some money to buy it with. He misses going with his cousins to the market and hawking their wares. Some of his cousins are talented woodworkers, hatching all sorts of ornaments, gadgets, tables and chairs out of the raw pieces of wood. Jakob has no skill with a knife. Jakob's job had been to help sell the items. Even as a child he somehow knew what to say, how to look, which passersby to pester. He could pull a smile from the most sour-faced tourist and, soon after the smile appeared, he could get them to part with the *kwacha* they had hidden somewhere in one of their pockets. They all had *kwacha*, even when they said they didn't.

Jakob misses his cousins and he misses his job and he misses the money they shared with him after a sale. But every time he thinks about going home his mother, without even looking, senses him nearby and says "*Aliyense,* you're here" so quietly that only he can hear. And then he again knows his purpose. He will have to make a life here, in this space.

It is one of the nurses who helps him find work. Maria. She appears there beside him when the head hospital custodian is looking doubtfully down at him—short, with eyes too big for his face, barely a neck, and legs and arms still too thin to be much use. "How old are you, anyway?" Jakob pipes in: "Eighteen," although he is only fifteen. "He carried his mother here when she could not stand on her own. He carried her for miles." Maria says this to the custodian, and it is true. Then she points at his club foot which he has been trying to tuck discreetly out of sight. "That foot," she says, "is where his power lies. It gives him great strength." The custodian turns his doubtful gaze to Jakob's short and twisted foot. "It better not bring me bad luck." Jakob stands on it to emphasize its wholesome and honest capabilities. The worker sighs and says he will speak to his manager. He warns Jakob that the pay is meagre—barely enough to cover a meal a day and Jakob shrugs this off, tingling all over with the possibility of money—a regular stream of it. And, later that day, the custodian hands Jakob a mop, and tells him where the buckets are, and which room to begin his work.

*

Jakob is rolling a bucket of clean water behind him when he sees the redheaded doctor rushing down the hall and this is the next thing that sets this doctor apart: no one rushes around here. Jakob feels the push of air as the doctor moves past and then watches his long white coat flap behind him down the hall. Jakob, still dragging his mop and bucket behind him, follows.

When Jakob enters the ward where the doctor has gone, there is a cluster of people standing around a bed in the middle of the room. Around this cluster the rest of the ward spreads out flat, silent and still.

Jakob spots the thatch of the doctor's red hair. He is the same man he'd seen in the market and he is now bent over the patient who lies in the bed. Then the doctor straightens. He is so tall. And now his voice rises up above the cluster of people, above the beds, above it all: "Why didn't you get me sooner? A person shouldn't die from pneumonia." The doctor directs his pale-eyed gaze from one nurse to the next, then to the collection of people assembled around the patient who lies so still he is certainly dead. The faces that look back at the doctor do so defiantly, or so it seems to Jakob as he watches from the doorway. He is ashamed of their defiance. The doctor spins on a heel and stalks out of the ward. He brushes past Jakob—the sleeve of his white coat actually grazes his bare arm—and Jakob watches him go.

He fingers the spot where the coat sleeve touched him. It tingles there, with the doctor's angry energy. Jakob wishes, hopes, prays, that this man can be his mother's doctor. This is a man who knows how to fight.

Chapter 4

Somewhere in the darkness, hippos shift and rouse. Henry can see their large, formless shapes moving against the dark grey sky. At this hour of the morning, everything is shades of grey, but he can now tell them apart—the bushes from the hippos. And the river: he is beginning to sense its movement in the muddy pre-dawn glow. For some reason, with the increasing light, he can hear more, too. He is aware of the river lapping, of hippos wading and greeting each other with grunts and moans—a surprisingly porcine sound.

Ellison shifts to his right, arranges himself on a narrow log, and releases a long, satisfied sigh. Art Ellison: an Aussie surgeon, an ex-pat who has settled himself here so definitively, has planted his feet like a non-native plant species that thrives despite the foreign environment. Ellison wades through life like a cowboy—rough, unapologetic, land-loving—and Malawi is his Wild West. Henry has assisted him in the operating theatre. Ellison is fearless there. He forges ahead, creating a solution that usually forgoes aesthetics for function. Henry once watched him resect a tumour from the jaw of a Malawian patient. This man had lived with the tumour growing in his mandible for years. Not knowing there was treatment, he'd accommodated its growth—by then to the size of a tennis ball—without questioning it. Ellison had spotted the man during an outreach clinic and corralled him back to Blantyre and into his operating theatre. He'd chopped it out and wired in a hunk of rib to replace the mandible. The man woke up from his surgery without the mass, with a small, lopsided half-jaw in its place. Examining the man post-operatively, Ellison had frowned, then grinned, standing tall, his big frame filling the ward. It'll do, he'd bellowed, squeezing the man's shoulder with his large hand.

Henry is aware of Ellison sinking onto the log to his right, settling in like a boulder. Big, muscular limbs, face wide, ruddy and friendly, his body is as large as his personality. Henry hears him breathe in the marshy, muddy air with noisy deliberation. As far as Henry knows, Ellison has no wife, no children. His love affair is with the land.

Ellison invited Henry on this trip, to attend an outreach clinic in Mlela, a town he visits once a month. They arrived at the hostel the previous evening, were waved in by the cheerful owner and shared a drink with him before retiring for the night. Ellison promised a hippo sighting if Henry was willing to rise before dawn. They met in front of the hostel in the dark, just after the chorus of rooster crows, and walked around to the back, down a narrow, overgrown path a few hundred metres to the river's edge.

The hippos, farther away than he'd thought now that he can see them clearly, gather in the shallow water and nuzzle each other with wide, wet snouts. They are across the river, on the opposite bank. Closer to Henry, just a few feet away, a heron moves its stilted legs through the reeds. Closer still, a small spider picks its way through a tangle of grass.

Henry sits and watches the river, feeling like he should be feeling more. Beside him, Ellison grows with each breath, opening up to the African morning like fog dispersing in the sun. But Henry remains the same, a small tight fist of uncertainty. He stares long and hard at the heron, watching for a clue, for a hint of what is to come. The heron moves its head and an almond-shaped, unblinking eye regards him, telling him nothing.

Henry is the first doctor in a long line of carpenters, the first Bryce boy to stray from this calling, and his hands are proof of it—pale and smooth as they take an unearned rest now, clasped between his knees. He should have been a surgeon—a carpenter of the body—he would have derived some satisfaction from the simple and gratifying surgical approach to illness: take it out.

His father's hands had been large, rough and calloused. Hands that could fix anything. His father had watched Henry try, once in a while, to handle some wood, run it past the chewing blades of the saw. It hadn't come naturally to Henry and his father had in many ways been relieved. He'd nudged Henry to read, to do what he seemed to do easily: to study, like his mother. Like any parent, he'd hoped for a good life for him, and education was the key. Knowledge was freedom; this was the doctrine that had been uttered through the house as he grew up. But science has betrayed him and the trust, what it all hinges on, what everything hinges on, has been lost.

He knows what Sarah would think if she were here. She would think what he thought when he first arrived. She would think that he has come to a place where the magic of pharmaceuticals can be displayed in a dramatic and spectacular way, a fireworks of lifesaving glory. Even after what happened, she never lost her faith in the scientific method. She pressed her lips together and returned with new vigour to her job. Right now, he could use her unrelenting enthusiasm for pharmaceutical technology. Her staunch belief in the reliability of calculated treatment success. This is what she does for a living, and does it well. She presents the miracle of science to doctors, shows them how science can change the world by removing pain and illness. And where better a place to show the healing capacity of drugs than here?

And yet the opposite has been the case. The exact opposite. Here, more than anywhere else, he is reminded of the limits of things. He brings his gaze from the river back to his hands, examines the tortuous path of his veins under his skin. He knows exactly where he begins and ends, now. He is all too familiar with where he ends.

Ellison stirs beside him. Moves his hands and arms upward, pushes his chest out in a mighty stretch, as if he has just woken up. He turns toward Henry, smiles with heavy-lidded eyes. “Stunning, eh?”

Henry nods and squints at the sun, now above the bush, the heat from it penetrating the mist that still swirls off the river. “Must be getting close to seven,” he says. “What time are we expected at the clinic?”

“Whenever we arrive.” Ellison pats him on the back and then rises to his feet, starts up the path to the hostel.

*

Ellison’s car meanders along the road to the outreach clinic, a short bumpy ride down a single, unpaved lane. The crowd outside the clinic watches their arrival. Ellison pulls the vehicle to a stop beside the building—a concrete box with a rusty corrugated roof. Usually the town church, Henry was told. The crowd, though large, is surprisingly quiet as they part to allow the doctors to pass and enter.

Once inside, Henry waits for his eyes to adjust to the darkness. There are two small windows on opposite walls. The air is ripe with bodies: sour and pungent. Patients—mostly women with children—fill the pews in two rows of closely spaced benches. A man greets them with a large grin and a strong handshake. "Welcome, Doctors. Come, come." He wears a shirt with the black and white collar of a pastor or priest. He beckons them down the aisle between the pews, past the altar, and through a door in the back of the building. The brightness stings Henry's eyes as he passes through the door into the space behind the church. It is an outdoor room, walled off with mud, but without a roof. A bench on either end, tucked discreetly behind stick-walled screens: the examining areas.

"I held the first clinic inside the church. Couldn't see a damn thing, so we built this." Ellison sweeps his hand around the space. "Took a week."

"Nice work."

"I'm going to have to scare up some clear plastic for the roof. Otherwise first rain, we're in trouble."

Henry places the duffle bag filled with equipment—gloves, needles, syringes, medication—on the ground, swings his backpack off his shoulders and fishes around for his stethoscope.

"Rare'n to go, mate?" Ellison grins.

"Loads of people waiting out there. We only have two days."

Ellison shrugs. "You do what you can. And then you call it a day."

Henry ducks through the door and into the church, into the darkness and back to the pews where the crowd waits. They are more lively when he appears, tangibly expectant.

They watch him approach the closest patient, a woman with a baby bundled in colourful cloth and carried behind her. The baby sleeps, his eyes closed and cheeks slack against her upper back. The woman lifts her eyes when Henry stands beside her. When she stands up, he leads her through the door and into the sunlit clinic.

*

The clinic, the church, the people, all become indistinct in the wake of dust and exhaust that they leave behind them. A crowd watches them go; a few of them wave. The rest turn away and walk back in clumps along the road.

Henry turns and faces forward, presses his fist into the dash, tightens his jaw. The duffle bag in the back seat is loose and nearly empty. All the syringes, IV bags, tubing, needles, gloves, bottles of drugs used up on this group of people and who knew how long it would sustain them. One duffle bag. An embarrassingly paltry effort.

"Why do you do it?"

Ellison glances over at Henry. "What's that, mate?"

"Why do you do it? What brought you here?"

"Fame and fortune."

Henry looks out the window at the grasslands that shrug and twitch in the wind like the hide of a beast. Its power lies in its unpredictability, its random swings of fate. All he has is his rationality, the ability to string one logical thought after another, like beads on a necklace, his own rosary, which he uses to pull himself along, to move from place to place, decision to decision.

Out the window on his right is a field, cleared of tall grass and filled with stones organized into neat piles or cairns, and these organized into rows. Ellison glances over at the same view.

"Graves."

"There must be hundreds of them."

"AIDS." He juts a thumb backwards, toward the clinic they just left. "Whole villages orphaned. Like those kids we just saw."

"I thought it was a paediatric clinic."

"It was by necessity. That's mostly all there is."

They are silent after this. The grave field is gone, replaced with the waving grasses, a few low hills in the distance. He could imagine that this place is uninhabited, or inhabited only by the dead. When he sees two boys waving sticks at some cattle, and their mother with hips swaying as she carries an urn of water on her head, he is irrationally relieved.

Those who have survived this place have learned acceptance. Everywhere he looks, there is acceptance, eyes closing so easily to what is offered, to what is placed before them: illness, drought, hunger. Even Ellison, in his large-chested, hearty way, accepts things here, puts up with the lack. Now he sits there in the driver's seat so definitively, meaty fingers clasped around the small steering wheel, jerking it left, right, left, around potholes, people and animals. Farm fowl skitter faster at the roar of the engine, make half-hearted attempts to fly. Cattle roam at the same slow pace, unmoved by the threat of a vehicle approaching. And the people. The people walk, sway to the side, wave through the dust, lift up their baskets of fruit and meat. *Muli bwangi*, they mouth, smiling through the noise, dust, heat and exhaust. *Muli bwangi*. Henry looks through the window, presses his fingers to it, knows that from the perspective of the people on the road he is a ghost who is there and then is gone. A fleeting, wan visage, indistinct through the dust and the reflection of the sun off the glass, staring out at them with pale eyes and a grim mouth.

Mulanje Mountain. Henry had been able to see it from the clinic and now, as they drive toward it, it rises up off the horizon, grey and formidable like a hippo rising from the river, rivulets of water dripping off its back and catching the sun as they plunge to the plains below. It is an inselberg, a rocky massif that has resisted erosion over the centuries and stands alone, a granite island, surrounded by an ocean of featureless plains as far as the eye can see. A halo of cloud encircles the higher mountain reaches and the rounded peaks jut above them, grey-brown against the blue sky. "Island in the sky" it has been called locally, and it is regarded with fear and respect by the Malawians who live near it.

Before they return to Blantyre, they will climb it.

Henry and Ellison leave their vehicle parked on the side of the road close to the mountain, sling their packs over their shoulders, and set off on one of the trails that snakes its way up. Initially, they wind through a forest where gnarled trunks of ancient cedar and cypress trees twist skyward. The moss, clinging to stones and trunks, the heady scent of soil and chlorophyll, the sense of enclosure is strange to Henry now, having adapted to the exposed plains elsewhere in the country. They plunge through the stillness with large and heavy steps over rocks and roots, with grunts and effort. Occasionally a mist moves in and further darkens the mountain, muffling it, making the sounds of their breath an affront to the quiet of this place.

The muscles of his legs clench and push against the land and propel Henry upward despite the strong pull of gravity, the tangible effort to keep him low, to keep him down. His legs keep pushing, his feet keep their grip on the loose pebbles, jutting rocks, sliding mud.

Eventually the forest thins and then disappears altogether and they are above everything but the bald, treeless peak of Mulanje Mountain.

Legends circle the mountain: they are carried around and around it by those who live at its foot. Ellison had described them with a bemused smile earlier on the drive to the mountain. "You should know that we are embarking on a dangerous journey." He said this with a twitch of his mouth, glancing over at Henry. Nudge. Wink. "The locals say there is an evil presence there."

"Evil." Henry had said. "What sort of evil are we talking about?"

Ellison spread his hands in front of the steering wheel. "Oh, you know, mysterious winds. People disappearing. That sort of thing. The usual witchcraft and sorcery."

"Here?"

"Oh, it's here, all right. You'll see. The longer you're here, the more you'll be aware of it."

"Do you believe in that stuff?"

Ellison waved a hand in the air, vague, all-encompassing. "It's like all religion and superstition. It serves a purpose. Keeps people in line. Provides an explanation. Gives them a sense of meaning."

Henry and Ellison reach a plain as the sky begins to darken. From here, they can see the setting sun; it sheds hasty orange light before it sinks down out of sight. After climbing uphill for so long, it is strange, this new flatness to the mountain, as though the thing they walk on has grown weary and has laid itself down for the night.

They pass through the grassy field and as the sky darkens completely they make their way down a slope, a brief descent to a hut that Henry cannot see but can smell—the spicy sweetness of cedar wood burning in an open fire. The hut keeper greets them with a nod when they arrive and drop their packs on the wooden slats of the deck. By the light of the fire and with little discussion, Henry and Ellison prepare a stew; they chop the vegetables and meat they carried up the mountain and drop the food into a battered aluminum pot that they hang over the flames and then wait.

Fatigue settles over Henry. Ellison is a dark bundle beside him on the bench. Both of them stare at the fire, watch their pot as it chars in the flames. Ellison peeks inside, stirs the contents, then replaces the lid and sits back down.

"My ex would've hated this." Why can't he say ex-wife? The same reason he can't say daughter.

"Hmm?" Ellison shifts on the bench.

"At home. My ex—she would have hated this." Henry leans forward, closer to the fire until he can't take the heat on his face anymore and leans back. "She's very much a city girl. Lipstick and nail polish and all that. She's a drug rep."

"In bed with the devil, were you?" Ellison chuckles.

"Sarah." Her name is pulled into the smoke of the fire. He imagines black, charred wisps that are carried up the flue, then are swept away by the wind, scattered over the mountain.

Henry turns to Ellison. "You?"

"No, no drug reps in my past, although tempted many times."

"I mean, any girlfriends, anyone serious."

"An ex-wife. But she wasn't serious."

Henry watches the yellow flames advance along the wood, a steady consumption that leaves a trail of mottled black in its wake. He started planning the trip when he knew he'd lost her. When it was official. This is why he is here, staring at a fire on a mountain in Africa. One last lurching effort to hold on to things, aspects of life that can be grasped, like where you live, what you do, who you help. Not who you love, though. Or who you lose. This, he now knows, cannot be grappled down, held to the ground, fixed in place. And he feels less naïve in the knowing. As he sits here staring at the fire, Henry feels a strength, a freedom in the knowing.

"This place," Henry says. "Malawi." He pauses.

"Strange, isn't it? Old and new."

"It makes me want to do something for these people. Make a change."

Ellison looks over at Henry, takes in his earnest posture, his determination, staring into the fire like that. "I'd be careful about change," says Ellison slowly. "Change is hard anywhere, but this place in particular. Don't be too hasty."

Henry is silent.

"You've only been here, what… a couple of months?"

"Two and a half."

"You've only just arrived."

"Yes."

"You're just settling in. Takes a while to get used to the place." Ellison pauses. "It's a good place, this. Good people." Ellison looks over at Henry again, reads the stare. "One thing I've learned, is there's no point pushing against something that won't budge."

Ellison breathes noisily beside Henry and then gets up to stir the pot again; its contents are now bubbling and the broth is thick. "Looks like supper's ready."

They eat quickly and then lie down on cots piled with blankets. Henry falls asleep smelling of sweat and smoke, the taste of stew in his mouth, the sound of wind moving outside the single pane of glass beside his cot.

When he wakes, it is from a dream of wind, thick and black, that has pushed and pulled at the hut, moved it around the mountain. Wind moaning, laughing, crying. Dark tendrils of wind coming up behind him, curling around him, whispering something he cannot understand, nudging him forward.

He sits up in his cot and peers out the dirty window. The sun has broken the horizon and it feels hot, even in the protected shade of the hut. He puts on his shoes and steps out onto the deck. It is warm out here, too, but then a breeze picks up and he is suddenly cold, wishing he had thrown on his sweater. He steps down off the deck and onto the ground. There are no trees, just the ochre grass reminiscent of the plains hundreds of metres below. This is the highest peak in south central Africa, and he feels it, feels closer to the wide, enigmatic sky with the wispy clouds that streak across it but don't move, as though the sky were a painting, and he is now close enough to see the brush strokes.

To his left is a small hill with a narrow path bisecting it: the path they descended at the end of the day yesterday. To his right is the steep rise of the Sapitwa peak, the highest peak on the mountain. This is the epicentre of the legends, the realm of evil spirits, the basis of all bad magic and witchcraft in Malawi, the place he was warned not to go. When Iris learned of his plans to accompany Ellison to the Mlela clinic, and then to Mulanje Mountain itself, she frowned darkly, her face turning in. "Only fools climb the mountain," she'd said, and he'd felt like replying, *then it shouldn't surprise you that I will be going*, but held his tongue. "Don't go to Sapitwa," she'd muttered before turning away completely.

He looks at Sapitwa peak: impressive—a granite wall jutting skyward—but not threatening. He sees no shadow gathering there, no cloud of winged monkeys flying wildly around the peak. No fiery pits breathing, spitting, or cursing.

Henry gazes at it, drawn by something thrilling, a pull in his gut. He feels compelled to climb it, scale the rock face with his bare hands, pull himself up its flanks, dig his fingers into the fissures in its thick hide, stand atop the very tallest reaches of it, feel the power that he knows he'd feel there, accept the consequences of such boldness because it would be worth it.

A figure approaches from across the plain, initially indistinct and wavering in the heat, almost the same colour as the grass. Before long he can see that it is Ellison walking toward him along one of the paths that criss-cross the subalpine plain. He stops a few feet in front of Henry and nods.

"Morning."

"Gorgeous one, isn't it."

Ellison gestures to Sapitwa. "Feels good to be up there. Like you're king of the world." As though he had been privy to Henry's thoughts of a few moments before. "Too bad we won't be able to climb it on this trip. I have to be back in Blantyre tonight."

"Do you need special equipment to get up? Harnesses and holds and all that?"

"Nah. Some do, but it's manageable with nothing but your hands and feet." Ellison lifts his wide palms up, displays the intersecting crevices and the calluses, twin topographical maps.

"I'd like to do it sometime." Henry squints and looks at the peak again. A few scanty clouds move behind Sapitwa now, but the appearance is of the peak crossing the sky, as though it is already moving on, as though it won't always be there for them.

"We'll do another trip. I love this place." Ellison moves toward the hut and Henry follows reluctantly, knowing that they will be going in to pack, and to begin their descent down the mountain and their journey back to Blantyre.

Chapter 5

Dr. Bryce, that man with the impossible hair, is staring at her. Here she is, sitting with a chart, doing the work she is here to do, and he is hovering, staring his pale stare, breathing his quiet breath and sweating. She can smell him from here and he smells anxious, like he always does. No different than when he first arrived two months ago.

Iris lifts her eyes and sure enough his eyes are fixed on her. Not nicely. Impatient. As though she has already done something wrong.

She looks down. She will not receive what he is about to dole out. He doles it out anyway. He says something about the bedding. Wondering who cleans it.

She looks at the desk with its chips and scratches and scribbles. She shrugs. "If we remove it, the housekeepers will clean it. But if we remove it, then the patients have nothing to lie on. And nothing to cover them." Finally, she lifts her eyes to him. She can see him swell and then tighten with the effort of keeping it in.

"So there's not enough."

"Yes. Not enough. We clean them between patients."

"And what about bathing the patients? Not enough soap and water?"

Iris stares at a thick black ring of coffee or tea on the desk that has been there as long as she has. She rubs at it, feels its smoothness, then nudges it with a fingernail. It doesn't give.

"Bathe the patients? We do." She thinks about earlier this morning, when she'd run a cloth along Juma's arms, how he'd looked out the window, not at her, never at her. All of them look away.

When Iris looks up again, Dr. Bryce is putting on his lab coat, fiddling with the buttons, pulling his stethoscope out of one of the deep pockets and hanging it around his neck. Of all the doctors who have passed through these wards, Dr. Bryce is the only one who keeps wearing the lab coat, day after day. To keep the patients at a distance? To remind them of his stature? She tries to remember the original purpose of a doctor's white coat. A symbol of cleanliness, a sterile barrier to protect the patient from killing bacteria. She takes in Dr. Bryce's rumpled coat, brown at the cuffs where his wrists stick out. Spots and smears of body fluids on the front. Her fingers drift up to her nurse's hat that she pins on every morning. It is white and crisp with bleach and starch. Dr. Bryce marches out of the office, back stiff and straight, chin jutting forward. Did the man visit Sapitwa after all? It seems he has brought the darkness back with him. It trails after him: a dirty wake of bad luck.

She closes the chart, leaves it on the desk and follows him into the ward, keeping back a safe distance.

He goes to Juma first, even though his is not the first bed on his rounds. He picks up Juma's chart hanging at the foot of the bed. He frowns and flips pages, eyeing the graphs that show the fevers, the dips in blood pressure, the surges in heart rate. Now he looks over the beds, cranes his head around. He is looking for her. Why does he always look for her? There are at least two other nurses circulating on the ward. She can see one of them over in the corner, by the man with TB of the spine. Dr. Bryce finds her, motions her over.

"The blood test results? They were drawn before I left for Mlela."

"Positive." She is referring to the HIV test, and he knows it. It is the only one that matters to him. Dr. Bryce dips his head for a long moment, then finally turns his gaze out the window. Juma watches him and waits for the doctor to speak. Like a disciple gazing up to his teacher. Juma does not care about the test results, meaningless numbers and symbols. All that matters to Juma is that he is here, under the care of this doctor. This tall, white doctor with reddish-gold hair, who, now that he is in Africa has grown a reddish-gold beard. This doctor who bends his beard down over his patients when he uses his stethoscope so Juma can study the strange, wiry hairs. This doctor who must bring luck the colour of gold, luck from the shining places overseas where miracles happen every day. Where people do not suffer. Juma does not know this doctor has been to Mulanje Mountain. Iris would never tell him.

Dr. Bryce now smiles at Juma. How can he smile? But there it is, his mouth stretched side to side, cheeks pulled into tight bunches beneath his beard. He puts a hand on the boy's shoulder. He says something to him. He moves a hand to his belly and pushes in and Juma lets him even though it is painful; Iris can see the boy tighten with the pain, one of his hands gripping the mattress. He listens to Juma's lungs and Juma rolls over so he can place the stethoscope on his back. Then he takes the chart, scribbles something on it, hangs it back up, and moves on.

Iris goes over to Juma's bed. "*Moni. Muli bwanji?*"

"*Ndiri bwino,*" he says, and watches her scan his chart.

The doctor has called for more IV saline, although they are in short supply, and Juma has been filling his basin with urine regularly enough, by her estimation. She sighs and goes to fetch it.

*

Henry's heart pushes against his chest in a way that makes him feel nauseous and light-headed. He sits down on his bed beside the small, square table that holds the telephone in his apartment. It is an old rotary phone, the plastic yellowed where so many fingers have wrapped around the receiver, and over the mouthpiece where so many mouths have hovered. The holes in the mouthpiece are large, and he can see the shine of metal through them. He listens to the ring tone, loud and foreign-sounding. This is the first phone call he has made since arriving in Africa. The phone smells like tobacco, years and years of it.

He hears the phone on the other end pick up in a clatter, clumsy on the other side. "Hello?" The voice is sluggish with sleep, confused. He realizes, now too late, that he has miscalculated. It is 5 AM, not 9 AM, on Saturday morning in Toronto.

"Sarah?" He says this as a question, although he knows it is her. He is still familiar with her thick sleep voice. It is the voice that comes from her body when it is warm and soft, her limbs loose and relaxed under the covers.

"Henry?" She is sounding more clear now, more in focus. "What time is it? Are you okay? Are you still over there?"

Over there. This place is more than a world away. It is miraculous, this phone conversation, that they can still speak to each other. That they still have a language, a history in common.

"I'm here," he says. "In Malawi. Blantyre." He can hear her sitting up in bed.

"God. Malawi. What part of Africa is that again? What's it like? Are you okay?"

"I'm okay."

She says nothing to this, and there is a pause, as if both of them are understanding how far away they each are. How strange it is that they are talking.

He clears his throat and asks: "How about you? Are you okay?"

"Yes. Yes, I'm fine. Same old, same old. You know how it is." He hears her shift in bed, the click of a lamp being turned on. Her night table, he imagines, is cluttered with paperwork, and some of it has tumbled over the edge onto the thickly carpeted floor. He looks down at his bare feet, toes gripping cold concrete. "God, it's early. What time is it there? Is something wrong?"

Henry doesn't know how to answer. He says, "No, not really. The work is hard. More frustrating than hard. I feel like I can't do much to help here." He hears Sarah's quiet breaths, he can hear her listening. He knows what she is thinking.

"I'm sure that's not true. You're doing what you can, right?"

He pauses. "That's where you come in."

"Me?" Henry is taken by the solitude in this word, in the tone of it. For a moment he still longs for her. And in this brief connection across the line, he finds the courage to proceed.

"There's a patient here with HIV," he begins.

"Isn't the HIV rate something like ten percent?"

"Fourteen percent. Maybe twenty in the city. In any case, there's this one young man. Juma." When he says the name, he feels like he has ripped open his shirt and bared his chest, like there is no turning back. One world has been shared with another, and he is suddenly not sure if he is doing the right thing. Revealing Juma to her.

"Juma," she repeats. It sounds strange from her mouth.

"He's so young. A really good kid. I'd been hoping it was just malaria but the kid's got full-blown AIDS. And there are no antiretrovirals here. None at all. Despite the fourteen percent prevalence."

"Because of the fourteen percent prevalence."

"Yes. Well."

"By the way, I'd suggest giving that habit up," she says.

"Giving what up?"

"Hoping it's not HIV. With a prevalence rate like that. You'll be done in no time if you keep thinking that way."

Henry does not reply and Sarah fills the silence quickly. "So where do I come in here, Henry? This has nothing to do with us."

He wishes, just for a second, that it did. "Your company makes a few of the antiretrovirals."

Henry hears her sharp intake of air. "Oh, my God. Are you serious? You want me to supply Africa with antiretrovirals?" Now the receiver scratches her out-breath across the line. "Henry. I'm a rep. My job is to *sell* the stuff. And I don't even represent the antiretrovirals. What do you expect me to do?"

"Just a few."

"Just a few? Henry, the prevalence is fourteen percent. That's like... hundreds of thousands of people over there. Millions on the continent. Even if I could get some for you, where would it stop?"

Henry is quiet on the other end. Still clutching the yellowed phone, the plastic slipping under his sweaty fingers, heart still pounding. He looks at his empty room, at the firm and narrow mattress he sits on. The single bedside table. Mosquito netting knotted in a bundle above him.

"I thought you'd understand. I thought you *especially* would understand."

"Understand?"

"The chance to save a kid." He wonders if the pressure he feels rising in his chest is rising in hers. If those words are almost too much for her, too. There is a long, empty moment.

"It's just not realistic."

And these words, her words, shut him down, the pressure clamped off at his throat.

"Henry," Sarah says more gently, "you know I'm not the one being unreasonable here, right?" When he says nothing, she continues. "Is it . . . are you still missing her?" She can't say her name. He is relieved that she can't say her name.

"This has nothing to do with that."

"Maybe not directly, but—"

"Nothing to do with her, Sarah."

Her sigh scratches through the line. Stupidly and for no other reason than comfort, he wants to feel her body release that sigh. He wants to feel her ribs fall in as the air comes out. He wants to feel her skin on his fingertips. He wants to tell her yes, he is still missing Emma.

"So you won't help," he says instead. After a moment he adds, "This call is going to be pretty pricey. I'd better get going."

"Take care of yourself, okay?"

"Yep. You too."

"Bye Henry."

"Bye."

Henry places the receiver back on its cradle and stares at the phone, hates its dilapidated state, the ugly plastic, the bulkiness. Barely functional.

*

She still figures prominently in his dreams. In his dreams Sarah's mouth is always there, twisted into a smile or a moist pout, punctuating her small daily thrills and disappointments.

Also her lipstick and her deodorant, her clutch purses and her long, smooth hands that grasp them. Her elaborate, lacy lingerie and her body that fills it. Her belly when it was flat and her belly when it was round and tight like a drum. Everything sweet and succulent, red and spicy. Almost everything he is missing here exists in abundance in his dreams.

He had heard that dreams were chemically altered by the antimalarial tablet, Larium; it rendered them surreal, or perhaps just more real. So many ex-pats complained about their dreams here, their Larium Dreams—bright, neon-coloured, cartoonish versions of life. But what if it isn't the Larium? What if it is simply the contrast of the abundant neon past with this pale, austere present? Nothing works more powerfully than deficiency to bring his old life into garish relief. Henry has stopped taking the tablets, but his dreams remain alive, vivid beyond reckoning, and Sarah remains inside them, flicking her glossy red nails and wavy brown hair. Even Sarah's perfume is overpowering in the dreams.

But that quiet part of himself that watches it all from some far-off place knows more about how real she is, already suspects that all this sensory detail is an elaborate cover-up for something absent. Something that was never there in the first place. And he wakes up each morning reminded of why they never could have made it work, and why he is here in this dust-covered place of muted dirt and concrete, and she is there in that sped-up, bustling, loud, luxurious and confusing place that used to be his home.

*

When she arrives at work, Dr. Bryce is already there. He does not wear his lab coat. He does not have his stethoscope with him. And worse: he does not tend to patients. They watch him. They lie on their cots, propped up on their elbows, and look on with faces shiny with sweat. The doctor crouches in a corner of the ward, rummages through equipment of some kind. He pulls out a roller then starts rolling it back and forth in the tray on the ground. He is painting. The doctor is painting the walls. This trip to Mulanje Mountain is showing itself—the seeds of the doctor's undoing have been planted. He is forgetting who he is. Iris scans the faces in the ward as they watch him roll the roller on the tray, then roll the paint onto the wall. It is there behind the eyes, behind the tall arches of the cheekbones and the drawn, flat mouths. It is there: the fear. They all know how easy it is for evil to take root. Even here, in this white man's hospital, with the wooden cross affixed to the wall on the far end of the ward. She can see it now, hanging there under a thick blanket of dust. It is useless against the forces that roam here.

Dr. Bryce puts down the paint roller and stands up and stretches a long, satisfied stretch involving all the long muscles of his body. This is when he sees her, adrift among the beds, watching him. He smiles at her. A large, happy smile that she has never before seen break his face. The smile makes the red-gold beard glint in the early morning sunlight that now enters through an open window. Remarkable how those wiry strands can gleam. These white men, their brightness, their skin and hair that can catch light and then recklessly throw it back to the world; they are almost sources of light themselves, a blinding brightness wherever they go. She, Iris, swallows the light. Hoards it. It comes out in stingy flashes and only through her eyes.

"Do you like it?"

Dr. Bryce is talking to her, asking her something and gesturing to the wall behind him, where fresh paint lights up one small corner of the ward. As the sun enters the ward through the window, it makes the painted corner absurdly bright. The smell is strong; she can see some patients lying down with their blankets pulled over their noses.

"The paint?"

"Yes. The colour. Do you like it?"

Iris looks at the wall. The paint has been rolled on neatly, one smooth, thick line beside another. The colour is yellow. Unorthodox and impractical. Ridiculous, really, for a hospital ward.

"It's yellow."

"Yellow ochre," he says, still smiling. "I thought it looked like the savannah. It reminds me of it." He gestures to the window and Iris follows his arm, her eyes searching for the yellow somewhere out there, but all she can see is the red-brown earth of the courtyard with the occasional straw-like strand of grass pushing its way through. These strands are yellow, she acknowledges. Perhaps farther out from the city, where the grass has not been trampled to extinction by thousands of feet, perhaps there the grass grows long and thick enough to be seen, and appreciated. She has not been to the country since she was a child. She grew up there, in a village by the mountain, and although she does not remember much of her life there, she misses it. And for this reason, she smiles.

"Yes." She says. "I like it."

Now each morning, Dr. Bryce comes to the hospital early, well before the sun begins to brighten the sky near the horizon, and paints. He cleans up his supplies when the first sunbeam enters the ward. Then he puts on his lab coat, places his stethoscope in its usual place around his neck, and begins his rounds. The other doctors observe Dr. Bryce with flat, grim expressions. The surgeon, Dr. Ellison, the paediatrician, Dr. Campbell, the internist, Dr. Kumwembe. They come into the ward with their hands deep in their pockets, or tugging on the ends of their stethoscopes that hang around their necks. They scan the ward, look over the rows of beds to the walls that are gradually being transformed, the flat grey replaced with the colour of straw. They finger their beards, they scratch their scalps, and then they go.

*

"You've taken on a new hobby, I see," says Kumwembe during another of their lunchtime conversations.

"Yes." Henry digs into his rice, forces it down in large, soft, salty balls. He eyes the *nsima* that Kumwembe dips into the sauce of his chicken and runs around his plate, absorbing the juices and odds and ends of food before he pushes it into his mouth. He has never been offered *nsima* when he brings his tray to the cook in the small hospital canteen who takes a quick, surmising look at him before heaping his plate with the usual white rice and chicken leg. He would like to try it, but doesn't know how to ask. He shovels up another forkful of the rice, but then leaves it on the plate. "I thought it would cheer the place up," he offers this to the silence, to the appraising look of Kumwembe.

"Cheer it up."

"Yes."

"It needed cheering, then."

"Most hospitals do."

Kumwembe dips his fingertips in the metal bowl of water beside his plate. Grease shines on the surface of the water, picks up the light in oily rainbow circles. He presses his hands on his napkin then brings his fingertips to a peak in front of his mouth, leans in closer to Henry, a co-conspirator.

"And you?" he says. "Do you need cheering up? Are you, perhaps, a little down?"

Henry looks at his food—half a plateful. He hates waste, especially here, and so lifts another forkful to his mouth, then plucks away some meat from the chicken bone.

"No. I am not depressed."

"A little homesick, then?"

Henry sighs. "Yes. Sure. A little homesick."

Kumwembe moves the peak made by his fingers down from his mouth, places it on the table in front of him. His fingers now form an arrowhead that points at Henry, directed at his gut, where the truth lies. "Do you like it here? Do you wish to stay?"

Henry stares at the hands, at the fingers, pale on the palms and under the nails, dark brown on the dorsum. "Yes. And yes." He looks up at Kumwembe. "Is this some sort of interview? Are you going to report back to a committee? Are you going to recommend that I return to Canada?"

"Dr. Bryce," he says, quietly. "You think too much, my good man. Stop thinking and you will find yourself to be much happier."

He looks at Henry for a moment, and when Henry does not reply, he says, "Come on, then. What else do you think needs improvement?"

Henry decides that Kumwembe is not mocking him and starts to describe the things that disturb him the most. The unnecessarily neglected things, the things that would be easy to improve, with little cost. Like painting the walls or cleaning the floor and latrines. Lobbying for a few more blankets. Kumwembe listens, watches Henry's face. He nods as he speaks. And then, quietly when Henry is finished, states: "Dr. Bryce, I will not help you. But I will not stop you."

Henry returns his attention to his place, chooses not to think about Kumwembe's words. For now, he can do as he likes. This is what he decides to hear.

Chapter 6

Iris squats down in front of the cook pot. When the water is near to boiling, she sprinkles in cornmeal from the bag beside her and stirs—the trick is to be quick. This way it will not clot. She feels her mother watching, judging to this day her skill in the kitchen. As she stirs, Iris looks at the bag of cornmeal. It is a bulky white ten kilogram sack with blue writing on it. The writing says in English that it was made in Lusaka.

A tall clay pot, used together with a long wooden post. This is something plumbed from the caverns of memory. The women of Mapiri, her childhood village, standing, heaving the post, grinding it into the pot, pounding the maize in the pot until it had the same consistency of the meal in the bag beside her. As a child, Iris watched them do this as she squatted nearby with her sisters and they pretended to pound their own maize.

Her mother's legs are stretched out and her bare feet, pale and dry on the bottoms, obscure part of her mother's face from this vantage point. Her mother leans her head back against the wall of their home, and closes her eyes.

She addresses her mother in Chichewa.

"Do you miss home, Mama?"

"This is home."

"You know what I mean. The village. The mountain."

Iris's mother lifts her head and regards her daughter. "Life is better here," she says, before resting her head again and closing her eyes.

This is as far as the conversation usually goes with her mother. She will never admit that moving to the city was a mistake, or even that she misses her ancestral home. She will insist, until death, that moving here brought them only good fortune. "You are Educated now, Iris," she will usually remind her, as if she doesn't know this. "You have an Education. You work in the hospital, alongside doctors, amongst the bright and honourable minds of this country."

And where did this get her? Cooking *nsima* over a cook fire in the dirt behind her home, just as she would be doing if they lived in the village, preparing lunch. No different. In fact, worse. Because she is alone. Without a husband to share her bed with. Without children for her to care for. Instead she is charged with caring for the thousands of ill that stumble through the dark corridors of the hospital, day after day, year after year. No one wants an Educated woman.

Evil drove them from the village, as her mother tells it. They ran from *matsenga*, hoping that the sorcery wasn't quick or agile enough to keep up with the bus that took them here to Blantyre after all the terrible things happened. It was after the baby was lost that her mother decided enough was enough. She packed up the rest of the family and brought them all here.

But this is how it began. Her uncle came up the path to their home, his face broken into a thousand weeping faces, spilling a million tears, her father's blood on his shirt. Her mother rushed to the accident, just over a mile from their village. Iris and her sisters and brother hadn't been allowed to go; the arms of their relatives had enclosed them and ushered them back to their hut.

A white man from the city was driving the car, heading toward the mountain. He had swerved to avoid a flock of chickens. Chickens! (His mother had stuck on this; it kept her up at night for years afterwards). The man swerved to avoid a flock of chickens and killed her father instead. There was some talk afterwards, amongst the men. Money had been exchanged. And that was it. The men took the money and returned to the village. The white man returned to his car and drove off.

Samuel was next. Her brother fell and broke his arm. He fell from a baobab tree, from a branch he'd easily climbed to for years. There was no outreach medical clinic; the resetting and bandaging was done by the *sing'anga*. His arm recovered, but remains misshapen. When he removes his shirt now, there is a bone that juts out strangely, and Iris has seen her mother stare at it, as though confronting the forces that created it. Then she usually turns away and puts her mouth in a determined line, full of certainty that she did the right thing all those years ago by bringing them here.

And then Grace. Their father's favourite. One year older than Iris, and prettier. Large, oval eyes that were golden brown. She'd looked like their mother, a spitting image. Grace was stricken by illness: shaking, chattering under her blankets in the darkness of the hut, in the oven heat of their home, while the sun beat down on the roof. Her eyes hollowed out, her cheeks collapsed in. She remembers how her sister stared past her, to something in the corner of the hut, something distasteful by the twist of her sister's mouth and the harshness of her eyes, but something she had resigned herself to by the way she closed her eyes to it, ready for what it would bring, or take away.

Fever, rigors, nausea, vomiting, diarrhea. Now, as a nurse, Iris knows these are all the signs of malaria. If they had lived here in Blantyre, she could have been treated, maybe even saved. An intravenous line with essential fluids and electrolytes. Antimalarial medication. All the rituals, incantations, all the rubbings on her skin, the protective lines of yellow and red and the black blood of sacrifice slick on the floor. And all the Christian prayers that her mother muttered, while the village healers did their work. None of this chased away whatever was in the corner, what Grace saw. Unafraid, it hunkered down and waited. And then it took her.

And when, a few weeks later, Iris's mother's belly bloomed again, there was something dull in her mother's eyes. It was as though she expected the next lurching stab at her family. And when it came, when her mother's stomach became flaccid like a punched-out balloon and her mother was not holding a baby, even six-year-old Iris felt the deep chill of terror. The baby, she was told, had joined her father and her sister, Grace. *Matsenga*, they said, and Iris remembers not wanting to be alone, not wanting to be the next worm on the hook for those nameless, shapeless things circling the village, circling close in on her family.

Even now, almost 25 years later, Iris feels her skin prickle with the memory. Feels the lurch in her chest, as though something has wrapped its hands around her heart and now pulls at her in short, sharp tugs, letting her know they have not been forgotten, letting her know that running to the city will not be enough to hide.

Iris looks over at her mother. Her eyes are still closed. She is not well. Her mother does less each day, does each task more slowly. She coughs with a weak effort, swallowing down whatever she has brought up. She is losing weight. Every time Iris looks at her, there are more bones showing; her collarbones push up through her skin, the sinews of her hands and arms are strung tight. She will not go to see a doctor.

The *nsima* is thick now, and smooth. It must be served hot, so Iris spoons it out quickly onto a plate, beside the relish that has already been prepared. She picks up the plate and brings it, with a bowl of clean water, to her mother. Her mother, sensing her standing there in front of her, opens her eyes and smiles.

She dips her hands into the water to clean them and then picks up a small piece of *nsima* dipped in the relish. Iris settles down beside her mother and looks out at the view from their back porch. Here, on the borders of Blantyre, their house is made of concrete with a wobbly corrugated zinc roof, squashed in with a hundred others. In the village it would have been mud with a grass roof. The view would have been of a stick fence, and over it, Mulanje Mountain framed in blue sky. Their yard would have been bigger. Here, it was a few square feet, bordered by mud walls with a sea of rubbish beyond them.

"Is that crazy white doctor still painting the walls?"

Iris is startled by her mother's voice. It is stronger today than usual. She looks over at her; she has barely touched her food. Her mother is staring at the cook fire that smoulders before them, the smoke rising up through the hole in the roof, then pulled sideways by the wind.

Iris looks down at her own hands. There is a thin layer of yellow paint buried in the groove between one of her fingernails and her skin, which she scratches at with another nail.

She hides her hands in her lap. "Yes. He's moved on to the hallways, now."

Her mother shakes her head. "Crazy man," she mutters. "Why isn't he using his God-given skill to save lives?"

"You wouldn't let him save yours." Iris flakes off the last of the paint from her nail. Her mother is silent, which means that it is true.

"Some people want that type of medicine," her mother says, finally. "Some people like it. Some like their pills and procedures."

And yet. The pride in her eyes, when she speaks of her daughter, the nurse. She worked and worked and did unmentionable things to pay Iris's school fees. This alone created a guilt so insurmountable that Iris could only follow through and get her diploma.

"Knowledge," her mother has said to Iris, "will give you power. So you can fight with equal weapons, when the time comes." What time? Iris wonders. What are they waiting for? Who are they going to fight? She feels as though this is what they have been doing for years, ever since they left their village: waiting. It has been steadily draining all of them of their energy, all these years of anxious expectation. They have so little fight left in them, that if the time comes, they will only be able to lie down and succumb.

Her sister Hope is married and pregnant with her fifth child. One child per year since becoming a wife. She lives in a fine house with a living room and a couch and beds and a toilet because she is married to a lawyer. A mean lawyer, though, with narrow eyes and a powerful fist when he is drunk. And he has not shied away from using it on her sister. Yet her sister stays. For her mother. They all do it for their mother, who did it for them, once.

Whenever she visits her brother Samuel who tends bar in the city, she thinks of what her mother did for them. Her brother pushes Carlsberg bottles across the tables to his customers who never raise their eyes above the tops of the bottles of beer, or the cleavage of the women who sit beside them in too-small shirts, who take suggestive sips from the bottlenecks with moist lips, allow themselves to be fondled.

It began to happen soon after they arrived in Blantyre. The late-night trips out of the house into the dark folds of a strange city. The children were left under the watch of an ageing female neighbour who understood what needed to be done. What other options were there for a young widowed mother with three hungry children?

As children they did not understand, crouching together in the house around the kerosene lantern their mother allowed them to burn in her absence. Their faces twisted up as they whispered to each other. She's already forgotten Papa. How could she forget him so soon? Occasionally, during the night, there would be a quiet knock at the door, a low, masculine voice murmuring her mother's name. And her mother would get up off the mat, shuffle over to the door and shoo him away, whispering through the crack of the door, fed up, tired.

Eventually, Iris's mother found a job sorting laundry at the hospital, and this is where the idea struck her, that Iris should become a nurse. Why was Iris charged with this responsibility? Perhaps because she was the oldest, the most serious, did the best in her studies, was the least likely to marry. She had none of her mother's remarkable features: the light brown eyes, the long nose, the wide, full lips, breasts and buttocks. Both of her sisters and even her brother had some of these features: physical proof that they were all of the same stock. Iris was her father. Down to his dark and deep-set eyes, his serious brow, and his quiet, stubborn intelligence. Perfectly suited for a serious job like nursing.

Iris reaches over and places her hand over the bones and sinews of her mother's hand. She squeezes it gently. "You should eat, Mama. It's getting cold."

Chapter 7

Henry arrives at the hospital while most are still asleep. He enters the office, finds it empty and is mildly disappointed in this. After he hangs his backpack over his lab coat, he leaves the office and makes his way down the dark hallway to one of the smaller wards, to where he had been painting the previous morning. As he navigates the hallway, he sees a figure in a stiff, A-line dress approaching from the opposite direction. She comes closer and he sees her shape and posture, hears the way her feet fall with a sound that is both proud and angry. He knows it is Iris. "Doctor," she murmurs in greeting as they pass each other. She looks down as they pass. "Good morning, Sister Iris." He says this to her although it is not really morning; it is still a long way till sunrise. But he feels as if he needs to share a normal greeting, to make this encounter in the dark, late hours of the night less strange.

When he reaches the ward that has been partially painted, he sees that some of the walls are wet and the supplies have been recently cleaned. He stands in the room of slumbering bodies and smells the wet paint. This has been happening sporadically. Walls painted in his absence.

So the nocturnal painter is Iris. Iris, who fixes him with such a stern stare, who watches his patient-care decisions with undisguised disapproval, who often takes pains to avoid his presence altogether when they share care of the ward. It is she who is spending the quiet hours of her overnight shifts painting the walls. He has suspected this for some time but has tried to ignore the clues.

Despite his certainty that it is her, he has yet to say anything to her, or to thank her. He takes care to arrive at the same time each morning, so as not to catch her in the act. He looks away when she surreptitiously rubs a bit of paint off her hand or arm. He prefers the secrecy and the cleanliness of the silence by which they go about their tasks toward a common goal. He senses a fragile burgeoning friendship somewhere in the vacuum of their interactions, which makes him cautious and anxious; he doesn't want to risk acknowledging it, he doesn't want to risk trampling it with his clumsiness, his large awkward ways.

But perhaps he is just imagining it, this fresh green bud of friendship. Perhaps it is just a common desire, a silent pact to improve the conditions for these patients. Nothing more than that.

Today he enters the ward, nods to her sitting there at the desk, puts some new blankets on the desk in front of her, and leaves the office to begin painting. As he turns away and leaves the room, he senses her reaching toward the three new blankets sitting folded on the desk, feeling the coarse cotton, knowing what to do with them.

Henry moves his painting supplies to the TB ward. He has finished the corridor now. It glows in the early light as though the walls are lit from within. A few hospital staff shuffle down the corridor past him, blink in the brightness of it, having emerged from a shadowy room, their eyes adjusting in sharp spears of pain. They eye his tray, roller, and paint can dubiously, give him a wide berth. He enters the TB ward where patients lie in still bundles in the semi-darkness. As he sets up, he hears an exchange of rooster crows from beyond the windows and some patients begin to shift in their cots. A few heads lift up from the beds and spot Henry, track him as he moves in the shadows. They have no doubt heard about the painting doctor and now here he is, about to leave his mark on their ward.

Henry opens the can of yellow paint and breathes in the familiar smell. He welcomes it as he stirs the paint with a wooden stick. It is the clean smell of change.

When he reaches for a patient's wrist to take a pulse in the same ward a few hours later, the patient looks away, twists his arm deftly out of Henry's grasp. When Henry reaches for him again, the man releases a shout: a short, sharp burst of warning. Henry stands in front of him, puzzled. He looks across the ward and there is Iris, watching. She sighs heavily; he can see her chest rise and fall from here, so many beds away. She weaves toward him between the beds like a boat tacking toward the shore. When Iris stands beside him, he reaches once more for the patient's arm and again it is pulled from his grasp. The man, sitting heavily on his cot, looks down at Henry's feet. Iris speaks in brisk Chichewa; Henry can hear the no-nonsense tone in her voice. The man mumbles a reply and then lies down on his bed, pulls his sheet over top of himself in a weak attempt to cover up, to hide. Iris translates:

"He's afraid of you." Right now, Henry is grateful for her matter-of-factness, her inability to mince words.

"Afraid."

"Yes."

"Why."

"He thinks you are an impostor. He thinks you are not a real doctor."

Henry says nothing but lifts the bell of his stethoscope up and stares at it as though it will speak on his behalf.

"Because you paint the walls. This is why he worries."

Henry says nothing still, then reaches for the man's wrist again. This time the patient does not pull away, but stares darkly at Henry as he allows the touch, he allows the press of the doctor's stethoscope to his chest while he takes quick and shallow breaths.

"Tell him what he needs to hear," Henry mutters and then listens as the man's breath slows while Iris speaks.

*

There are the sounds again. The funeral wails, the ululations—rising, falling, rising. Like the waves of grief itself. But only the women. Why only the women? Why can't the men participate, shed their grief along with their women? Perhaps they can, perhaps they do somewhere else, in some other way. Their job here in the hospital seems to be to disappear, and to allow their women to grieve unrepressed.

Henry presses himself against the wall as the gurney, pushed solemnly by the men and followed by the crowd of wailing women, moves past him down the hallway. The body—long and narrow under the sheet—has been draped as usual, with a white sheet emblazoned with a red cross. He wonders if it is one of his.

Henry's first experience with death was on the medical wards. "Check the pupils for reactivity," the senior medical resident had said, yawning, for it was 4 AM when he received his lesson in pronouncing death. "Feel for a pulse in a big artery, like the carotid. Auscultate for breaths and for heart sounds." She'd turned to face him then, away from the body on the bed whose mouth still gaped open, whose eyes were not quite closed. "It's all a silly formality, making us do this. The nurses know perfectly well when a patient is dead." And then she'd led him out of the room. Following her out, he had brushed open the curtain that divided the dead patient's bed from her roommate. The woman stared back at him from her pillow with an expression he has ever since tried to forget.

He didn't know then what loss feels like.

Now he knows that loss is having the lower half of his lungs fill with something thick and immoveable so he can never again take a satisfying breath. He wanted to do all sorts of things when Emma died: throw himself down on the ground. Pound his fists. Scream until his throat ached. Release the violence.

But he kept silent.

Here where he stands pressed up against the wall long after the gurney has passed, silence makes no sense. You have to make noise, you have to yell and complain. You have to be outraged. Your voice has to follow the soul, up and up and up. And as he watches the procession disappear around the corner the women's wails echo even more, reiterated by the corners, the long halls, the maze of this place that contributes to the fury. Yes, he thinks. Make noise. Make it matter.

*

Henry is stretching up, reaching the highest recesses of the walls with his roller on an extension pole, when Ellison comes into the TB ward. He stands behind Henry for a few minutes and watches him. Then he clears his throat and shifts noisily. Henry turns around, sees him, and smiles. "Hey there," he says.

Ellison nods. Tilts his head toward the hallway. "Can we chat?"

Henry wraps up his tools and follows Ellison's broad shoulders out of the ward and into the hall. Ellison stands off to the side, touches a hand to the wall, and then leans up against the yellow. "You've been hard at work," he says, folding his arms across his chest.

"Yes. No more dingy grey." Henry looks down at his hands that are chafed and calloused. The sight of them pleases him. He adds, "There were years of grime on the those walls. Nice to cover it up, start fresh."

Ellison looks down the hall. "I'll bet," he says. He shifts position, shoves his hands in his trouser pockets. "Listen. I've been asked to share some concerns with you. About all this." He waves a hand out, gesturing vaguely around them. "What is all this, mate?"

"I'm just doing what should have been done years ago."

"Well, that may be, but… " Ellison pauses then continues. "We're just not sure what you're trying to do here. You're trained as a physician, not an interior decorator, for Chrissake."

"I'm just trying to improve the lot for these people," says Henry, "by doing whatever it takes."

"Well, frankly, it's bizarre. And you're scaring the patients."

"Scaring them?" Henry thinks of the patient who pulled away.

Ellison sighs. "They think you're lost. They think the real you's been kidnapped and an impostor is in your place. Or worse—that you're possessed. They're nervous to be treated by a man who's only pretending to be a doctor. And who can blame them? To be honest, I'm starting to wonder myself."

"It's cleaner now. Less dark. Less depressing."

"I'd hazard a guess that it being depressing here has nothing to do with what colour the wall is. C'mon, man. Think. When you come in here fighting for your life, does it matter whether you're staring at a yellow wall, or a grey one? It could be purple, for Chrissake. You're dying. And maybe, just maybe, one of these white guys will drop his paintbrush and turn around and help you."

Henry studies Ellison's implacable face. "Have you noticed the new supplies coming in? I've managed to convince a few organizations to be more generous with us. More drugs, blankets, gloves."

Ellison twists his mouth. "That's great, mate. But again: not your job." He sweeps his hand around again. "You're not God, Bryce. You're not here to wave a wand and—ta-da! A whole new, better place. One thing at a time, man. One thing at a time. Focus on what you're best at. What you're trained to do. This," he gestures to the yellow wall, "is a waste of your very expensive education."

Ellison places a large, warm hand on Henry's shoulder.

"Let's head back to the ward, eh? Painting smock off, lab coat on. Let's try to help these poor sods. Get them better." He steers Henry down along the hall and Henry walks.

*

Henry's mother often brought him to her workplace after picking him up from school. He would follow her down elevator shafts and through long corridors all the way to her subterranean lab. She was a medical pathologist and her lab smelled of harsh things. A pungent, eye-stinging smell of formalin and other fixatives. She never showed him a body. She showed him parts, though. Tiny slices of flesh, frozen then carved by a delicate knife into transparent slivers one cell thick. Human tissue viewed under the microscope was beautiful—cotton-candy swirls of pink studded with blue and purple gems. Like a painting. He would have liked to enlarge them, frame them and hang them on his wall they were that beautiful. They were slices of a secret life.

Down in his mother's lab, he learned all about this microscopic universe of hustle and bustle, how well mannered and coordinated it all was, each cell doggedly contributing, pumping out messages, receiving others, obeying instructions. All these were acts of pure altruism, down to the cell's own programmed death. This cellular world was a sliver of nirvana, each single act in harmony with every other.

It was his mother's job to look for war deep down in the tissue. And she found it. Rogue cells which as a boy he imagined as pirates. His eyelashes brushed against the lenses of the microscope while she told him what he was looking at. The idea of such a tiny battlefield frightened him. Pirates, hiding in the body. Lawless and brutal. Greedy and mercenary. They slashed through the nirvana, ruthlessly sought immortality. They refused to die. And in this Peter Pan quest, they brought the whole organism to its knees.

Under the microscope they looked disturbed; somehow their gluttony was visible through the magnified lens—their cytoplasm bloated, their mitochondria crooked. They even took more stain; they soaked up the pigment like blood. These were the cells that ballooned into a tumefied, disorganized mass, or they attacked their own trusting neighbours.

Even as a child he could pick out the slides that contained pathology: the swirling pink slashed and pockmarked, the chaotic spill of purple-celled armies, row upon threatening row of them all squinting their single-nucleus eyes and turning them on the pink cells bleeding cytoplasm, the red cells punctured and deflated and eviscerating, the ferrous stain of waste and cellular rubble. Henry gripped the microscope with small cold hands and stared down at these scenes.

He would lie in bed after coming home from his mother's lab, close his eyes and see that advancing army and wonder if there was a dissenter in his own ranks, waiting quietly in an organ, plotting an uprising. An irrational seed.

Chapter 8

Henry feels a tug on his sleeve. He looks down and sees a boy—short, dark, slender—staring up at him with an urgency he doesn't often see in this place. It is the urgency, not the boy delivering it, that catches his attention.

"Yes? What is it?" He tries—albeit a weak effort—to hide his impatience. He bothers less and less these days with hiding this sort of thing.

The boy stammers but manages to get out that there is a very sick patient in another ward.

"Where?"

"This way, Doctor." The boy limps off and Henry follows. The nurse whom he abandons in the middle of the ward watches them leave, not a smudge of curiosity on her face.

Henry hears the patient as he turns the corner into the ward. The woman —young—another one too damn young—breathes as though underwater. She is surrounded by the usual mass of sick patients, no hospital staff. The boy points needlessly to the patient in trouble, then bows his head and ducks out of the ward. Henry mutters, "Need a crash cart." As though there were one to retrieve. He scans the room anyway, hoping to see its familiar red bulk. Nothing. He represses the urge to say, "Call a code blue" to the space where there should be people—nurses and other doctors—milling, trying to organize their rising panic into something productive. He moves over to the patient. He grabs her arm—slippery with sweat—feels for a radial pulse, then reaches for the shallow groove in her neck and under her jaw where the carotid pulse should be, then shoves aside a wet sheet to feel in her groin for the femoral pulse. Nothing. Pulseless. Fingers cold, nail beds blue. The woman's underwater breathing sounds have stopped. When did they stop? Couldn't have been more than a minute ago.

Feeling a rising energy and nowhere for it to go, he crosses his hands over the woman's sternum and plunges down. Pump. Pump. Pump. There is a nurse—over by the clean utilities. "Get me some oxygen, and an endotracheal tube—#7, and a laryngoscope. A clean one." He hears his voice—hoarse, tight with the excitement of this attack on impending death. Crack. Crack. The ribs break beneath his hands as he compresses again. Pump. Pump. Pump. He stops for a moment to feel for a pulse. Nothing. He grabs the oxygen mask from the nurse, fits it over the woman's mouth, pulls her jaw forward, opens the valve on the tank. "Continue the CPR," he says to the nurse and she stares at the woman's chest, puts her hands over her sternum and leans forward, unsure. Henry moves the mask aside and picks up the laryngoscope. He snaps open the blade, tilts the woman's head back, slides the blade into her mouth and uses it to push the bulk of her tongue over. The light shines down on her tonsils, then on her esophagus, then on the reedy, white triangle of her larynx. He passes the thick plastic endotracheal tube through it and into her trachea, removes the laryngoscope, and attaches the oxygen supply to the blunt end of the tube that now sticks out of the woman's mouth. He compresses the black bag, squeezes some air into the tube. The woman's chest rises with each compression.

Henry looks at the nurse—Maria, he thinks her name is. "Let's take her to the ICU."

Euphoria moves through him like a current of energy. He has been shaken awake. He forgot how it feels. He looks over at Maria and she smiles back—shy, tentative. They transfer the patient to a gurney and then push the gurney, weave it squeaking through the beds, run it along the hallway. They rush. People shuffle out of their way. Orderlies hold open doors. They ride this tide of urgency and it carries them all the way to the intensive care unit.

*

Jakob tells his mother later about the woman that he saw in the ward he was cleaning, how he had noticed her struggling with her breath, and how no one else seemed to notice, or didn't care. And he knew she was going to die. He told her how he ran over to another ward and summoned Dr. Bryce. And then how Dr. Bryce did some wonderful things and saved her all by himself.

His mother listens to the story. He waits for her smile, for pride to break through her face like it used to do for lesser accomplishments. Instead she clicks her tongue and turns away. "This isn't right, Jakob," she says. "You are toying with God's plans. God organized this woman to be alone in that ward. You meddled."

"But Ma. She wasn't alone. Nurses were there. And they looked away. They left her."

"They are Sisters. And they knew God's plans." His mother fumbles for his hand. And weak as she is, she manages to clutch him hard. "You are *aliyense* to me, Jakob, but you can't be *aliyense* to everyone. Only God is that." She crosses herself, says nothing more. So Jakob gets up off her bed and returns to his work. Despite his mother's words, he feels that this job, his world here at the hospital is growing out and filling in like a lush green garden. Each day feels bigger, more elaborate and robust, more like the future he had imagined this place would bring.

*

Jakob moves his mop beneath the bed. An enormous clot of dust comes back with the wet strings. Also insect carcasses and plastic wrappers. An empty syringe. He lifts the mop with the debris clinging to it over to the pail and dunks it in. He presses the mop into the wringer and squeezes the water out. The trickle of water into the pail disappears into the other sounds in the room: the repetitive hiss of the breathing machine, the regular beep which is accompanied by a green dance of light on the screen above the bed: the patient's heartbeat, represented in sounds and patterns, so that the nurse at the desk on the other side of the room need only raise her eyes to confirm that the patient's heartbeat has slowed down or sped up or stopped.

The woman whom Dr. Bryce saved lies in this bed. There have been a parade of visitors into this room: a husband, parents, aunts, uncles, children—six of them ranging from toddler to teen, two of them still taking from the breast. They all come to the bedside, touch her hand or arm, then recoil as though surprised to find her skin warm. They watch her chest rise and fall with the bellows beside her bed. They study the clear tape that holds her eyelids closed, how her lashes are pressed down and fan out over her cheeks. They stare at the circles of milk that darken the sheets over her breasts. They frown at her hands because they look different, swollen with the fluid that snakes into her from plastic pouches that hang over her like pregnant flags. Through all this their faces are flat, but Jakob knows what they are thinking. They are wondering if they should mourn. The children know, though. The children cry while the adults stand respectfully aside.

*

"We should pull the plug."

This is Dr. Ellison, the one who took Jakob's mother's foot. The two doctors—Dr. Bryce and Dr. Ellison—stand beside the bed of this woman in the ICU. It is a one-bed ICU. There is only one machine to give breath, only one machine to watch the heartbeat, to record the pulse, to measure the oxygen in her blood.

Dr. Bryce just stares at the green pattern moving on the screen above her. It is a regular pattern of peaks and waves that repeats itself over and over again. Jakob finds it comforting. The nurse sitting at the desk in the corner—Neva—glares at him; he has not managed to coax a smile out of her, not even with the biscuits he brought her from the doctor's lounge. He looks away and resumes his work organizing the supplies cupboard.

"Bryce. Listen. If we knew what it was, if we knew what to fix, it would be a different story. Have you seen her lungs? A mess. And she keeps coming back culture-negative."

"It's a simple pneumonia. She just needs time."

"You saw the x-ray. Total white-out. It's ARDS. And we don't have the resources."

Dr. Bryce uses the suction to suck up some liquid in the woman's throat, does not speak.

"What's her HIV status?"

"Negative."

Dr. Ellison purses his lips and frowns as though a ready excuse has been stolen from him.

"What if we need the ventilator? For something temporary, something reversible. Someone we could actually help."

" 'Actually.' " Dr. Bryce barks out an ugly laugh. "I've always hated that word."

"You know by now, Bryce, that practising medicine here has nothing to do with heroics. It's the exact opposite of heroics."

Jakob can hear the doctor's sigh across the room. He looks over. Dr. Bryce has placed a hand on the woman's swollen leg and stares down at it. He says, "What a fucking mess."

*

Jakob remembers as if it was yesterday, as if it was now: when they turned the machines off, the family was there. They stood too far away in an respectful huddle. Jakob can still see his own arms moving down then up, from box to shelf as he listened. He did it over and over; he must have filled two shelves with clean syringes. He can still hear the crinkle of the plastic wrapping, although he tried to be silent, he tried to be invisible. He felt as though it could have just as easily been his hand that pushed the button to turn off the breath machine.

He heard the bellows stop, half-compressed. Her lungs half-filled with air. And then he heard death arrive. Her delicate heartbeats—those dancing green lights—were stilled to a single line of sound. To hear aloud the very moment her heart stopped. To know her death in this way—broadcast through the room like this—such an angry sound. It should have been silent and mysterious and greater than a straight green line. It should have been a secret, passing between only the woman and God. It should have been allowed to be beautiful—as beautiful as birth.

The sound was turned off and the silence moved in.

The silence was thick and full of wanting—wanting her to move, wanting her chest to rise—but then the strong grieving women pushed it aside with their wails and when Jakob turned around, he could see that the women had finally closed the gap; they were hugging her body, grasping her arms, stroking her hair. The buckles on their grief had been unclasped.

But the children stood back. The children watched with empty faces and dry eyes and silent mouths.

Hands shaking, Jakob stood up and placed another package on the shelf. It slipped off and fell to the floor and he did not pick it up. He closed the cupboard and left the room. As he left he realized that he never learned the woman's name. And, not knowing her name, he didn't know how he would ever be able to apologize to her spirit for meddling. If it weren't for his intervention, she would never have been brought to the ICU and the doctor would never have said, with his hand on her leg and loud enough for her sleeping ears to hear: what a fucking mess.

Outside and behind the hospital, the men's laughter comes loud and raucous from around the corner. They are smoking and spitting and chewing tobacco leaves. They are scratching themselves and criticizing their boss and arguing about the nurses' bottoms, and who has the nicest. These are the real men of the hospital: they do all the heavy lifting and deal with terrible things like the corpses and the used-up needles, the body fluids and the blood-stained bandages. These are the men who can truly laugh—a full, belly-shaking laugh—and Jakob thinks it is because of their job, and how they must live in this sadness of the hospital full-time and how this is their only escape.

"Eh, here's the Robin Hood."

The men turn, smiling at him.

"Robin Hood—steal from the doctors to win over the nurses, eh? I've seen you pass them those biscuits."

The men break out in another chorus of laughs, this time at his expense. Jakob's face gets hot, but he doesn't really mind. Soon, he finds himself laughing along. Soon, he can't stop. His belly aches. His eyes are wet. He slaps his legs, pushes away the joking prods from the men.

And now, after laughing a real laugh that comes out of the exact place that his tears came earlier, he feels it again as he wipes dry the corners of his eyes: some sort of weightless peace that he tries not to hold on to. He knows this feeling is like a bird; the instant you try to catch it, it is gone in a flash of feathers.

*

Juma still smiles when Henry comes around. Still looks up with reverence. Points to the paint smears on Henry' hands and laughs out loud: a strange sound in the ward. When he laughs, it feels like the ward is empty.

Henry arrives at Juma's bedside one day to find a woman kneeling beside his bed. Her head rests on his abdomen, and she holds one of his hands. Henry stops a few feet away and looks over at Iris who pushes the cart silently behind him.

"His mother. She comes every day, usually when you are not here." Iris rearranges vials on her cart as she speaks. "She worries because he is not improving."

The woman lifts her head off her son and unfolds herself to stand beside Juma's bed. She maintains her grip on Juma's hand. Now standing stiffly, she directs her gaze to somewhere over Henry's right shoulder, something Iris used to do when she had to speak with him. He interprets it as evidence of disrespect, and dislike. Iris, thank God, no longer does this. She regards him directly with her hard gaze, and at least now she makes him feel like she wants to be here, working with him.

Juma's mother says something in Chichewa and Juma looks away. Iris steps a foot closer. "She asks why her son is getting worse. She says he is rotting in this bed. She says nothing is being done to help him."

The woman looks directly at Henry now, which means she is giving him an opportunity to prove himself. It is his job to reassure, and so he tries, knowing that, even though she will not understand the words, she will detect the real truth in the tone. He can see the look in her eye as he talks. He hears Iris translating his words behind him. Her tone is better, more solid and comforting, but it will not help.

Henry watches Juma's mother as she listens to Iris's translation. He looks at her face: intelligent, angry. Something has been destroyed in this culture, amongst this people. The injury has started here, and will become severe enough to affect them all. It is only a matter of time.

He has stopped speaking and Iris has stopped speaking and there is silence. And then Juma's mother speaks.

"She wants to take him to a traditional healer. She wants to take him out of the hospital." Iris says this quietly beside him. Juma looks at him calmly, knowing what he will say. Knowing Henry will rise up with the authoritative protection of a medical institution. Flash his badge of Western authority, spread a protective wing around his charge.

He looks at Juma and feels the exquisite pain of love overwhelm him. So unexpected, to feel it here. In this place. For this young boy. And here, right now, his love will be tested. My God, the resolve this will require, the mind- and heart-steeling resolve. He almost grinds his teeth with the effort of it.

"Take him to a healer. Take him home." And before the wound in Juma's eyes can infect him with doubt or regret, he moves on to the next patient.

"You don't know what it's like to lose a child." This is Iris's voice. She is speaking Juma's mother's words in his ear.

Even before Henry turns around to see her, he knows Juma's mother is shaking her fist. Not at him. At the world. At God.

He goes back to Juma's mother. He looks at her as one parent to another.

"Yes I do."

*

Henry can tell from across the ward that the new patient has meningitis. The arched back, the neck that is so rigid that the upper body pushes up off the gurney in a stiff bowstring. The struggle; God, the struggle that Henry can see from here, eight rows of beds away, the sweat and agony of it. A few months ago, this textbook scenario would have moved him; he would have felt his heart pound faster at the idea of seeing such a classic presentation. Because he would have known what to do. Lumbar puncture. Send the fluid off to the lab. Cover with broad spectrum antibiotics, cover every bug, just in case. Modify the antibiotics when the cultures came back. But here. But now. Something clenches tight inside him at the sight of the man, wheeled in fresh from the streets. He pushes the thought away. He pushes the thought behind him as he makes his way over to him. When he examines him, he tries not to look for evidence of HIV, and when he finds it—in this case, a small, blue patch of Kaposi's sarcoma on his right ankle—he tries to be surprised, he tries to muster some sympathy in the gaze that he exchanges with the woman who clutches the man's hand—his wife? his sister?—and she looks back at him briefly, with a flatness that says it all.

*

When Henry was choosing his field of practice he never considered his mother's work. Pathology. The pure dichotomy of that world depressed him. There, the truth was bared and unembellished. The impossible conflict of cellular wisdom and selfish genetics. It was much easier to float above this simple wisdom in the world of the whole organism where one could live by ideals so complicated they could never be proven wrong, or right. Here, one could set his sights on manipulating the unseen world so that blood pressure could be controlled and body fluids could be balanced, cholesterol could be measured, the risk of disease could be reduced. The considered and worthy goals of your typical doctor.

Now he understands his mother's choice. At least in her work there was peace. At least there was no sense of futility. There was no roller coaster of hope and disappointment. And there was quiet, deep in the stillness of those rooms. Peace and quiet. What we all want, ultimately.

*

Jakob had thought what Dr. Bryce had done for the woman in the ICU was a miracle. But what happened afterward—the warm body already emptied of the person it housed—was much less than a miracle. And somehow they all ended up paying for it, for interfering.

The button on the ventilator was a plastic square and it lit up with a dim red light when the machine was turned on and when it was turned off, the red light went out. It didn't seem right that this button—any button—was so direct a link to death. And Jakob is now sure that it wasn't. He is certain that in the last few days they had all fallen under the spell of a masterful hoax spun by the Western machines. Death did not happen with the press of this button after all. It happened that day in the ward while Dr. Bryce was pushing on her chest and making her body lift and fall, squeeze and expand, when her blood flowed only because Dr. Bryce forced it with his pushes, and air moved only because the machine insisted on it. That's when death happened, and all the rest that followed was just a story. An invented story about a life that had already passed.

*

"You'll get used to it."

These were the worst words Henry heard the first day he'd worked here. It was a pronouncement made by the pharmacist, a Dutch woman who has since left and gone back home to the Netherlands. She had said it in reply to his angry shock over the antibiotic supplies. "Only Penicillin." He'd said just before: "That's it? What do I do for a gram negative infection?" He'd asked this, thinking of the four or so patients right then in the ward who were harbouring this. And her answer had been: you'll get used to it.

The worst part about it was that it was true. He is used to it now. He doesn't even pause to consider his lack of choice. It doesn't even register as lack anymore, it's just the narrow confines of the space he is working within. Adaptation is the death of progress, he thinks. Getting used to something is the reverse of evolution, it is devolution, it is our undoing. Here he has adapted, and he no longer despises the system, or the lack. He doesn't need change anymore, and so will not force it. And things will stay the way they are.

Chapter 9

"Oh-oh-oh." Solomon, one of the orderlies, elbows Jakob. He speaks more quietly than his usual loud, boastful talk. "Over there, under the tree."

A few yards away in the shade of a tree, Dr. Bryce is eating a sandwich. His usual lunchtime ritual. But now the sandwich lies forgotten in his lap because he is looking at a boy who stands before him, just a few feet away. The boy is a few years younger than Jakob—maybe twelve or thirteen years old. Old enough to hold dangerous things, like the sharp-edged rocks he grips in both hands. And he is old enough to feel dangerous things—like anger, hurt, hate. All this Jakob can see in the boy's eyes.

And now, looking up at the boy, Dr. Bryce does the worst thing he can do: he smiles at him. But surely the doctor must see what he and Solomon can see all the way from here. He must see how fiercely the boy clenches the rocks, and his arms: how spring-like they are, two bows pulled taut. Surely he must see what the boy needs to do, where his anger must go.

The doctor doesn't know how it feels to have your rage answered with a smile.

Jakob now begins to feel the same anger; it burns in his throat and he feels his hands clench along with the boy's hands. He stares at the rocks and wills his own boiling energy into those hands, that they may release enough power to hit hard, strike bone, draw blood. The boy draws back one arm, the energy of so much hate tied up in a single, tight limb.

"Hey!"

All at once it is gone. With the shout, a flock of birds has lifted out of the tree and now dissolves into the blue sky. And the boy has released a rock but it only tumbles weakly to its target, rolling and then stopping a foot away from where Dr. Bryce sits. Solomon is walking over to the boy, gesturing angrily with his arms, telling the boy off. "He is a doctor, you stupid kid, a doctor!" He hears Solomon's words in Chichewa, aimed at the boy. Aimed also at him. Jakob looks down at his own clenched fists and opens them up, feels the cool air dry the sweat off his palms. It cools off his anger, too. It cools him down until all he feels is the low simmer of shame deep inside.

*

As Dr. Bryce approaches, as the wind swept by the doctor's long, white coat—stale, rotten from the wards—moves into him, Jakob turns away from him to the open window. He busies himself with the corner between the floor and the wall which he sweeps back and forth, moving the dirt here then there, until the doctor is long past. Then he turns and watches the doctor stride away. From here Jakob can study his posture, the way he holds his shoulders, the tautness of the muscles of his neck. Then Jakob lifts his shoulders the same way, feels the tension, feels it all the way up to his head where he imagines so much information is stored, information that he can use any which way he pleases: to remove pain or let it linger, to end disease or allow it to fester and progress, to ward off death or to invite it into a body where it can wiggle and worm its way into all the hidden areas, all the unseen secrets exposed in the moments before death moves in. He has seen this so many times now, when an orderly is called to shift another of death's many residences to the morgue, away from the searching eyes of the living. Jakob wants, like the doctor, to use what fills his head to make these sorts of decisions, to decide the fate of another. As it is, despite his head being filled with thoughts, ideas, plans, he cannot decide anyone's fate. Beyond whether he gets up in the morning off the pallet on the floor beside his mother's cot, whether he shows up for work or whether he gives up altogether, he cannot even decide his own.

And this is perhaps where it came from. That feeling that bound him, in that moment, to the boy under the tree. He knows the boy's need to shatter fate, to take control. The need to snatch just one decision from the doctor's hands. The need to be important. And the boy's actions stirred a wretched and bilious sense of injustice within Jakob. This doctor makes so many decisions—several decisions a minute, thousands an hour, a million a day, all affecting others—a flick of his fingers and a family grieves or does not. And he, Jakob, is left deciding nothing. He knows, logically, that it is not as simple as that. They were not all present at the table when the pie was cut. But he is beginning to understand that his own buried anger is what brought them here to the hospital, what saved his mother, what got him this job. The shame he felt that day has now been replaced with something harder, more adult and certain. He is done with being a boy. He is ready to take on the harsher things, the ugly things, and he is in the right place to do it.

*

Henry leans over the patient who has just been wheeled in. The man breathes with difficulty, and there are a lot of secretions: his lungs are wet, his mouth is wet, his skin is wet. He thinks it might be OP poisoning, just like the case he'd seen with Kumwembe when he first arrived. He is trying to wrap a blood pressure cuff around the man's arm and he is having little success so far—the arm is slippery and the man writhes. Henry feels a grip on his own arm now and the man's clutch is tight. Henry drops the cuff and works at prying the man's fingers off his forearm but they won't budge. The patient's gaze and hand are fixed on him and Henry is beginning to feel a rising panic. He looks at the man's bloodshot eyes and sees the boy, or rather what the boy had in him when he looked at Henry that day under the tree, which was hate. It was a hate that had a maturity about it, as though it had been fed a steady diet of something merciless that would enable it to flourish in the hidden recesses of the boy for years. Not just years, but lifetimes, generations, all of the depraved and deprived and depressed history—all this was packed into that boy's narrowed eyes. And here it is again seeping out of this man as he fixes him with that stare.

Henry plucks at the man's fingers uselessly, feels his own fingers grow numb. The man needs medical attention or he will die gripping Henry's arm and gripping Henry's mind with that look. And now the man is hissing something at him: "sss .. ayyy .. fff." It is drowned in all the saliva, he can't make it out. The man spits on the floor and repeats it: "Save my life."

Henry stops. For a moment, it is a threat, what he has said. Save my life or I'll take yours with mine. But then Henry sees what is in the man's eyes. It is not hate at all. It is fear. He says to the patient: "Yes, I will. I will." And the man lets go of him and closes his eyes.

Henry gets the blood pressure cuff on the man's arm now, and compresses the pump until the cuff is squeezing his arm tightly enough to stop the blood from flowing. The cuff deflates as he slowly releases the air and allows the blood to flow past the cuff and back into the man's hand, as he listens for his pulse to break through and thump in his ears. He looks at the red finger marks on his own arm and feels his own blood throb there as he listens to the rush through the patient's brachial artery.

They have the same pulse.

It is a shared beat of hope and fear, fear and hope. Two sides of the same coin. Emotions spent on possibility, never certainty. He wonders how many times he has confused them.

The man turned around remarkably fast. A single dose of atropine and the secretions stopped, the confusion improved and soon he was standing and walking and talking and the next day he left the hospital. Henry watched him go, his eyes now hardened again, the fear tucked back inside. He'd flashed Henry a quick look as he gathered his sandals before leaving the ward. Hate, or anger, or at least dislike.

Now Henry is finding it everywhere. What was in the boy's eyes has been appearing like a phantom, a flicker behind every other pair of eyes, buried beneath smiles and kind words. And it is there in the mirror when he is brushing his teeth, or splashing water on his face. His whole face is contorted with it.

Part II

There is a field

Chapter 10

Iris sits in the back seat of Dr. Ellison's car, along with a bag of medical equipment. They are on their way to the Mlela outreach clinic. Dr. Bryce sits in the passenger seat in front of her, and she can see the back of his neck, where his red-gold hair narrows to a soft, fuzzy peak that points downwards to his spine. She can see Dr. Ellison's hands as they casually grip the steering wheel. She can see Dr. Bryce's face, just a piece of it, in the side-view mirror. He is gazing out the window, his brow tight and dark.

Iris told her mother over dinner the night before they were to leave. She told her mother she was going to Mlela, that one of the doctors had asked for her. That she was needed to assist the doctors in their work. That to say no would be to turn away from her position as a carer, turn away from her Education, turn away an opportunity to help close to home. Maybe she would even be able to help people from their village. Imagine that! Helping their own villagers, their own family.

Her mother had squeezed her eyes closed. You won't come back, she said. You will be lost.

Iris left early the next morning while her mother lay curled up on her side of the mat, pretending to sleep.

She kissed her mother's shoulder and whispered *ndapita*. Goodbye.

Iris has imagined the reunion with her villagers many times. She imagines that when they appear, her head will be bent over a patient in the clinic, perhaps applying a bandage, and she will hear her name, pronounced in the thick tongue of her people, pronounced with amazement and joy. It will be a homecoming, with laughter and hugs, and she will finally feel that her longing, that constant hunger, is fed. No one will say anything about *matsenga*, or bad luck, they will only say that she has been dearly missed, that they, too, have dreamed of this reunion, that the village has been incomplete without her.

As Iris imagines this again, as she tries to conjure the faces of the people of her village in the shrubs and grass of the fields that float by beyond the window, she feels the car slow. Dr. Ellison gears down and jerks the car sideways, over to the edge of the road and half on the grass beside it. He pulls the car to a stop. Iris now sees the man—a local man but not a villager, a medical man—outside the vehicle, running alongside the road toward them, arms waving high above his head. Ellison cranks down his window and leans his arm and head out.

"There is a child," says the man as he comes up to the car. He leans on the car with both arms, heaves a few more breathes before continuing. "He fell and broke his leg. Very sick." He chops at his femur with the side of his hand. "Broken." He says. "Terrible."

Dr. Ellison, very calm, asks where he is.

The man has caught his breath and stands straight. He points down the road. Toward the late morning sun. "A mile or two further, then right on the first road you come to. In a village there. You will see."

Ellison nods again and says thank you. He rolls up his window and the man steps back. Thank you Dr. Ellison, he says as the window moves up, closes the gap. He wears a blue surgical cap, and a clean, white shirt. She wonders what he does at the clinic, what sorts of minor procedures does this man perform, what does he treat, what does he cure, how many ill does he see in a day? Someday she will run a clinic like this, near her village, saving her people from things that the *sing'anga* cannot. Then she is ashamed by her ambition.

Dr. Ellison turns to Dr. Bryce. "A fractured femur, from the sounds of it. If that's the case, we'll probably have to return to Blantyre." He starts the car and they move off the grass, back onto the road where they pick up speed and leave the man far behind.

Iris tries to stifle the disappointment that rises. It is no use and the tears come. Her dreams of reunion with her villagers dissolve in an instant; they were held together by mere threads of hope, anyway. Of the fifty or so villages near the clinic, what were the chances someone from her own village would seek western medical aid?

The road unwinds in front of the car. Grasslands stretch to the right and left, ahead and behind. There is a diagram in her nursing textbook that shows how an image passes through the lens of the eye and becomes inverted on the retina. Right now half of a blue sky illuminates the bottom of her retina, and the dry grasses brush overtop of it. Then it flips back upright as it passes deeper, into the rear of her brain where her visual cortex is coiled like layers of fat sausages. This swinging, spinning, half-blue, half-yellow image sweeps through her mind, brushing away the last 25 years, clearing the dust in her cortex, waking it up. A memory now shines as clear as the day it occurred—that final day in Mapiri. The day they left the village.

We are leaving.

Her mother came into the *khumbi* and said it. She was sweaty from carrying the water from the well. Two miles she had walked with so many litres of water balanced on her head. Her older sister Grace used to help her, carrying her own smaller jug. Then her mother went alone.

All the children were there when she said this. All looked up at her, not really understanding what leaving meant. This *khumbi*? They will have a new one? A bigger one, perhaps? A child's mind always leaps to the hopeful possibilities. It was her brother who asked: When?

Soon.

Just an hour later the group of them walked down the main path of the village. The whole of Mapiri village came to watch them leave.

During that walk her mother gripped her hand and her younger sister Hope's (her brother followed them carrying their only bag of belongings) and looked forward—proud and determined—like they were going toward something, not leaving anything behind. Iris spent most of the final walk out of Mapiri village looking at her mother, at the firm, half-smile on her face. And once they were through the field and on the long red road that would take them to their new home, her mother filled their heads with stories of their future. What they would do, where they would live, who they would meet. A wondrous life awaited them, just down the road, just around the next bend.

And now she has a thought: not new, it has lived in those coiled, fatty sausages of her cortex for years, just now setting off a string of neuronal firings to a sudden awareness, a truth. This new life was not a choice. Those faces, lined up along the path as they walked, they weren't the faces of well-wishers. And the way her mother held her head that day—stubborn—like a proud walk to the gaol. The village wanted her family to leave, and to take their darkness with them. Three consecutive deaths and an injury could only be a terrible sorcery. *Matsenga, matsenga.* How could she have forgotten the whispers, the accusations? Their village was stricken by evil, and the nest from which the darkness roamed was within her family. Of course this nest needed to be expelled, for the greater good, for the safety of the village.

Iris's eyes flick back and forth, back and forth they move across the landscape that flings by outside the vehicle. She is a spirit, fleeing at inhuman speeds through air. She flies past fields, past baobab trees with their heads buried in the earth, their feet frozen in the sky, past villagers swathed in *chitenjes*, balancing baskets of food or firewood or water on their heads, past flocks of chickens, stray dogs, goats and cattle. She, in the flesh and bone body she still inhabits, was not meant to return to this. The world out here, the village life, the life that engages with magic. Her villagers never meant for her to come back here, and the ritual that escorted them out of the village saw to that.

Iris dries her tears and stares out the window. It is more blurred now, a whirl of yellow. Like Dr. Bryce's walls. They are both trapped, she and the doctor, walls around them closing in.

Iris sees something out the window, miles beyond the glass that traps her. She moves back and forth, up and down to get a better view, to get the glare and dust of the window out of the way so she can see it better. A grey hump in the distance. A small, benign lump of land from this view; a meaningless, nameless mole on the smooth skin of the land, with no sign of its power and danger. But Iris knows it is much more than this. It is Mulanje Mountain.

She watches as they hurtle down the road toward it. They move toward it so quickly, so recklessly, and she worries. The mountain should never be approached in this manner—so directly, so wickedly fast. She watches as Mulanje grows in size. It is now no longer just a blemish on the horizon; it rises and gains height and mass as if drawing on the land itself, pulling the land up its haunches, adding to its bulk so that it soon towers over them, darkening the sky, blocking the sun entirely. They are now in its shadow. She hears Ellison and Bryce murmur in the front seat. "It's beautiful," they say, as though they have no idea, as though it were a piece of art, a sculpture to be admired, nothing more. She cannot understand how two intelligent men can be so oblivious to what is so clear. How can they not notice that the mountain smoulders? How can they not feel its rising heat, its anger collecting above it in the steaming, roiling clouds? Instead they chat happily about their last trip to Mulanje, their hike, how they climbed up and slept on it as though it were a hotel. How do they not know that this is further enraging the spirits who are surely listening to this mindless banter?

Iris sits in the back seat and tries to breathe—long, deep breaths—and she watches what is happening outside the vehicle. People are waving to them, shouting, gesturing. Iris has had her eyes fixed on the mountain for so long that she hasn't been paying attention to their immediate surroundings. She now looks at the road and the trees and the fields nearby. The landscape collides, smashes together in her mind, an ocean wave crashing to the shore. She is at Mapiri village. She is home.

The crowd outside the vehicle comes closer and Dr. Ellison is forced to slow his speed until he eventually comes to a complete stop in the middle of the road. He cuts the engine. People surround them. Many are children, curiosity getting the better of them. They kick the tires, touch the hood and jump back, laughing, surprised at the heat. They peer in the windows, cupping hands around their eyes to see inside. The adults stand farther back, look stern.

"I guess this is the place," says Dr. Ellison and he reaches into the back seat, grabs at the bag of supplies beside Iris. Iris shrinks away, tucks her head down. Dr. Bryce peers back at her, frowns. "You okay?"

"I'll just stay here," she says. "I'll look after the car."

"We'll need your help to translate," says Ellison. "The car will be fine." They both look at her. "Come on, then." Ellison is anxious and impatient. Iris can see the crowd milling outside, Ellison's large shape between her and them. The glare off her window prevents her from seeing much beyond the shadowed faces of the children who press their noses to the glass. She does not recognize the children. They are too young. It would be the adults she would recognize, and who might recognize her. She presses herself back into the seat, makes herself small, shakes her head at the doctors. "I'll stay."

Sighing, Ellison reaches around to the handle of the back door and pushes it open. In the sudden bright sunlight, over the heads of the children, Iris sees a woman. Her face—round, dark, gentle—is familiar. The woman sees her. As Iris tries to recall her name, pulls back into the mind of her childhood, searches for a name, she sees the woman's face change. Her eyes widen, her mouth draws open into an oval, but then her lips peel back, spread across her teeth. Her eyes tighten in fear. Iris hears the sound coming from the woman, who she now knows is her aunt, her father's sister: first a moan, low but slowly rising, gaining pitch until it is a scream and someone, another villager, a man, pulls her aunt into him, buries her face and Iris hides her own. She folds forward into herself, covers her face with her hands, and allows the wrenching emptiness to split her open.

Chapter 11

Iris is sitting with the women and Henry feels sorry for her, so uncomfortable and stiff and silent in her dress while the women talk and laugh and sway and hum some tune as they work. Her movements are quick and rough while theirs are smooth and fluid. Even though she seems to know them, she doesn't belong. She is like a duck squatting among swans.

There was confusion when they arrived. People running, people shouting, even screaming—a woman in the crowd wailing that frightening sound as though someone had died. The sound that always accompanies a white sheet, a red cross, a body beneath and Henry immediately worried that they were too late. But there was no such tragedy. There was Iris, huddled strangely in the back seat of the car, and the injured boy still lay with a fractured femur not far from the road in the village.

Ellison had gone to get the boy and Henry had tended to Iris. He urged her to leave the vehicle but she refused and remained curled up on the back seat, staring ahead with strange eyes. It took a woman from the crowd to go to Iris—she hugged her and rubbed her back and murmured things to her—and Iris eventually sat up and then stood on shaking legs and looked around blinking like a newborn calf. She has not spoken to him since they entered the village, and Henry feels her humiliation. He will not ask her.

It was Ellison who decided the father must accompany the boy back to the hospital. The child was so young—no more than eight. Henry agreed that he couldn't leave the village alone. So the father and son went and Henry and Iris stayed. And here they are. Waiting for Ellison to return tomorrow with the car and take them to the clinic.

It is all that had to happen to bring him here, standing on the dirt in his tan chinos and blue button-down T-shirt, hot and uncomfortable in the sun and dust and wondering what to do. At least there is nothing to say. No one here speaks English. He is released from that obligation, the obligation to reassure, to make peace with words, and the tricky business of choosing the right ones. He has never been good at that.

*

The men stand. Toe the dirt. Look off into the distance. As though there is something they are waiting for, as though someone is due to arrive.

But it has already happened. All in one instant they are here, the two of them: the white man—the doctor with the hair like a flame and her—bad luck in the form of a woman who left as a girl named Iris. For the moment, the men seem more concerned with Dr. Bryce; Iris sees their eyes drift to his hair and his expensive-looking rucksack slung over his shoulder, then the quick look away, as though they have caught themselves showing an interest they do not want to admit. None of the men look at her.

She feels a touch on her leg—gentle and brief and she follows the hand to her auntie's smile—also brief. It barely hides her trouble—the trouble she is having with their arrival. It was an event none of them had expected, least of all Iris.

"Iris," says her aunt. "Would you like some water?"

She is being handled carefully, like a guest. At first, her aunt wouldn't even let her help with preparing dinner but she insisted. She shifts in her tight, constricting nurse's uniform. The cut of it and the fabric does not allow her to sit easily on the ground. It is too narrow and stiff. She shakes her head, murmurs "no, Auntie." Then she returns her gaze to Dr. Bryce.

This is something she has never been able to do—watch him like this. In the hospital she was always too busy, and it was not her place. Her place was to listen, and to carry through an order. Order after order. With her head down. Now he stands with his hands tucked into his pockets, and she knows this is what he does when he is uncomfortable or unsure. He looks at the men who speak to each other in Chichewa. They ignore him, and he tries to look friendly—she can see the strain of this in the lines of the doctor's face, the twist of his half smile. He is uncomfortable with people. This is something that never occurred to her before, he was so busy trying to save them. But he cannot just be with them. He cannot just stand and be in the presence of others without something to do, something to fill his hands, or his mind.

Iris knows that the women are watching her as she watches Bryce. They are experts in the language of the body, the language before words. No doubt they are speculating as to their relationship. Perhaps they think they are a couple and this gives Iris a little tingle somewhere inside her. She studies his face, his angular limbs, the looseness of his clothes, the self-conscious slouch of his shoulders. From this view where she sits on the ground he looks kind, she decides. Kind and earnest and he is trying too hard. It is strange how just now she is able to decide these things about Dr. Bryce. He wore the hospital like a cloak, and only now, far away from it, can she really see him.

One of the younger men is talking to Dr. Bryce now. He speaks of the game *Bao* in mostly gestures. Dr. Bryce leans in, effort to understand all over his face. She turns back to the group she is sitting with. Many of them look quickly away when she turns to face them. Her bowl of peeled cassava is nearly empty compared to the other women. She picks up another of the vegetables. She feels their judgement hot on her face.

In the hospital, it is impossible to survive HIV. It is impossible to overcome a deadly disease. In this village, it is impossible to return when you have been sent away. It is impossible to disobey the wishes of the elders and the ancestors. Or it is very stupid and dangerous. And so she is a risk to them all, inflicting her bad luck on the whole of them. It is a selfish thing to do, to stay here. Just by staying here, she has proven that she is *mutu umazungulira,* she has a spinning head. She is not taking into consideration the greater needs of the village. If there was no room in the car that dropped them off and took away the injured boy, she should have walked back to Blantyre.

Looking down into her lap as she peels, she knows all this. She catches her aunt's gaze and says, quickly, before she can look away: "I didn't choose this." Her aunt washes the peeled cassava and doesn't say anything. Iris doesn't really know what her own words mean. She didn't choose so many things. When she thinks about it, she realizes that she has never chosen anything.

*

Iris motions to him and when he goes over, Henry sees a pale, half-peeled cassava in her lap. It makes her look so domestic, so different, more like a wife, a mother, more like a woman, and he shifts back a little, averts his gaze. She tells him that they have been invited to her aunt's home for dinner and before that, they will meet her grandfather. He nods, then walks back to the group of men. He struggles to keep the neutral, nurse image of Iris in his mind. Good old Iris. Good old Iris who has an aunt and a grandfather in this village. It seems that Iris has come home.

*

They enter a yard through a fence. The hut that the fence surrounds is rectangular, mud-walled and windowless. The roof, as with all structures in this village, is made of straw from the vast grassy plains that surround them. The doorway opens wide to the interior darkness. There are no doors. Just smooth, wide doorways in all the homes they passed on their way through the village. They stop and stand in the yard, look at the hut in front of them. The hut has its own presence, a stolid brown homestead, warm and strong and welcoming despite its unremarkable structure, its plain mud walls.

Iris, still beside him, just an inch or two away, trembles and brings her hands to her face. She takes her hands away and Henry can see the slick shine of her skin. He places a tentative hand on her back, just his fingertips. He touches her over her right shoulder, feels the starched stiffness of the cotton, and her warm skin beneath it.

A man appears at the doorway. He rests one hand on the door frame. He stares outside the hut, deep-carved lines of his face in shadows. He looks at Iris, brings his hands together and up to his lips. "Iris," he says.

Iris steps forward toward the hut and falls to her knees just before the doorway, before her grandfather, who moves his hands from his lips to her head.

They remain like this for a long moment. Eventually, Iris stands, clasping the old man's hands and she is led inside the hut. Henry remains outside the hut, on the well-swept dirt yard. He stands there and waits.

When Iris reappears, she does not smile. She steps down into the yard and reaches out for Henry. "Come," she says. "You will be welcomed." His knees ache, muscles stiff and tired. He would like to lie down under a shady tree and have a nap. But he follows this new Iris. In the hospital, she had been a soldier, all edges, hard and unforgiving. There is a disconcerting vulnerability in her now.

And her new face, this new Iris, is turned up to him, tremulous with anticipation. He follows her through the doorway, moves past a heavy curtain that hangs over the doorway and into the darkness of the hut.

At first, Henry cannot see anything at all. He has to relinquish control to whomever is there with him and Henry wonders if this is by design. He feels warm broad hands press onto his shoulders so he succumbs to the pressure and kneels down. The floor is cool dirt, but smooth, not dusty, like it has been lacquered with something. It smells of raw, deep earth. And there is another smell. Fresh and fragrant like wind, perhaps herbs that might be hanging somewhere to dry. Above him, pins of light pierce the layers of straw like stars. He hears Iris position herself behind him. Someone is in front of him, probably the old man, Iris's grandfather. Henry can't see his face now, but recalls all the fissures crossing it and obscuring his bones, his most defining features. His face is broad like hers, their noses a similar shape.

After a moment, Henry can see that the old man is in front of him, sitting on a low stool, watching him. As an elder in the village, he clearly expects respect. Henry looks up at his face, at the eyes that are studying him grimly, and then Henry feels compelled to look down, he cannot bear the weight of that gaze any longer. The man wears sandals made of old rubber tires.

Iris's breath is on his neck as she leans forward and whispers in his ear, "Do you have a gift? Visitors usually offer a gift. Anything will do."

Henry sits for a moment, his mind empty of ideas, irritated by this expectation revealed to him just now. Is he supposed to create something out of thin air? He slides his hand into his trousers pocket and his fingers find smooth metal. He grasps the object and pulls it out, looks at it in his hands. His reflex hammer. A thick red rubber arrowhead attached to a metal handle. The blade of the handle is smooth and flat, the tip pointed. The handle shines in the dim light of the hut. Henry extends it to the old man and he reaches down and takes it, holds it in both of his hands. The old man laughs out loud, his few teeth gleam like the blade of the hammer.

The man becomes quiet again, but continues to smile. He reaches behind himself and brings out a small object which he holds out to Henry and Henry takes it. It is oval, hard and smooth and cool to touch. The underside reveals an opening that has a corrugated edge. Hollow inside. A shell. Just smaller than the palm of his hand. He runs his thumb across the surface. Henry smiles and looks up at the man who grins back at him.

"Thank you."

He and the old man look at each other for a long moment, the old man fingering the blade of the reflex hammer, Henry the shell. The elder reaches behind himself again, and then brings forward a small basket. He tips the basket toward Henry and Henry can see that it is filled with shells and carved bones of various shapes and sizes. The man points a finger to Henry's shell, and then the basket. Henry places his shell back amongst the others. He must have failed some sort of test. He hears Iris inhale behind him, disappointed, perhaps, that he did not meet the elder's approval.

The old man then hands the basket to Henry, and motions to him to tip it over. Henry hears Iris's breath coming out in one long stream as he does as he is requested and spills the contents of the basket onto the floor. The elder places one hand on each knee as he leans forward over the spilled shells and bones. He studies them and Henry watches. Henry sees the shell he was given, lying half on top of a long bone, tipped up, catching the small amount of light filtering in from outside. Its underside is exposed, the slit-like aperture like a heavy-lidded eye and turned on him in a steady gaze. Finally, the man reaches down to the shells, picks up the one he had given to Henry, and hands it back to him. Henry accepts it again. The man no longer looks at Henry. He rounds up the remaining bones and shells, returns them to the basket, and Henry has the sense that he has been dismissed. He feels Iris's hand on his shoulder. She leans toward him. "We can go now."

Henry unfolds himself reluctantly, hoping for more. He leaves the hut, widening the slice of sunlight that marks the threshold by pushing aside the cloth that is obscuring the doorway. He glances back one last time before stepping into the light, and the old man is turned away from him, rummaging through his things.

Chapter 12

Iris walks through the fence and out of her grandfather's yard and Dr. Bryce follows her, his brow wrinkled and staring mostly at his feet. She moves through the village without seeing. She walks past fences and large shade trees, past all of the villagers who go about their daily business but who follow her progress without watching her. She feels all this. The *khumbi*, the trees, the nearby mountain, the well, the shrines and the graveyard. She feels the villagers and what flits on the surface of their minds as they attend to their various tasks. They are thinking that she is all fire, that she is burning up with the heat of the city. That her distance from spirit can only have made her brittle—a dry, dead twig—more liable to leap up in flames. Dr. Bryce beside her is a blaze. What effect would the two of them have on this place? The health of a village depends on the balance of all of its members. This is what her grandfather whispered to her when she reunited with him in his hut. This is the warning he gave her.

The sun has dropped. Dusk is about an hour away. People are preparing dinner, slowing down so their stomachs will be ready for the final meal of the day. She glances over at Dr. Bryce who walks beside her in his loping gait.

In the low evening sun, Dr. Bryce's beard glows the red and yellow of firelight. His mouth behind his beard is grim, set in a straight line. His eyes, she realizes, are circled with fatigue. She softens and slows down.

"We will go to my aunt's home for supper. It is not far now."

Iris's aunt stands at the threshold of her yard, just outside the fence. She smiles when she sees them approach.

"Here you are," she says to Iris in Chichewa. "You must be hungry." They both look at Dr. Bryce who stands there rumpled and quiet.

"Is he okay?" Iris's aunt asks her this quietly, as though he can understand.

"He's fine," says Iris. "He's just tired. And hungry. Westerners are always tired and hungry, no matter how much they eat and sleep."

"He is a doctor?"

"Yes."

"You work with him?"

"Yes. I work with him."

Iris smiles at her aunt and takes her hand. Her hand is cool and soothing. Her aunt's touch feels so good that she moves closer to her, and her aunt responds, wrapping Iris in her arms before pulling away out of respect for their other guest.

"Let's go in. The children are waiting." Her aunt touches Iris on the small of her back, guiding her into the yard. She waits for Dr. Bryce to follow Iris, before she follows them.

Once in the yard, the children shriek and laugh and run to them. They stop short by a few feet then press up against each other, shoulders, bare arms, elbows all criss-crossing.

They study her with their eyes open. They are not coy. And they stare at Dr. Bryce.

"My, what beautiful little faces and round little tummies you all have!" Iris prods the protruding stomach of one of the children with a wiggling finger and receives a chorus of laughter in response. The children all wrap their arms around their bellies as though she has tickled them all. She tickles a few more before standing up again and smiling at Dr. Bryce. The children have moved in, and press up against them, fingering Iris's blue nurse's uniform, and the doctor's trousers. Some reach up to touch the rucksack that is slung over his shoulder.

"They are very curious about you," says Iris. "Especially your beard."

Dr. Bryce squats down among them. He looks out at the group. They have grown solemn and watch him with round eyes. He rubs his fingers in his beard. "It's rough and prickly. See?" One girl reaches a tentative hand out and makes brief contact with a few of the wiry hairs before snatching her hand back. Soon more of them, overcome by curiosity, reach out and Dr. Bryce closes his eyes and smiles as his hair, face and beard are touched, poked, prodded and tugged.

"It's like fire!" they shriek. "But it's not hot."

"It won't burn you," says one of the older boys to a younger one who has until now held back.

"His eyes are strange, too. Wait until he opens them again and see."

Eventually, Dr. Bryce stands again. "What is it about children?" He asks, his tired eyes turned on her. "How are they always so perfect?"

"They are the closest to spirit, and the ancestors. They have only just left that world. When they are very young, they still remember it."

Iris's aunt begins to shoo the children out of the yard, shepherds them out the gate, instructing them to go home for supper. They crane their necks around, gathering one last look at Iris and Dr. Bryce before disappearing into the darkening night.

Yellow light brightens the doorway and windows of Iris's aunt's hut. Henry is not expecting anyone to be inside when they enter, but two pairs of eyes are fixed on him when he ducks through the doorway.

A woman stands across from him and a child stands in front of her, pressed against her legs. The woman has her hands placed on the child's shoulders in a protective grip. They stand in the far corner of the room, as far from the doorway as possible. It is the woman's eyes that startle Henry, so light a brown that they seem to glow, and trained on him as though he is a hyena nosing his way into her home. He sees her tighten her hold on her child's shoulders. She nods curtly at Henry.

"*Muli bwangi.*" Henry offers this and stands there at the threshold, not aware that he has blocked the entrance to Iris and her aunt until he feels Iris try to slip between him and the doorway in order to enter. He shifts over for her. Her aunt is the last to enter, and she sighs loud enough for all of them to hear.

Iris's aunt speaks. About him, most likely, because she lowers her voice, speaks in hushed tones as though he can understand. He listens to the meaningless words, tries at least to pick out the general tone. He watches the face of the woman in the corner, for evidence that she is softening with Iris's aunt's words, but she remains stony and clutches her daughter's shoulders as tightly as ever. It is hot in this hut, and his body here seems oversized, overgrown from the excesses of his Western existence, barely held together by his fragile skin.

After a long exchange, the woman and her child move forward from the corner, come a few feet closer, and stop. Iris's aunt gestures toward this woman and says, "Alile." Then toward the child: "Mkele." When Alile fixes her yellow gaze on him, Henry feels his pulse beat through to his skull and when she murmurs "*Muli bwangi*" to him, he cannot respond with anything but a nod of his head. "*Dili bwino*," he finally manages when she has already moved on, when she has already moved past him. He whispers it to her hair, which is cropped to follow the curves of her skull and which he can still smell, a strong scent of herb and smoke.

They all follow her to another corner of the room where an array of food has been laid out on a mat. Bowls of tomato and kidney bean relish, chicken meat, small flat fish piled up like silver dollars on a plate. They all settle in around the food. Iris hands him a small plastic bowl containing water and instructs him to use it to wash his hands. A plate of *nsima* is placed before him, somehow still steaming hot. He looks at it, a creamy mound of cooked maize, perfect in its smooth roundness like the shell in his pocket.

At first they eat in silence, sounds of chewing and swallowing and smells and flavours of tomato bean relish sour and sweet fill his senses. A chicken was also cooked for the meal and the picked-clean bones pile up on a plate in the centre of the circle. Gradually the women begin to talk and Henry listens to the cadence of it, busies himself with the task of eating this good food. Following the lead of the women, he uses the *nsima* to soak up the remaining relish. He is suddenly and overwhelmingly grateful for this meal and he blurts out, "Thank you," and none of the women respond. They acknowledge it, though, with a brief pause in their conversation.

Henry and the child have been stealing looks at each other. Each studies the other when they are afforded a chance, when the other is busy with food. She looks to be about six years old by his estimation, although he has found that he is terrible at guessing age here. Time, in general, eludes him and confuses him.

The girl sits there with a dancer's poise and looks knowingly at him, like she understands something about him that he doesn't. She lacks the playfulness of the other children from the village. Iris had said earlier that children and elders are the closest to spirit, and now he feels it: the familiar deep pang of anguish. The first in a long time. His food sticks in his mouth.

The girl is about the age Emma would be, had she survived. This thought, appearing so suddenly and before he could suppress it, comes and then goes. He reaches for some water to force the food down and the thought is already gone.

He watches Mkele's narrow fingers reach down to pick up the last of the *nsima* from her bowl and then her mother's hand reaches over to place more food in it. Alile touches her daughter's hand. A brief, reassuring touch and a gentle reminder that she is here with her, that they are here together.

Iris sits beside him remarkably quiet. She has returned to her prior self, the Iris he knows well—surly and silent. He almost reaches over to touch her hand or her shoulder, but holds back. He looks over at her, tries to catch her eye but if she senses it, she does not let him know. She stares resolutely at her empty plate.

When the meal is over, Iris's aunt and Alile begin softly singing as they tidy up. He remains sitting, not sure what else to do. Iris has risen and has joined the other women in the clean-up, but not in the song. She has that stubborn look on her face again, Iris of the old days on the ward, and Henry is swept over with warmth. He watches her move around the hut as though she's always lived there and maybe for a good portion of her life she has. He knows almost nothing about Iris. He did not even know she was not born in Blantyre until today. How long has she lived there? When did she leave the village? He wants to ask her all these things, but here is not the place, and now is not the time, and she has shut him out again. Him and everyone else, it seems. She has curled up into her self, showing only her hard back like a cowrie shell, and with this thought Henry places his hand in his pocket again. It is there: round, smooth and reassuring.

Strange for a shell to be here, in a landlocked country. Henry squeezes the shell, closes his eyes briefly and imagines its history. How many generations, how many tribes, how many villages, how many hands have passed it on, how many stories has it told, how many decisions has it made, how many fates has it sealed?

The shell, still in his pocket, begins to feel warm, as hot as his hand. Henry places two fingers on the shell, as though taking its pulse. He feels its heat through his fingertips, he feels like he is touching someone's wrist, or hand. The shell almost has the texture of skin. He pulls the thing out of his pocket. His hand is trembling. It is still just a shell and it gleams in the light of the lantern. He closes his eyes, leans back against the wall of the hut, feels the shell throbbing in his palm, and waits for the women to finish.

Chapter 13

Iris goes behind the hut with the dirty dishes. She knows there will be a basin there, a place to wash the bowls, and when she arrives, she finds it where she expects to. The rhythm of village life has begun to beat within her. She has mechanically joined the beat, joined in the dance with the other women. But she cannot bring herself to join the songs. The feeling of union would be too much and she would be overcome. She does not wish to lose control. This she has inherited from her time in the city. This stifling self-awareness. But this seems a strange concept here, and if it were not for Dr. Bryce, sitting there in the corner, she would have already succumbed. She would have joined the song. She would have fallen to her knees, melted into the earth of this village, bathed in the blood of her ancestors.

She wants to die here. This thought comes suddenly and here, alone in the yard of her aunt's home under the moonless sky, she nearly buckles under the weight of it. The idea of dying in the city and being buried among a wide spread of nameless graves. She has never been to one of the city graveyards, but she can imagine the feeling she would have there. The numbers of unsettled spirits, shifting and moaning in their graves, forever separated from their ancestral homes.

It would be bone-chilling. Dangerous, even. Who knows what the discontented dead can do?

Her ancestors are buried here. Generations and generations of them, and they all remain a part of the village life. They watch the goings-on, react to the behaviour of the villagers, communicate if they are pleased or displeased, and advise where necessary. They share the wisdom of the beyond with those who struggle through the hard tangibility of this existence. How vital this wisdom suddenly seems.

Her grandmother's grave is here, just beyond the borders of the village, in a wooded thicket. Her father's mother died when she was only five, and yet she still feels her pull. Stronger since she arrived. And she has not yet had the chance to visit her *kachisi*. She has not had a chance to pay her respects, to offer a gift. Today, her grandfather had been kind and understanding and welcoming. He treated her as though she were injured. Without speaking it, made her feel like her mother had made a terrible mistake, and she has been cast adrift.

Iris continues to scrub the bowls. She squats beside the hut in the semi-darkness. The goings-on of the village are all around her. She can hear her aunt's neighbours in their nightly routine. The women singing, the men talking, laughing, the children murmuring to each other in bed, nearly asleep. All of this is happening around her, within her, above her and below her. Soft, barely audible, but there, part of her and she, with the gentle clink of her dishes, the pouring of her water, with her sighs and rustlings, is part of it.

She puts down the last bowl and rests for a moment. There is no moon tonight and the stars shine astonishingly bright. The past, what led to the path her mother took, remains in darkness. Yet the memories since their arrival in Blantyre return to her in sharp painful jabs. The home they moved into and the maze-like alleys they had to navigate to find it, tucked in and abutting all the others. And the gangs of city children—skinny legs and smeary faces and narrow eyes snickering behind their hands at all the men their mother bedded. And the ritualistic paint on her mother's face—the bright red on her lips, blue over the eyes like two shiny bruises. Iris dreaded this ritual because it meant the the door would be closed behind her mother when she left and the lock would be turned and she would be trapped in a place where she did not feel safe. Her brother and sister felt the same—she saw the size of their eyes, how they huddled together despite the heat.

All this is still so acute, as if it happened a few days ago. But the village life—all these memories are gone. Iris gathers up the bowls and moves back into the hut. The light of the paraffin lantern shifts and changes the shadows on the walls and the hut is filled with its pungent smoke. Everything is more vague inside the hut. Iris's aunt and the woman Alile sit in one corner on a straw mat, chatting in hushed tones. The girl is curled up in the corner of the mat like a cat, asleep. Dr. Bryce is slumped against the wall, eyes closed, his breath coming in large, patient heaves of his chest.

Alile turns toward her, and her eyes fix on Iris's face through the haze. It is in this look, in the eyes that take her in, deliberately unapologetic. This is when Iris realizes something important. Something she must have known all along. Iris feels her face twist and brings her fists to her forehead. She turns and runs out of the hut, through the yard, and into the darkness of the village. She hears her name being called, now faint and far behind her.

When she has run out of breath, Iris slows down. Her shoes are slipping off her feet, her toes and heels raw where the shoes were rubbing. She stops to remove them and carries them as she continues to walk. She takes in the appearance of the village at night. The huts are spread far enough apart for privacy, but close enough together to maintain a sense of safety and community. Trees spread a weave of branches above the huts. She walks past one hut and then the next, trying to remember who lives in each. Sometimes she recalls a face, sometimes a name, sometimes nothing. Even though there is no moon, she can see enough to navigate the village. She walks until she arrives at the thicket, just beyond the final group of huts. The graveyard, the spirit-place. Yes: she knew she would arrive here tonight. She stops in front of the low grass fence that marks her grandmother's grave and her *kachisi*.

She can't see much beyond the fence. A warm wind pushes past her face, originating from within the thicket, moving on to elsewhere.

Iris steps in through the fence. She knows she is breaking protocol, but the urge is too strong, she has been away too long and so she takes a few more steps. It is even harder to see within the compound; the wood is dense and only the fallen branches are harvested. She takes five more steps and then stops. Breathes. Waits. There is the sweet and sharp odour of *ku-konda mowa* souring inside the offering pots buried in the sand. Remnants of previous offerings, food and drink left by others before her. Villagers who have paid their respects and deposited their *nsembe* in the pots.

Iris kneels down on the ground. The burial site of her grandmother is beneath her and she can feel its energy warm the ground that touches her folded legs. The smell from the clay pots—two of them, buried almost completely before the heap of rocks—is stronger now. She leans forward and places her hands, and then her forehead on the earth in front of the pots.

She feels tears roll off the bridge of her nose and drop onto the ground. They come from the blackness of her mind, from the burning emptiness there. She is an endless landscape of fissured, cracked scales, and the last drops of her are for her grandmother. They join the earth, they sink between the kernels of soil and slip underground to nourish her. This is all she has to offer.

Eventually, she pushes herself up, stares at the *kachisi*, and the rocks that form her burial site, now a place of prayer. Iris stares, waiting. Nothing. Her grandmother's *kachisi* is pale and unresponsive in the starlight. She has been away too long. She can no longer go beyond the mind, let its cloth fall away. It remains on her, tied around her head, a hangman's hood. This is Education.

She misses her grandmother: her crooked body and her soft whispers. She almost feels the warmth of them now, the tickling feeling of breath just a hair away. Her grandmother used to pull her close, hug her and tell her things. This was always out of earshot of her mother, who would not approve of what was being said. It became a game, telling her these things when only she could hear them, listen, believe. When she was still very young, she just listened to the sounds that hissed near her ear. She heard: "sss … ss … sssss … ss." And she would close her eyes and imagine that important things were being moved into her body in this way, secretly, through her ear and into her heart and mind. When she was older, she listened more carefully and knew that her grandmother said she was showing signs of a healer's ability, like her grandfather. And her grandmother felt the openness in her, the vulnerability that was required to hear the whispers of the *mzimu*, the ancestors. A few times her grandmother pulled away, looked at her slyly: "Those were not my whispers.

You know that, don't you, sister?" Sister. This is what her grandmother called her, as though they were twins.

There is a rustle. Close by, deep in the thicket. Movement through dry leaves. Soft as a whisper and she sees the tail of it before it disappears into the undergrowth. A python. Iris hugs herself and begins to cry. It was right there, right beside the *kachisi*. It might have been studying her, smelling her with its flickering tongue. *Kantu ndi aka kawa mu maso.* What she sees with her eyes is a real thing. She is frightened by how much she wants to believe that her grandmother came to witness her return.

Iris stands. She kisses her hands and then places them gently on the stones of the *kachisi*. She turns and leaves the compound. She walks until she reaches her grandfather's hut and he is standing at the threshold, waiting for her when she arrives. Without speaking, he leads her into his hut and to a mat he has laid out for her where she lies down, still in her nurse's uniform, and falls asleep.

She dreams of flightless moths. The creatures bat their useless wings and crawl in patterns, around and around in lines and loops, and if Iris could only get far enough away, if she could only gain enough distance from the crawling moths, she would see the pattern described in their moving paths, she would see what they are trying to tell her.

When she wakes, she is bitterly disappointed in her dreams. They communicated none of the symbols, none of the prophetic messages she was hoping for. All they told her was what she already knows: that she is lost.

Chapter 14

Henry wakes up to the cries of roosters. Loud and self-important, they boast to each other across the village, first one, then another and another until all are roused, the whole group of them joining in a cacophony of rigorous, excited calls. Henry listens in the darkness of the hut. He is lying on a mat by the wall, probably the very same mat where they shared dinner the previous night. He must have fallen asleep while the women were cleaning up. The roosters fall silent and Henry shifts on the mat and looks around. He sees the sleeping forms of the women and the girl, over on the other side of the hut. Iris's aunt lies on her side with her back to Henry. Her rib cage lifts and falls with the deep breath of sleep. Beside her, Henry can see the girl, tucked in the concavity of her mother. Her mother's shape rises behind her, her hip and shoulder the highest peaks. Her arm curls protectively around her daughter. Moving his gaze up past her arm, past the slumbering face of Mkele, Henry now sees Alile, eyes open, watching him with a steady gaze. They lie on their respective mats and watch each other in the dim light. And then her child stirs and murmurs and they are far away when Alile tucks her head into her daughter's hair, hugs her closer and whispers something Henry can barely hear. But still he strains to hear it, to hear the soft, reassuring murmurs. He rolls on to his back, lies there for a moment, and then gets up and leaves through the open doorway of the hut.

The sandy ground of the yard is white. He steps into a patch of sunlight. The sun off his skin is blinding. He squints to the piercing pain in his eyes, then keeps them closed, stands there and observes the red glow of sunlight through his eyelids, the wafting, flickering lights that drift across his visual fields.

Beyond the yard, he can hear the goings-on of early morning village life. His watch is inside the hut, with his backpack, and he stifles a compulsion to go back to the hut to check the time. It is the thought of the woman Alile, with her light brown eyes, that stops him. And so he starts for the fence, feeling her gaze hot like the sun on his back until he is on the other side.

He walks past women carrying bundles on their heads—water urns, woven trays of vegetables, bundles of sticks. They smile warmly at him. "*Muli bwanji*," they murmur as they pass. One child races up to him. "*Muli bwanji*!" He shouts and then joins Henry in step, trailing him by one pace. Soon he is followed by a throng of children. They burst into laughter whenever he turns around, so he does it again and again, puts a mock expression of surprise on his face each time and each time they burst out in laughter. They pass a group of older boys kicking around a football. They kick it over to him and he hoofs it back. It is made of plastic bags, bound up with twine and it bounces heavily off his foot. His shot is poor; it misses the boy he'd sent it to by a few feet, and the boys laugh. He shrugs his shoulders in apology.

He hears a shout and sees someone wave, over by an enormous baobab tree with generous branches and plenty of shade. The children grab his hands and direct him over to the tree. "Mister, mister, here!" They lead him to the tree trunk and pull him down so he sits.

The man who waved them over approaches Henry with a broad smile. Henry recognizes them; he was in the group of men greeting them when they first arrived. He holds something in his hands, a wooden box which he holds out to Henry. "This … *bao*" is all he manages. The children move in, their hands on the box. They open it up, reveal the carved holes, the round, dried seeds nestled in the holes, two to a pod. A game. The man gestures to Henry, then to himself, then to the game.

"I don't know how to play."

The man smiles broadly and nods. His long, lean fingers reach for the game and Henry hands it over. Henry places his hands over his chest. "Henry." Then he points to the man. "You are … "

"Elias! He Elias!" The children chime in, bouncing back and forth between the men, delighted to be witness to their awkward introduction, thrilled to be able to chaperone the exchange as knowledgeable intermediaries. The man smiles again. "El-i-as," he pronounces with some pride. He says it slowly, exaggerating each syllable. He turns his attention to the game, points to the board, "*Bao.*" "Ba-wo," Henry copies, sounding it out like Elias had, and Elias nods perfunctorily.

Elias places the game between them, opens it up. He accounts for all the pieces, and then places the pieces, hard round wrinkled seeds, into the holes in a specific pattern. Henry watches carefully. Elias leads. He picks up seeds from one of the holes and disperses them into the adjacent holes.

He sits back, smiles, and gestures for Henry to follow suit. He reaches out for a hole containing two seeds. Before he can reach them, Elias makes a loud tsk and the children are laughing. "No, Mister!"

Not allowed, then. He reaches for seeds in another hole, but again the loud, disappointed tsk and the laughing children. He selects from another row, and there is a hopeful silence. He feels the group willing him to make the right move. He moves the seeds over, places them in two other holes, one in each. The children squat down, pleased, and Elias leans back, touches his fingers to his mouth, smiles.

And so the game progresses, Henry fumbling through, guided by the children who react to his every move like irrepressible ripples through a pond. Elias, with his stern tsks, and his pleased smiles, his encouraging chuckles. Eventually, there are just a few seeds left on the board, and Henry watches as Elias scoops them up, moves them into one of his pods. He smiles, bows again to Henry. He packs up the board, pieces locked inside and stands up.

"*Tionana.*" He says and walks swiftly away.

"Tionana," replies Henry after him, not sure if this is the correct response. He looks at the children, and they beam back at him. He wants to remain here, under the tree, saying nothing and doing nothing and, when Iris's aunt finds him there and beckons him to follow her to her hut, presumably for breakfast, he follows reluctantly.

*

Iris eats with her grandfather. They are both silent. Iris knows how her grandfather feels about talking—that it is a distraction, a winding path that leads one away from the truth. The more talk, the further from truth one wanders, until there is no way back. Writing is even worse. The finality of words on a page. Like a cage. A trap that reinforces the notion that things can be known, that things can be permanent, fixed in place and time. A trap that pushes the unknown to the boundaries of consciousness, that causes one to fear the unknown, and to cling to what is written as though it will keep one safe. In years past, her grandfather has shaken his head sadly at her books, the books she brought back from school when she was a child. Even when she lived here, in the village, she read books. She learned to read in a one-room schoolhouse that was built by missionaries many years ago. She recalls the school being quite far from the village. It seemed she spent more time walking to and from the school than she spent in the classroom learning. Not all of the village children attended classes. There was only one school and one teacher for many surrounding villages and, on any given day, there were only a few children gathered in the room, peering at the blackboard, trying to make sense of the dusty white scratches that the teacher made on it.

Iris's mother insisted that her children attend the classes. When they were young, she would walk the long way with them, but as they grew older, her mother would wave to them from the hut, confident that they would keep going, all the way to the school. Eventually, Iris was the only one who kept going, her brother and sisters would break away, run off to play with their friends from neighbouring villages. Iris, on her own, continued to attend. She studied the chalk markings until they were no longer mysterious. Then she turned to the mysteries inside the pages of books. There had been a modest collection of books at the schoolhouse, presumably dropped off over the years by charities. Some were written in English, used by Western children, their names printed in pencil at the top right corner of the first page. William. Alice. Maude. Harry. She imagined these children, dressed in fine clothes, reading under the shade of a large, leafy tree near a river, as often depicted in the stories the books contained. She sought out similar places to read, or as best she could get to them. She felt a connection with these children who read the same words, somewhere across the world, where there were oceans of green lawns and gardens.

Iris looks over at her grandfather with his head bent to his *nsima,* focused on the food. Her father's father. What would he think of her medical textbooks? What would he think of all the diagrams of the microscopic cells that make up the body, and all the molecules that communicate with these cells, numbering in the millions? He would shake his head. He would say it was a dream, a fantasy cooked up by minds who feel so compelled to know things, and who feel so compelled to show others what they know. And even if it were true, what good could come from knowing it, and from documenting it? Only the finality of a closed door. Only stagnation. And, eventually, only decay. This is what he would say, gazing regretfully out at whatever was in front of him: the bark of a tree, the progress of an ant, the skeleton of a leaf. He would shake his head.

He shakes his head now, looking down at his plate. He is smiling.

"You are a good cook," he says, "just like your mother."

"Thank you."

She waits. "I'm sure the boy will be well taken care of in Blantyre. There are good doctors there."

"Hm."

She watches him move the *nsima* from plate to mouth. He has a tremor now, whenever he uses his hands. He has not been washing. She wonders who has been helping look after him. This would have been her job, or one of her sisters. Surely her aunt helps out.

"Are you well, Grandfather? Is there anything I can help with?"

"I notice you have become important. And ambitious. Just like your mother."

"I'm just trying to help."

"Is that all you need to do? Just say it?"

Iris does not reply. For some reason, she doesn't feel the shame she is meant to.

"Your head is hardening." He leans over, knocks on it twice. He nods, as though he has confirmed his suspicions. "Hard." He sighs. "Your grandmother must be so disappointed."

Iris holds her tongue. She doesn't mention the visit to the grave, or the python. She doesn't because it would seem disingenuous, and perhaps it would be. Perhaps his accusations are true.

"What did she do?" she asks. "Why did she leave?"

"Who?"

"My mother."

He chooses silence and she does not press it.

"She is not well. I'm worried."

Her grandfather sighs heavily. "Yes."

"She will not seek help. She won't go to the hospital and she won't see the *sing'anga*."

"Yes."

"She won't see the doctors that I work with. The ones she wanted me to learn from. The ones she says have so much wisdom and knowledge. She says that type of medicine is good for some people, not for her." Iris begins to scrape at her bowl with quick, rough movements. She struggles to contain her frustration in front of her grandfather.

"She lost her way a long time ago." This is muttered into his *nsima*.

Another long moment passes and then he says: "But she prays, doesn't she?"

Iris hesitates. Surely he must know which God she prays to. "Yes." She refrains from elaborating. As she finishes her meal, she wonders if her grandfather has answered her question.

Chapter 15

Henry watches Alile's girl, Mkele. She sits in the corner of the yard and plays alone, with a cloth doll that she dresses and undresses, chatting to it in the nurturing tones of a young mother.

Mkele's mother is not here. Iris is not here either. He wonders where she is, hopes that she is safe, and then feels silly for the worrying—after all, this is her home, not his. These are her people. He is the strange one, the stranger.

So far, they seem to expect little of him, smiling at him with such benevolence, perhaps even a little pity, or is he imagining that? Iris's aunt moved around the hut, tidying up after his breakfast. After completing his meal, he stood and offered to help but she waved him away, shaking her head, smiling. Always smiling.

Henry wonders how the boy with the fractured femur is doing. No doubt Ellison has already operated, and he is probably lying in the recovery room, coming to from the anaesthetic. He wonders when they will return.

In the rush to take the boy to the hospital, Ellison left with all the medical equipment still packed away in the trunk of the car—everything Henry would require to be of use. And all around him he has seen the need—Kwashiorkor babies, TB, bilharzia.

Over in the corner of the yard, Mkele coughs. A wet, productive cough and he wonders if it could be TB. She has that look about her—somehow sallow despite the warm brown of her skin. She swallows whatever she has just coughed up and continues playing. He goes inside the hut, rummages through his backpack and returns with his stethoscope. From the shade in the front of the hut, he calls her name. The girl looks up at him, squinting into the sun. Her features are bright and sharp in the sunlight. Her long nose, the angles of her clavicles above the neckline of the loose blue dress she wears, a dress that is much too large for her narrow frame. But her eyes are hidden, screwed up tight from the squinting. Henry beckons her over and she stands then walks slowly over to him, her doll abandoned in the dirt.

He places the earbuds of the stethoscope in his ears, feels them press in and seal sound out. He gently pulls her a little closer from where she stands still a foot away. He places his stethoscope on her back and tells her to breathe. When she does nothing, he takes big deep breaths himself and encourages her to do the same. She looks at him. A moment passes and then she takes in a mouthful of air. He cannot hear the breath over the scratchy movement of the cloth of her dress. He squats down and reaches under her loose dress and places the scope directly on the warm skin of her back. He takes another deep breath and she does the same. They breath like this, in unison, in and out. In. Out. In. Out. Beneath his stethoscope, beneath the warm skin of her back, beneath her birdlike ribs and the muscle stretched between them, her lungs fill then empty over and over and he can hear the echoing cavities, he can hear the air pop and whistle and squeeze through the swollen passageways. In. Out. They stay like this, longer than truly necessary. He knows it. And he thinks, I never listened to her. I never held her and listened to her. And when he finally looks up and sees Alile across the yard, when he hears her voice, sharp, calling her daughter's name, and when Mkele runs from him over to her mother, he stands and takes his stethoscope out of his ears and the sounds are much louder now, and the sound of Mkele's voice as she tells her mother what happened is shrill and accusing. It is not the sound, not the voice he was hoping to hear.

He clears his throat and says something. He says, "I think she has TB." Alile takes Mkele's hand and leaves the yard, leaves him standing there with his stethoscope dangling from his hand, alone.

Henry moves along the fences, grateful for the shade of trees that he passes under, patches of bright sunlight dappling his face in quick succession as he walks. Dark, light, dark, light. It feels good to be walking. He should have done this hours ago. As he passes villagers, they are quick with a greeting and he responds, trying to imitate their cadence, trying to suppress the natural tendency to inflect upward at the end of the reply. They laugh, good-natured, at his attempts, wave as he passes. Henry walks past the tree where he played the game of *bao*, but Elias is not there. A few women now sit in its shade, weaving mats out of long, thin, green palm leaves. They sing together as they work: a quiet, low melody.

For the first time today, Henry notices the mountain. It rises just beyond the nearest trees; the village nestles at its feet. He had forgotten how close they are to the mountain, and he stops walking, stands and looks at it. His eyes climb its flanks appreciatively, take in the scrabble of brush along its lower haunches, then rise up to the bald, rocky massif above the trees.

He feels something, a tingle in his scalp, and he turns to see a villager looking at him in a way that is neither friendly nor hostile. Somewhere in between, still waiting to pass final judgement. Henry raises a hand in greeting. "Moni," he says.

After a deliberate pause, the man lifts his hand. "*Moni.*"

This is the man who attended the child with the fractured leg. Perhaps he is a healer of some sort, a herbalist. The man watches Henry's face, and sees the recognition dawn. He turns and begins to walk through a space in the fence large enough for one man to pass. The man stops midway through and looks back at Henry, gestures with a wave of his hand to follow him, so he follows, sidling through the narrow opening in the fence and into the space beyond it. It is just a yard like the others, with a hut positioned at the far end of it, except there is a garden within this yard, off to the side. A herb and vegetable garden, with plants of different varieties planted in orderly rows. The leaves spring up from the ground, robust and impossibly green. The man walks across the yard, along the side of the hut then behind it. Henry follows him.

Behind the hut it is cool and shady. A man lies on the step—a raised platform of mud which serves as the foundation of the hut. The man—alarmingly thin—is slumped against the wall of the hut. This man is ill. Critically ill. He breathes with his intercostal muscles—the short muscles that run between the ribs—and his abdomen pulls in with each breath rather than filling out, a sign of diaphragmatic exhaustion. End-stage respiratory failure. His limbs splay out, no longer struggling, already succumbing to the fatigue, every ounce of his energy dedicated to the task of breathing. His eyes roll up toward Henry, then to the healer beside him. He lifts a hand an inch off the ground then drops it.

The healer turns to Henry and then holds his hand palm up, out to the man on the step, as if to say: "He's all yours."

Henry kneels down and curls his fingers around the man's wrist to feel his pulse but doesn't find it so he moves his hand to the crook of his neck, just under the angle of his jaw, to feel for his carotid pulse. It is a fleeting whir under his fingertips, rapid and weak. Henry moves his hand away. He has no stethoscope, but even if he had one, what would he do with it? Listen to his laboured breaths? The cataclysmic contractions of his heart?

The man's wishbone mandible strains upward and below it his neck is all taut strings and the raw machinations of breath, the trachea tugging down with each heave of his lungs, with each stingy mouthful of air sucked in. It's too damn difficult to watch so Henry fixes on the man's right hand. The veins are flat down, the hand as smooth as a young boy's. At home he'd be putting in a line by now, shoving plastic into a vein in the neck or a leg, and a bag of fluid through that to get some volume into him. The man's legs are loose and limp and already forgotten, already irrelevant. His trousers—faded black cotton, are worn thin at the knees as though he spent his days praying, the waistband loose and gaping over his stomach. His abdomen draws in, draws down. His ribs spread a fraction on each side then collapse in over and over in gasps, striated like gills.

Henry feels the jagged impatience of the healer on his back, the vacuum of this man's death before him. He stretches out his hand and places it on the man's chest, slides it over the ribs on the left side, spreads his fingers over the spaces between the ribs so he can feel the apex of the man's heart tapping against his fingers. After a moment, the man's eyes squeeze shut and his right hand flattens against the earth. His fingers tighten around a fistful of dust. Henry holds his heart and the man holds the earth and the earth does what it always does—stays hard and ungraspable and his heart keeps squeezing bolus after bolus of blood out to the edges of him despite the pull of gravity getting stronger and stronger.

The steady tapping beneath Henry's fingers now changes, it becomes erratic and disorganized and Henry pulls his hand back. Fuck oh fuck oh fuck. He looks up at the tree branches hanging uselessly down and at the sky between them and at the fence that hems them into this dusty yard where there is nothing, not a thing here that he can use to change this heartbeat back to a good one. He stares at that chest tugging down and in, down and in, and at those eyes that have opened again and roll from him to the healer, him to the healer, and at that hand that claws at the ground. Henry looks anywhere but at his face but feels the glare of the whites of his eyes and he wants him to close them so he cannot see all this, so he cannot see the culmination of the moments before his death. So he won't see Henry sitting there bearing witness to it and doing nothing.

Lay on your goddamn hands. Do something. He forces himself to look, finally. From the trousers that already seem empty and from the man's closed fist, Henry drags his gaze up to the man's face and he sees his eyes still with the fight, still staring at Henry, still waiting. Still filled with the fucking hope.

Henry looks up at the healer. Shakes his head.

"It is no use."

The healer does something with his mouth. The lips move into a smudged line—not a smile, but something akin to one. Affirmation. He flicks his hand at Henry and Henry stands, moves back, feels the nausea rise up, the world close in.

The healer kneels in Henry's place, puts his hand on the man's chest, not over the heart as Henry had done, over the centre of it. His other arm reaches behind him, flaps at Henry: *go*. Henry turns and leaves. Once outside the fence, he begins to run.

His legs push hard, move mechanically and his breath forces his tight chest open. He moves forward, forward, into the bright white space in front of him that peels open as he pushes through it. His breath comes fast and tight in sharp, irregular heaves but as he moves it starts to slow down into large, deep lungfuls of air and becomes regular again, the smooth regular inhalations of a healthy man with healthy lungs and a healthy heart.

Henry slows down to a walk and then finally stops. Beads of sweat coalesce and then slide down his face, his chest, into the cleft between his buttocks. His clothes are discoloured with sweat and dust. He is wearing long trousers, as most men do here, and the feel of the fabric against his skin is unbearable. He sits down on a boulder and leans over to roll up the legs of his chinos. He unbuttons his shirt. The cool air on his skin slows down his breathing, allows him to take bigger, calmer breaths. He looks around.

Somehow he has made his way to the foot of the mountain, on one of the trails that leads upward, through to the sky which now gazes on him with benevolent indifference. The wide, blue sky. This sight is supposed to reassure, to be calming, hopeful. But he is panicked by it. It serves as a reminder of how trapped he is, of how damn expansive this place is, no matter how far he runs, swims, crawls, he will always see it.

There is no one here at the trailhead but him. There is an unearthly quiet about the place, considering the bustling village only a mile or so away.

He leans forward, rests his forearms on his thighs and gazes at his hands. His veins bulge. The last thing his hands touched was the man who lay dying, who is probably already dead.

How many deaths has he overseen? How many times have his efforts to revive patients in some variety of cardiac arrest failed? God, the temerity with which he used to battle death when he worked in the hospital in Toronto. After compressing the chest, administering IV drugs, establishing an airway, assisting breathing, all performed relentlessly on the lifeless body, someone inevitably uttered: "Let's call it." At this point everyone stepped back, away from the body, and gazed at the clock. Time of death. Synonymous with the time at which the resuscitation team agreed to give up, although death had been in the room with them long before this. There, death happened in the midst of a flurry of activity, death wasn't acknowledged until the medical team agreed to acknowledge it, as though the medical team had the final say, and not death itself.

Here in the village, death had its grip on the man's body. It was squeezing the breath out of him. And Henry retreated from the challenge. Somehow he felt like he was in its territory, he was stepping on its ground. He was an intruder in death's workshop, not the other way around.

He still feels the tapping of the man's heart on the pads of his fingers, the strain of muscle moving from regular to erratic, from control to chaos.

He thinks now, of the things he could have done. He could have done a throat sweep, even tried the Heimlich manouever. Or a makeshift tracheostomy. He could have looked for signs of a tension pneumothorax which can be treated with a simple needle puncture, the creation of a release valve. It was endless, the list of possibilities that were still relevant, even here, in rural Malawi. He could have tried.

Henry folds down on himself, cradles his head in his hands. In those moments, looking at the dying man, he felt incomplete. Without devices, medications, an ICU nearby with all its infrastructure. Without a hospital attached to him like a placenta, what is he? He is just a man with knowledge of anatomy, and illness, and how terribly wrong it can all go.

Suddenly cold, he pulls his shirt closed, fumbles with the buttons, succeeds in doing up one or two before he shakes with rigors and senses the world pulling away, floating grey spots where there used to be something solid. He plunges his head down between his knees, tries to stave off what seems to be coming. He sure as hell cannot afford to pass out now.

Sitting there, leaning forward, feeling the nausea rising in him, spitting out the water-brash that accumulates in his mouth, there is a flare of colour in his periphery. He looks up. Nothing. And then again: a streak of pale blue in the surrounding browns and greens and greys of the trees, the path, the stones. Over to the right, he sees it again, slipping behind a tree, and then between the tree and the boulder. A blue shift—the hem of a dress? He stands up, holds onto a tree for another wave of nausea, and scans the forest, takes a few steps closer toward the grove where he last saw it. He listens. He still sees nothing and so returns to the path and the boulder where he had been sitting.

Now his head pounds and he wipes his brow. Slippery with oily sweat. He sits down, rests his elbows on his knees again and stares at his hands—white, shaking. He clasps them together to keep them still, tries to stare at something immoveable—the carpet of dry leaves and twigs, a sharp-edged rock, a broken branch.

When he sees a glimpse of colour again, he springs up. He moves closer to it. Once he is standing where he is sure he saw it, he looks around. This time he sees a girl, or at least the shape of a girl; she is so far away it is difficult to be certain. He takes a few steps more and then sees her more clearly. She leans into a tree and gazes back at him. She smiles. At him. Then, swift and silent, she is gone again, farther up the mountain. Henry follows.

He climbs upward, his breathing coming fast and regular, the heat in him rising again. His trouser legs slowly unroll until they cover his legs, the cotton heavy and scratchy on his skin. When he gets to the next rise, he stops to catch his breath. The girl waits for him, sitting on a boulder just like the one he had been resting on farther down the mountain. The lightness about her, the ease with which she breathes, the dryness of her skin, all seem to mock him with his large, sweaty bulk that fights everything in his path, his footsteps obliterating everything beneath. The girl smiles at him again. Alile's daughter? He is still not close enough to know for certain. Henry wonders if she followed him here, if she followed him from the moment he stepped out of Iris's aunt's yard. He feels somehow guilty for bringing her here, although he did nothing of the sort. He feels responsible for this child. It is like feeling responsible for the welfare of the mountain itself.

Now the girl stands up. She waves to him and then, swift as a bird, she is moving again, she is gone, disappearing into the mountain.

Henry lumbers onward, in the direction she went. His energy is spent by now, and he has little reserve to keep going, to keep pushing uphill. He slows down then stops at the next rise, leans against a tree, looks around. The girl is nowhere to be found.

Chapter 16

Iris leaves her grandfather's hut after breakfast. By now, the sun is high and hot and she wishes she could discard her nurse's uniform. She watches the women in their *chitenjes* with envy. How comfortable they must be, how cool despite the rising heat. Most of the women keep their heads low when she passes. She tries to place names with the faces she sees but she can't. These people are strangers to her and today they behave like strangers, look away quickly. Some of the women eye her uniform with an unpleasant expression—a mix of dislike and distrust. Similarly her hair. She has seen them looking at it. It is longer than the style in the villages, where women traditionally crop it close to their heads. Over the last few years, Iris has been growing it a little longer, more like the Western women—visiting doctors or nurses or students who come through the hospital—women who wander in from Europe, or Australia, sometimes America. Women who breeze through the wards smelling of herbs and flowers and freedom, women with soft, clean skin, women who never sweat, women who wear the cool, calm smile of suppressed shock and disgust, women who were never meant to see the things they see here, women who eventually acknowledge this, women who quietly slip back to the airplane that purrs on the runway and waits to lift them up and away, back to their homes, back to the safety of the West. Iris's hair is long enough now to fit into a ponytail, which is how she is wearing it now, pulled back from her face with an elastic band, a short tuft of it protruding from her head, just above the nape of her neck. She cannot see it, but runs her hand over it, feels the stiff wiry strands, feels how it doesn't flow like the slippery strands of the white women's hair. No, nothing like those women.

A woman brushes past Iris on her way somewhere. "*Pepani*," she says, as she moves along the main path toward the centre of the village. Iris wonders where she is off to so urgently. As she makes her way to her aunt's house, she becomes increasingly aware of the village swept up in something.

She slips into her aunt's yard and finds her aunt sitting on the back step shelling peas. Just like her mother would be doing. Iris wonders if her mother and her aunt were friends. They are sisters by marriage only. She cannot recall if they sat together, doing tasks like this in each other's company. Her aunt's lap is filled with the green shells. She looks up at Iris and smiles, shading her face against the sun. "*Moni.*" Iris sits down beside her and takes a few pods, begins to shell.

"What is going on in the village?" She asks her after a moment's hesitation, unsure of whether she wishes to reveal her disconnect, her unfamiliarity with village life.

"They are preparing a feast for the harvest." Her aunt continues her work, pea after pea dropping into the bowl beside her. Iris feels heat on her face: of course. Now that she has been reminded, she feels shame from her forgetting. All the memories of these routines and rituals, at one point integral to her existence, have gone missing, and she must retrieve them, one by one, from where they lie. She must reassemble her life here.

"I'd like to come," says Iris.

"Of course," says her aunt who then pauses in her shelling to glance at her. "You should cut your hair. You don't want to confuse the ancestors. You don't want them mistaking you for a *mzungu.*"

Iris nods. She feels her ponytail like an absurd growth; it moves along with her head, up and down, punctuating her acquiescence.

*

Henry leans against a tree and catches his breath. He looks down at his trouser legs, dark with sweat and dusty with the red-brown dirt of the mountain. His shirt hangs open and his chest feels cool while his back is sticky and hot, so he removes his shirt, drapes it over the bend of the tree trunk. He wants to take off his trousers, too, but decides against this, as wandering the mountain in boxer shorts, deserted as it is, is still beyond him, even now, even in this state.

He looks around. He can tell how far up the mountain he is by the sweeping vista to the plains below, the fields that fluoresce white-yellow in the noon-hour sun. He must be more than halfway up by now. He cannot see the peak. He can't see Sapitwa up there, not yet. He remembers his climb with Ellison, weeks before. They started from a different side of the mountain, a different trailhead. Nothing is familiar here, not even the plains below.

And he is off the path. In his chase after the girl, he followed her deeper into the bush, higher up the mountain, and farther off the path. He can't even hazard a guess as to where he might go to find it again.

There are no boulders to sit on here, so he lowers himself down to the grass—short, tough, wheat-coloured grass that prickles against his palms. He looks out at the plains below. He can't make out any sign of a village. He wonders how far around the side of the mountain he has gone. He is not even sure if the village is to the right, or to the left. He acknowledges now, with the hot noon sun making white whorls in his vision, that he is lost.

Henry looks out and sees the flat pallor of the sky above the horizon. It gives no clues, remains as blank as the first day he arrived here, the day he touched down on African soil. The blue has been filling him, sweeping in on him like a rising tide. Soon it will be all he is. Impassive like the sky. Nothing surprises him anymore. It is impossible to feel the usual sentiments that his days at home had been crowded with. Even the prospect of being lost, alone on a mountain in hot sun without food, water, or shelter, does not jolt a reaction in him. He contemplates his running shoes—reasonable footwear, he thinks. The logo is obscured by dust and he can't remember what it is anymore. His trousers are too hot. Cotton is idiotic in this climate. He wishes he'd worn his hiking trousers—the kind made of some quick-to-dry synthetic material and converts to shorts—these are the conveniences he'd scorned when coming here. He'd wanted basic. And here he is. Man against mountain. As simple as it gets.

Henry stands. He looks down the mountain at the emptiness stretching for miles. He turns around and looks up. Just a hundred metres or so and he will be above the treeline. There are rest huts there, planted up on the highest reaches of the mountain, and maintained by hut keepers. He recalls the welcoming scent of the cedar fire. The hot broth of the soup he and Ellison had cooked. If he were to climb farther, if he were to aim for the peak, he would be close to the hut where they'd stayed. From Sapitwa he would be able to see everything. From Sapitwa he could find his way home.

Chapter 17

Iris and her aunt join the crowd that flows along the main village path all the way to the centre where the feast is being prepared. As a child, Iris did little to participate in these rituals. She was too young, not yet initiated. Her role was a supportive one—fetching food and water and doing other menial tasks. As Iris moves along with the crowd, she brushes past a goat that canters away from the group, eyes rolling, nostrils wide. Somehow it knows it is at risk.

The crowd of villagers press toward the village centre, already wearing the mood of the ritual—jubilation, hunger. There are still hours to go before the event will begin but the collective energy swells in anticipation. Rituals to celebrate the harvest are joyful events, a time for music, dance and rest after many months of labour, and Iris is pulled along, feels the energy trill inside her.

When she first arrived in the city, Iris felt each missed ritual as a dull, lonely emptiness. She and her siblings once tried to recreate a ritual by making a fire in their small, urban backyard after their mother left for her evening work. They took turns approaching the fire, close enough to be uncomfortable, staring into it with their eyes fixed and wide like they had seen the adults do, and they practiced dancing like the fearsome Nyau. They fell asleep in the yard, and left the fire burning unattended. Iris remembers waking to her mother screaming. She looked like she was walking in fire; fire lit all around her, her hair smoked and flickered and glowed red, orange, yellow. Her eyes, though, were black. At first Iris thought her mother was burning, that she was the sacrifice that they, her children, had unintentionally submitted to the spirits. Their mother was who the spirits wanted, and so the spirits were taking her, consuming her in one enormous, burning swallow. But their mother was safe, untouched by the power of the flames. She walked through the fire without even feeling the heat. And then she doused it unceremoniously with bucket after bucket of water, her mouth a thin, straight line. For weeks afterward, their backs felt the burn from the switch their mother used on them. They never attempted a ritual again.

Iris and her aunt have been recruited to help prepare food and they join a group of women sitting under one of the baobab trees. Iris is handed a pile of long, thin palm leaves and asked to weave some platters and baskets for the food. She begins winding the leaves clumsily, large holes appearing between the leaves and then the whole weave slipping apart despite her best efforts. After some time spent struggling with her first project, one of the women clucks and takes the leaves away from her, points her in the direction of the cooking. She spends the next few hours staring into pot after pot of boiling cassava, her eyes red and her face wet and swollen with sweat and vapour. The women sing and chat. They tell stories. They laugh. Iris stares into the pot and listens. Then she closes her eyes and listens. She lets the harmony and melody of the songs and the chatter fill her up with their goodness. She begins to have that feeling again, the one she has missed for so long, the awareness that they are all from this small patch of earth, birthed from this soil, the soil they sit on as they sing, the soil from which their cassava and groundnuts and tomatoes grow, the soil that will welcome them all back when they are dead, the soil where their ancestors lie in watchful silence. How can she possibly remain a stranger here, when she has this undeniable connection to all of them?

She avoids touching her ponytail. She wishes she and her aunt had cut it off before coming here. She wants the smooth nape of her people. She admires them all, bowing their beautiful heads over their work, their generous smiles, their kind eyes. She steals these glances, these quick glimpses of her people before returning her gaze to her pot. She avoids looking up from her pot for too long, in case she is called upon to contribute something. A story or a song. This is the last thing she wants: to have all these women who know each other like sisters, staring at her, she the non-sister, the lost sister, the one with the Bad Luck. She just wants to spend some time with these women, here under the tree, she just wants to be with them for long enough that they will see that she will not bring back the luck that her mother took with her. That luck will stay in the city.

And then she hears her name. *Iris. Iris.* They are chanting it, sing-song. *Iris.* She looks up and the women are looking at her. They are smiling.

"How about you, Iris?"

"Do you have a story? Tell us something about the city. Tell us about the people there."

"What about the hospital? I hear it is so big, so big, you can't know everyone. Is this true?"

Iris looks at them all, paused in their chores. They keep smiling. They want to hear.

"The hospital is so big that you can't see across it. There are walls everywhere. Tall ones. And doors that block everything—noise, people—everything. There are many different rooms for all the different patients. There are beds for some patients, but many people lie on the floor. The floor is cold and hard like stone. There are more patients than you can count in each room. None of the patients know each other. It is a place full of strangers."

The women watch her for a moment. Their smiles falter as they absorb it all.

"And this doctor—Bryce? What is he like? Is he as strange as he seems?"

Iris finds herself smiling. "Yes. And no." She pauses. "He is strange in his ways, he makes strange decisions, but when you understand why, then he is the only one that isn't strange."

"So you understand him?" The women watch her face.

"No. Only once in awhile I understand. I understood the painting." This last statement she says quietly while looking down at her boiling pot, and she realizes the cassava are probably overcooked. She pokes at them with a spoon. Yes, it pushes through the roots too easily.

"Is he a good man?" One of the women asks this and the group becomes more quiet, as though they know the answer.

"Yes," says Iris. "He is good. I wouldn't let him into the village, otherwise."

The women remain quiet.

Iris adds, "He means well. He wants to help." She knows this is still not enough. But she can't think of anything else to say. She gets up and goes to pour out the boiling water. It is thick and white with the starch of the cassava. She returns to the group with her pot of overcooked cassava and they have already moved on, they are singing a song. It is an old song, a fable about a lion and a monkey and how the lion tricks the monkey. Iris can't remember the words.

*

Henry has been climbing uphill for hours. The sun has tracked across the sky a considerable distance, or is his perspective changing? Is he cutting across the mountain more than he thought? He stops and looks out from the mountain. He can only see the far-off horizon, now, and he tries to gauge where the sun is in relation to it. It has moved across the sky, but has it begun its downward arch yet? He can't tell. It still sits high up, a bright white affront that makes his vision spotty and his head feel like it moves even when it is still.

He is so goddamn thirsty. He hasn't found a single stream yet. When he came with Ellison, it seemed they traversed several different streams as they climbed, or were they just switchbacking across the same one? He remembers the appearance of the streams on the mountain from a distance—silver threads stitched into the rock.

He still hasn't found a path and has been contending with scratchy, low-lying brush. Keeping his trousers unrolled to his shoes, although hot, at least protects his legs from the scratches of the small, sharp branches of the bushes that he must step through. His progress has certainly been slowed by the bushwhacking, but he has moved above the treeline, so the going has become a little easier. Some of the shrubs have berries on them and he has sat down, picked a few and looked at them in his palm for a long time before deciding the risk was too great. He let the firm, red fruit roll off his palm. He pressed his shoe onto them and then removed it to see the red stain on the soil.

Henry reaches a plateau—the first yet—and he finds that the high subalpine plain is almost a desert. Sparse patches of low grass wave in the welcome breeze. The air feels light and de-oxygenated. He folds his knees and rests on the ground, first kneeling, then he rolls over and lies in the grass. Odd that his legs don't ache. They feel light, barely touching the scratchy grass beneath him. He rolls his head to the side and watches a small spider pick its way up a strand of grass, then cross over to a neighbouring strand where it moves its legs in a mysterious pattern, rubbing them together then feeling down the blade, plotting its next move. There is plenty of insect life here; he has seen beetles, ants, spiders, mosquitos. But little else. No rodents. Not even a bird has flitted overhead. And it is so quiet. If he strains, he can hear the wind passing through the grass, but even this is a softer sound than usual, almost muffled.

Henry looks across the plain, between blades of grass. He sees the yellow of the grass and the blue of the sky. Why can't he see Sapitwa yet? He knows it is there. He can feel it watching him. He tries to recall Iris's warnings. What was it that she warned him against? Only fools climb the mountain. She'd been particularly concerned about Sapitwa. Ellison had mentioned bad spirits. Henry looks up at the sky. The only bad spirit here is him. A dark stain on the mountain, lying here seeping into the soil like the juice from the berries.

He feels the sting of a mosquito on his arm and reaches across to slap at it. He looks at his fingers—they are red with his blood. That's it, he thinks. Now the mountain will smell my blood. Now it will come after me. He closes his eyes and waits. He sleeps.

*

A crowd gathers near the prayer tree. Offerings are placed around it. Most are food—millet flour—or beer. Some are personal, handmade. Something for the ancestors who are buried beneath. Something that will please the eye or the palate.

Iris watches the villagers approach the *kachisi*, kneel down, place their offering nearby, back away from it. One final admiring glance back and then they depart, satisfied with their work. She considers what she should offer. And then she knows what she will do. She returns to her aunt's hut, anxious to begin.

Searching through her aunt's belongings, Iris finds what she is looking for: a pair of scissors, their blades kept sharp with a stone. She removes her clothing.

When her aunt returns to the hut, Iris is crouching inside it, naked except for her underwear, looking at something, turning it over in her hands.

"Iris!" Her aunt stands in the doorway.

Iris stands up straight, looks at her aunt, and smiles. "Hi Auntie," she says. "I have my *nsembe*." She holds up the piece of cloth. It is a flower, a large, bulky flower with many petals. Blue in colour. The petals have been sewn together in the centre. "It's my uniform."

Her aunt stares at the remains of the dress on the floor of the hut—messy bits of cloth. Her nurse's pin gleams where it lies, still attached to an unused scrap. Her hat, remarkably white, thrown overtop.

"It was a nice dress," she says. She stays in the doorway, blocks the light. "So you've made your decision. You won't be returning."

Iris looks at the flower in her hands. "I don't know." She walks to the doorway, looks out on the yard. "It seems right. To be here now."

"Don't be rash, Iris." She looks at the flower in Iris's hand. It is large and bulky and droops sadly. "Will you get in trouble for ruining that?"

Iris tightens her jaw. "It's mine. I paid for it. I earned it."

Her aunt sighs. "See? You talk like a city girl now. Maybe it is too hard. Too hard to come back." She reaches out for Iris's face but doesn't touch it. She drops her hand. "You are so closed, now."

Iris moves away. She steps out of the hut and into the yard. The sun on her skin feels warm and reassuring. She can see Mulanje from here. It is bare and bald and hard as a diamond. It is angry. That much she can feel. Ever since they catapulted toward it in Ellison's car. It remains angry. But tonight, she thinks. Tonight is her chance to offer something. To offer what is left of herself, and to see what the spirits wish to give back.

She reaches to the nape of her neck for her hair and grasps it. She turns back to her aunt.

"Will you help me with this?"

Her aunt nods, and they re-enter the darkness of the hut together.

Chapter 18

When Henry wakes, it has cooled off and the sun is low. The sky has taken on a darker hue and he can see the moon, a thin crescent hanging up in the blue. Henry rolls over in the grass and feels the ache in his muscles, the emptiness in his stomach, and the dryness in his mouth. There are a few large welts on his neck and arms that itch. He suppresses the desire to scratch at them. The itch is almost worse than the hunger and the thirst.

He sits up. There is Sapitwa, the peak is just visible across the plain and under the moon. It has been there all along, watching him sleep. He stands up and faces it as he struggles to find his balance. He starts to walk.

If Sapitwa is there, within such an easy reach, then there must be a rest hut somewhere nearby. His pace quickens at the thought. He sniffs the air for cedar wood smoke but smells only the clean mountain air, empty of fragrance. He stares at the peak, tries to determine whether this is the face that he had seen when he stayed in the hut with Ellison.

His body moves amazingly well without interference from himself. The orchestra plays on without the conductor. But with each hour that passes his effort rises, and his body tells him increasingly of the dwindling reserves. Warning signals are being sent up from below and he is suppressing them all, exerting his autocratic power. Like a war-primed youth, he is blind with a desire to carry on, to fight, to win.

Kumwembe's words: if you are not able to fight you will struggle. There is wisdom in this advice. Being bloodthirsty but satiated was infinitely better than the alternative. To struggle is to be weak. To struggle is to be overcome.

He should know. He has struggled with and lost to his memory—a terrifying opponent. He can restrain, repress, stifle, smother, submerge, but it is there, it is all there. Of course it is there, how could he think it is somehow separate from him, it is what makes him who he is. Memory is him and he is memory, an overlapping Venn diagram of consciousness, trick rings that never separate.

And now, as he walks up here so close to the sky, that slice of moon must be tugging on them because they rise inside him again, flood his arid mind.

Emma stomps after the mouse that had just made him jump. It had appeared suddenly, it bolted from behind a garbage can outside the restaurant where they had just eaten sandwiches. They were hearty sandwiches with thick, crusty bread, and she'd struggled to bite into them with her front tooth missing.

The creature has scurried back behind the can and Emma turns to him and smiles. A stark cut-out on the wilderness of the graffiti-decorated brick wall: her wide pale face, brown eyes, freckled cheeks, skinny legs under baggy shorts, looking over at him with that child-adult look.

You were afraid of that little mouse? Daddy! Her tone is scolding but she runs on those gangly legs from the mouse and into him with a fierce hug. *I'll protect you.* Her breath on his chest is humid and smells like mustard. She lets go and he lets her go and watches her run over to where Sarah is sitting to tell her, no doubt, of his cowardice.

Now she lies at the foot of the stairs. Her head on her arms, her body spilling over the steps, white skin between strands of sweat-darkened hair. *I can't climb them Daddy. My legs won't go.* He hurries over to her and touches her shoulder. Heat flares from her, burns his skin.

Sarah is here. They are here together; they continue to have a common purpose, a thread of love still stitches them together. She sits across the bed from him, silent. Emma sleeps fitfully between them. Beside him, plastic tubing climbs to the bag of medication.

He knows he should speak but he has already said too much. He already told Sarah what he did earlier in the day. He told her that he signed the consent form but he did not tell her how fear drew those lines—the thin, spidery script. He did not tell her that his scrawl on the page looked careless but when he handed the form over to the oncologist the page was buckled from the sweat of his palm.

He wants to tell her all this but he won't. He won't because it is his job to know what to do, his job to understand the drugs, the treatment options, the evidence. But even though he knows it, every last word of it, he has a sick, sinking feeling that it is all meaningless.

He lifts his eyes and sees Sarah watching the drip of fluid, falling one sphere at a time into the reservoir and then down the line and into their daughter's hand. From there her body will welcome it, allow it into her marrow where it will methodically and dispassionately destroy her blood cells, line by line. From this wreckage, it is hoped, she will replace them all. Flowers from a wand. Something out of nothing.

It'll be okay.

Sarah looks over at him and knows that he is lying.

And then, with the spin of himself on his own axis away from this, the memories recede.

Fight or flight. Along with food and sex these are the basic survival responses. For the last few months he has not lifted himself from the lowest levels of human experience but sure as hell he has secured his own survival. Obscurely driven, plunging forward. If he wasn't so afraid of what he has done, he would laugh.

Why did you have to be so aggressive? You can't always win. You can't control the world.

And her eyes when she said it: dry and hopeless and hard.

God Sarah, I wanted to cure her. It was our only chance.

Chance? You left it up to chance?

He hears the sobs as though they are coming from out there, and if he walks on he will stumble across the creature responsible for them—half man, half beast, staring into a pond of his own tears.

For a while after the sun has sunk below the horizon, the sky remains lit with a colourless glow, enough to see by. He finds a narrow footpath and joins it as it crosses the plain, but when he realizes it is taking him away from Sapitwa, he leaves the path and crosses through the grass again. Once the sunlight goes altogether, he relies on the meagre light from the thin sliver of moon and the stars.

He looks up at the night sky and does not recognize it. Of course there is no North Star to find. But maybe something else to grab hold of: the Big Dipper, or Cassiopeia. But there is nothing familiar about this sky. The stars gather in patterns that are mysterious to him. Everything here evades him. Everything remains beyond his reach.

And then he receives a gift. He hears a rushing sound, the sound of movement. He stands and listens. It is beneath him, this sound, this movement. He crouches down and puts all he has into the listening. He feels the funnelling of sound to his ear, the fine-tuning of his attention to this, just to this. He places his hand on the ground and feels it. There is movement under him and it is the movement of water.

Henry scrambles along the ground, feeling in front of him, looking for it. And then he sees it and feels it all at once. Cold and wet on his hands. Bright in his eyes, moonlight coming up at him from the ground. A mountain stream.

He dips his hands into it, between the rocks and pebbles. It is shallow, maybe two inches deep. He scoops at it, brings it to his mouth. He wets his lips in it, lets it slide over his tongue and down the back of his throat. My God, it is a gift. A miraculous gift. He splashes it on his face, scoops handfuls of it into his mouth, feels himself return.

Crouching down, something presses against his thigh. He stands up, reaches into the pocket of his trousers and finds it. It is still there. The old man's shell. Did it find the water for him? Did it guide him to it? Or was it Sapitwa? Was the mountain tossing him one last scrap? Or Emma? God, Emma, is her sweet soul up there warming that strange sky, blowing kisses, fulfilling wishes? Regardless of who or what or how, he is grateful and he says so out loud: thank you. He kneels down, dips his forehead in the stream and says it again.

*

The village darkens with the setting sun and Iris joins the throng of people moving downstream to the centre of the village. The celebrations have been ongoing for hours, and now the firelight is visible from where she is, still many huts away. She can see the glow cast on everything around it and the village shrinks and grows in the changing light. Iris allows the crowd to move her along, closer to the ceremonial fire. She feels the heat from the bodies around her and, as she gets closer, feels the heat from the fire itself. There is a drumbeat; at first it is outside of her, a regular pulse, and as she gets closer the pulse becomes indistinguishable from her own, the one inside her, the one she can't stop.

She goes first to the prayer tree and places her flower just in front of it, along with all the other offerings and kneels down in front of the tree. Her throat tightens with each beat of the drums. She bows her head and tries to think of something to say to the ancestors. Something honest—there is no use lying to them.

She comes up with nothing so straightens and looks at the shrine, at the offerings people have left here. A bowl of millet flour. A rough wooden carving of some animal with a large snout and teeth. A piece of cloth, rolled up and tied with a piece of string. A bundle of hair.

As she looks at the offerings, she cannot ignore the fear, the grief, the anger and the powerlessness. This is the other side of the spirit. This is the side that her mother feared but did not discuss. Iris saw it in the way she looked at Mulanje Mountain, where the dark spirits were felt to roam free and were not bound to the rules of village life, and in the way she eyed the *sing'anga* in her village.

Those who are afraid are the most susceptible, her grandfather once said to her as he prepared a remedy for someone. Her grandfather is a *sing'anga*, but not the most respected. He often refused to mediate an act of revenge, and people interpreted this as a sign of weakness.

Iris stands and leaves the shrine, moves closer to the heat of the fire. People are dancing. The drumbeat throbs, low and guttural. A few men crouch around their drums, muscles taut, skin shiny in the firelight, beating down on the stretched skins with effort and in synchrony. Some people approach the fire, stare it down. And there, in the circle of bodies around the fire, she sees her grandfather.

He immediately looks over to her. He mouths something. Iris shakes her head. He says it again: *mzungu*.

Iris looks around for Dr. Bryce. Her immediate thought is that he must be here, participating, but she doesn't see him. He isn't here. She sees her grandfather again across the fire and he is looking somewhere else, looking up. He is looking at the mountain, or where she believes it is, as she can't see it now in the darkness. She can't see anything beyond the glow of the firelight. Her grandfather continues to stare at the mountain, wearing a grim expression.

Bryce is on the mountain.

Iris feels the beat on her ears, in her chest and fingertips. It is muffling everything, it is muffling her. She is having trouble thinking. She'd warned him. Weeks ago, in the hospital, she'd tried to warn him. And it seems to her that Bryce had turned strange immediately after that trip to the mountain with Ellison. And now the mountain is finishing what it has begun.

Iris looks at the fire. It swims up the sky and licks at the mountain. She steps forward and feels the threat of it on her skin. She stands there until she does not feel it anymore.

Chapter 19

Henry wakes to the heat on his skin: morning sunlight already so strong. He hears the gurgle of the stream beside him and rolls over toward it, dips his hand in the water. He feels it rush over his fingers. The stones under the water are rough and sharp. He has cuts and scrapes on his knuckles from scooping up the water from the shallow stream the previous night and the cold water soothes them now.

Something sharp stabs at the palm of his other hand. He peels open his fingers to see the object: the shell. The slit-like opening on the belly of the thing gapes open slightly like pursed lips and Henry runs his fingers along the corrugated edges. He moves onto his knees and crouches over the stream. The sun wavers on the surface of the water, flits between smooth curves of current.

Henry takes the shell and dips it in the stream. He scoops water into it and then raises it to his lips and drinks. He pays close attention to the feel of the water moving down his throat, all the way to his stomach. He does this many times until he has no more room for water and then he lies down again, beside the stream, closes his eyes to the brightness above him. The undersides of his eyelids are red with transient, hazy spots.

When he opens his eyes, he sees something up in the air. Something white. It has white wings. No. It couldn't be a dove. His mother saved one, once. Or rather, tried to save it. They were on their way to a wedding, the three of them, when Henry was still quite young. He and his father dressed in their stiff collared shirts and jackets and his mother wore a thin, loose and fluid dress that lifted and billowed in the wind like a sail. It was pale green. When she saw the bird sitting in the grass beside the trunk of a tree, she went over to it and picked it up. She pulled it in, close to her body, cupped it in her two hands like a child holding a communion wafer. She went over to a bench and sat down and clucked at it softly. The thing was stunned. The pink-rimmed eye that Henry could see looked vague, not at all the sharp, quick gaze of all the rest of the birds he had ever seen. Eventually, it tucked its head down, looping its neck in, toward its chest. "He's going," his mother murmured, and he wondered what she was feeling in her hands. Did she feel the last flutter of the heart against her finger? Did she feel it shudder as the soul shook loose from the body, slipped out from between the wings?

There were a lot of loose feathers, and some blood, and one of the wings had been broken. Probably from the jaws of a dog, or a fox. Henry could see a pale spear of bone among the blood and feathers, and he pointed to it. His mother didn't let him touch it. "Some bird bones are hollow," she said, "so they are light enough to fly. Just think, Henry, how close these birds are to the sky. They are mostly air, inside their bones and all around them, just air. Just empty space." And how young he had been then, because at that age and at the time when she said it, he felt nothing but pity for the bird.

Emma's marrow had been depleted by the chemotherapy. Her bones emptied out. As hollow as a bird's and she felt that way when he picked her up—as light as air.

When Henry opens his eyes again, the white bird is gone, and the sky is vacant. He rolls over and listens to the flow of water over rock.

He would prefer to stay here by the stream until he is found. But there is the risk—he may never be discovered here, so far off any path. He could last for days with water, but what's the use if he remains lost?

He knows that he will need to move on and continue his search for a rest hut and so he wills himself to get up. After some time, he reluctantly pulls himself to standing.

He feels unsteady on his feet, despite the rest and the water. He wavers a little; patches flit across his visual fields. He steadies himself and then looks around, tries to locate Sapitwa: his compass point, his goal. He cannot see it now. Henry turns in a circle, scans the field around him but just sees the grassy plateau arching away from him in every direction as though he is on a parched, grass-covered ball. Nowhere to go but over the edge.

*

Iris wakes up and recognizes the smell of her grandfather's hut: the fragrant scent of drying herbs. She brings her arms up to cover her face, to block out the bright stars of sunlight piercing the weaves of the roof and then smells the traces of fire on her skin—the salty smell of sweat and the sweet smoke of cedar wood embers.

She recalls being pulled away from the fire. Arms gently tugged her backward and into the cool darkness of the surrounding village. All she is able to retrieve from before her dreamless sleep is a memory of a dry, yellow landscape. It was not a real landscape and she was not really there. She could see the rough brushstrokes of yellow ochre, layered on in thick sweeps. And then blue above the yellow. Meaningless.

She sits up abruptly when she remembers Dr. Bryce. She gets up and leaves the hut. Her grandfather is there, he is just walking in through the fence. She goes to him, takes one of the heavy jugs of water out of his hand. He smiles briefly. The two of them walk across the yard, place the jugs near the cook hut.

Iris pours some of the water into a pot. She coaxes a fire with twigs and one of the hot embers in the cook hut. She encourages it with waves of her hand until the flames are high enough for her to put the pot over them. She leans back on her heels and watches tiny bubbles rise.

"How will we find him?" She says this into her arms that are crossed over her knees.

Iris's grandfather heaves the bag of maize closer to her. It is the same large rough weave with the same white script on it as the one in her mother's home. He says, "We will let the village know. Ade will help."

When the water reaches a boil, Iris scoops out some maize and lets it drift into the pot from her cup. It spills like sand and congeals like mud in the water. She stirs quickly.

"Ade knows." Says Iris. Ade: headman and *sing'anga*. Of course he knows.

"Yes."

"Bryce was driven out." This comes out more as a statement than a question.

"It is better to walk than curse the road. We will leave soon. After breakfast." He eyes the *nsima* that is thickening in the pot, then stands and walks back into the hut where it is cool.

When Iris and her grandfather leave his yard, it is still early but the village bustles with activity. The energy is always greater the day before and after a ritual. People smile and nod at them as they walk the short distance to Ade's hut. They enter through the fence. The yard is empty and so Iris and her grandfather go to the step in front of Ade's hut where they sit in the shade and wait.

Ade steps out a few minutes later. Iris and her grandfather rise. Ade eyes Iris's new garment, borrowed from her aunt and then her hair so neatly cropped. This man had been present to negotiate her arrival in this world so many years ago. He was the *sing'anga* who chaperoned her from the spirit world into this one and he knew the purpose of her journey. Traditional names are given to reflect the individual's purpose, the meaning that will propel them through the world. But Iris's mother chose not to bestow this name upon her children. Instead, she chose her children's names from a book left by white missionaries, a book left in the classroom that Iris attended. The place where all the Western books were kept. Iris had found this name book once, perched on the bookshelf among the storybooks. She'd flipped through it and found her name there. No meaning was given. (In nursing school she learned it meant the muscular coloured ring around the pupil of the eye and she'd cried over this—that her name was tied to something so anatomical and ordinary.)

Her mother had done this with all her children—assigned them Western names. Grace. Samuel. Hope. As though she knew, even at the time of their birth, that they would be foreigners here. Now, standing here in front of her grandfather and Ade, she feels ashamed of what her mother did. She feels the sting of the insult.

"The doctor is lost." Her grandfather wastes no time.

Ade looks at Iris. "You lost your guest?"

Iris enjoys for a moment the implication: that she, Iris, is not a guest. "My guest lost himself." She replies.

Ade smiles.

"Where shall we look for this *mzungu*?"

"Mulanje." Her grandfather says. "He is on the mountain."

Ade's smile broadens. "Mulanje. A fine place for a *mzungu* to wander. How are you so certain?"

"Alile's daughter, Mkele," says her grandfather and Iris looks at him sharply. He had not told her this. "Mkele told me yesterday that she saw him climbing the mountain. He was carrying no food or water."

"He'll burn the whole thing down before he's done with it." Ade looks over at the mountain now, as if he expects to see a curl of smoke rising from it. Iris looks too, but it is the same. It always looks angry to her. It seems no more angry today than yesterday or the day before.

Ade turns to her grandfather. "So we let him find his own way down. How about that?"

Her grandfather stares back at him, his hand trembles on his walking stick.

"We cannot leave him there."

Ade barks a laugh. "Why not?"

"We cannot."

"He is a *mzungu*. What do we owe him?"

"He is a doctor."

"So what?" He looks around, like there are other people to see. "Everyone running to him like he is a god. They enjoy that, you know? That is why they come here. To feel like gods." He spits on the dirt and starts to walk away. Then he stops. "I think we should do nothing."

Iris's grandfather walks to him. He raises a long, bent finger and points it at Ade's face. "You will get him and bring him back here. You will do the decent thing." He pauses. "I have been a *sing'anga* for a long time. Many years. And I have not dealt with the bad magic. But I can." He lowers his finger slowly and Ade looks away, at the mountain, before spitting one more time then then stalking off, into his hut.

Her grandfather stands beside her. She turns to the mountain and feels for an instant like she can see Bryce there, scaling its side, moving across it like an insect.

Those who fear are the vulnerable ones, her grandfather has said. She has never seen Bryce afraid.

*

He sees Sapitwa for a moment, just a moment, and then it is gone. It could be the shifting clouds that rearrange themselves in the sky as it has been doing this, or he has been doing this, for hours, now. Seeing Sapitwa and then losing it again. Just those glimpses, though, keep him going, keep him thinking he must be getting nearer. So he keeps on, keeps at it, walking over the grass, trudging, at times stumbling. He has not found a path again, not since the prior evening and he curses himself for leaving it. It would have gone somewhere, eventually, wouldn't it? Not necessarily. There were a lot of paths that criss-crossed the mountain, especially at the top. Henry remembers passing a number of them last time, when he was here with Ellison. They intersected the main path, and seemed to go nowhere but the horizon, although how to know? At least it was a path, a place people walk. Not this Godforsaken plain. Not even animals walk here. He still has not seen a creature more evolved than an insect. Things with exoskeletons. He could use one of those right about now, so that when he falls it doesn't hurt so damn much.

He has walked into countless webs, stretched across the grass waiting for him. Most of the spiders have been small and seemingly harmless. He has seen larger ones in the city, though. As large as his fist and ominous looking. Carnivorous. All legs and eyes. Henry laughs and the sound is lost quickly. He thinks of Sarah: all legs and eyes and, come to think of it, not unlike a spider in many ways. Especially after Emma died—she withdrew, wove a tight web around herself. If she could see him right now, she would be skittering across her web to immobilize him with her words, inject him with another of her venomous looks. Why the hell did you decide to climb a mountain? She would say. Why alone, without food or water? What got into you? Guilt again? Then she would sigh, pierce him with one more look before slipping back to the edge of her web where she would wait for him to make another mistake.

But God, she was beautiful. And she loved him, back then. Even when she was angry. And afterwards, after their fights she would wrap those legs around him and squeeze, squeeze him with all those long, smooth limbs and he would relax into it, relinquish himself to the pleasure of it. The pleasure of her.

He knows how he and Sarah lost their way. Trust of all kinds was ruined by what happened. When a couple loses a child ... It does not need to be figured or explained, does it? When a couple loses a child. That is all.

*

Ade has gone back into his hut. Iris and her grandfather wait outside, and Iris wanders over to look at Ade's garden, lets her eyes rest on the soothing green of the plants. She spies the orange of ripening tomatoes among the green. Cassava leaves spring from the ground in robust clusters. There are other plants, many of which she does not recognize. She remembers Ade's garden from childhood. It has always been larger, more fruitful and lush than the others'. What magic does this *sing'anga* employ, even in the garden, that allows him to do what others cannot?

"These colours look nice on you," says a woman's voice beside her. Iris turns. It is Alile. She is smiling and reaching out to finger the cloth that Iris's aunt had given her to wear. Iris looks at her, forces her gaze to the woman's face, to those eyes. Unmistakable. Her mother's eyes, and all her siblings. Iris looks away, down at the fabric draped across her body, where Alile's fingers still linger.

"Thank you," says Iris, feeling simple. "My aunt lent it to me."

"What happened to your dress?" Alile keeps her golden eyes on her, moves her hand away. "It was so lovely."

"It fell apart in this heat." Iris turns back to the garden, stares at a tomato plant.

"I imagine the city is much more comfortable." Alile says this softly. She turns to the garden, bends down and lifts a leaf with her long fingers. "Do you like my garden?"

"Oh." She says. "I thought it was Ade's. Being here, in his yard, I just assumed ... "

"Yes, it is Ade's," Alile smiles. "But he has let me tend it lately, so I am feeling more and more like its mother." She caresses another leaf, cradles a young tomato in her palm for a moment before she lets it slide off her hand and dip gently on the vine. "We are good, this garden and me." Alile looks at Iris. "And you?"

She says this and Iris is aware of her own barrenness. How incapable she is of producing anything.

"I don't garden."

Alile keeps her eyes on Iris's face for a moment longer, then says, "That is a shame. Maybe I can teach you."

Before Iris can manage a response, Ade reappears. He goes to Iris's grandfather who is sitting on the step of his hut, in the shade, with his eyes closed. When Ade returns, he stands and the two men talk in low voices, their hands on their hips. Alile watches the men for a moment, then turns her attention back to Iris.

"So your *mzungu* is lost?"

Iris nods.

"He went to Mulanje?"

"Yes."

"Alone?"

"Yes."

Alile looks over at the mountain. "So many *mzungu* go to the mountain now. They climb all over it. Like ants. So many of them." She turns to Iris. "Why?" As if Iris understands, as if Iris could explain it.

Iris sighs. "I warned him last time he went. He knows. But I can't warn them all." She toes the dirt under her foot. "Hopefully he will at least avoid Sapitwa."

Alile is quiet for a moment. "Maybe he should go to Sapitwa. Maybe he should finally understand."

Iris says nothing.

Alile has been holding her hand over her brow to shade it as she looks out at the mountain. In the shade of her hand, her eyes have darkened and seem deeper set, more like Iris's own. Alile continues.

"Mkele saw him yesterday. She said he was running like a *mafunso*. He was all sweaty."

Iris tries to imagine this: Dr. Bryce looking crazed, running inexplicably, running into a certain threat. Completely illogical. She is beginning to assume that whatever changed when he first went to the mountain has progressed, set irrevocably in motion, something that will move forward despite anything anyone does, or tries to do. Including Bryce himself. In a way, this thought releases her. Knowing that something is beyond one's control alleviates worry. And guilt. She smiles and looks at Alile.

"He is strong and resourceful. I'm sure he will be a formidable opponent to Sapitwa."

Alile smiles. There is a new understanding between them. After all, they share blood. They both turn and watch Ade and her grandfather talk. Something flashes between the two men, an object that her grandfather passes to Ade. It is Dr. Bryce's reflex hammer. Now Ade has it. He slips it into his pocket. Then they watch as Ade waves to them, walks across the yard and slips through the partition in the fence, heading to the mountain, heading out to save the *mzungu*.

*

There. He opens his eyes and sees Sapitwa again. It looms in front of him. The sun is high and bright but somehow Sapitwa remains dark, a jutting stab of obsidian on the white-blue sky. He gets up, stumbles forward, trips, falls. He is on his knees in front of it. It is still there. Sapitwa. He says the name out loud. Sapitwa. It glowers at him.

Henry struggles up again. He doesn't feel his legs anymore, but they are down there, below him, propelling him forward. He runs across the field, no longer stumbling, no longer tired. He moves so fast, so fast he is not running but flying across the field. He soars over the grass and Sapitwa grows until it is all he can see. The blue sky is consumed by the dark peak of the mountain and he feels its shade on his face. His legs fling him forward and then the earth drops off. The field falls away from him. He is in the air for a moment. For a moment he is suspended, exhilarated, part of the sky. He soars toward Sapitwa.

But the mountain reaches up, paws at him with clawed swipes, rough jabs of pain as bushes grab at his skin and clothes, grapple him to the ground and then, abruptly, he stops.

His head throbs because it is downhill from his legs. He pulls and rearranges himself until he is sitting up. It is a steep slope and he didn't see it coming. He can see the sharp drop from the plateau where he had been running when he fell. And there, in the opposite direction and just a few more metres ahead of him, Sapitwa rises, more enormous and impenetrable than it had appeared from afar.

He is now in its shade. It is cooler here, but not breezy. The air stagnates in this little pocket of space between the plateau and the peak. He closes his eyes, just for a moment. He needs to regain some strength and energy if he is to proceed. And he will need to go further if he is to orient himself on this beast of a mountain. He will need to scale Sapitwa. He looks up at it. It is no longer a peak on a mountain, it is a wall.

It seems to rise straight up out of the ground. Yes, there are cracks and crevices that he could use as handholds, but to do so without a harness would be an outrageous risk. He remembers Ellison remarking that some people climb it with gear, but others have done it with nothing. Ellison himself has climbed it without ropes or harnesses.

He looks at it again. Straight up, for God's sake. Maybe there is a gentler slope by another approach. After resting here for a while, he will walk around its perimeter. He will find a safer approach. He leans back on the side of the mountain and watches Sapitwa out of half-closed eyes.

*

The village is quiet—most are in their huts preparing for the dinner meal—as Alile and Iris walk together, hands held behind them, heads down, watching their dresses swish in front of them with each step. Although they could not look more different, they are the same person. This is what Iris is discovering. And Alile's existence alone verifies many of Iris's suspicions.

Alile is younger than Iris, six years younger. Alile was born the year Iris and her family left the village. Six years was the age Iris was when her mother lost the baby, a baby that would have been her last sibling, a baby that Iris was told was stillborn, dead in the uterus before it could take a breath of air.

Iris looks at Alile.

"Your eyes ... " Iris begins.

"They are strange. No one has them."

Iris realizes that Alile has never borne witness to her maternal lineage, has never seen her own eyes on any other face. She wonders what Alile has been told about her mother.

Alile, too, must feel adrift. This is what unites them, she and Alile, this feeling of floating without an anchor.

"They are remarkable." She finally says, arriving at a truthful statement she will not be ashamed of.

Alile looks down and that bright glow disappears under her eyelids. Iris looks away, ashamed anyway.

"Ade says they make me special. He says that when he saw them for the first time, he knew I would be a great *sing'anga*."

Iris looks over at Alile again. She thinks about her own unremarkable nursing career, how lacking in greatness it is. Pushing the medical cart after silent doctors. Helping them collect body fluids: blood, spinal fluid, ascites, stool, urine. Helping them give medication. Helping them find reasons to give up: resistant infection, AIDS, poverty. "Bad Substrate" as they sometimes said in conversations she stood at the edges of, shrugging their shoulders. There was nothing anyone could do about Bad Substrate. And this land is full of people with Bad Substrate.

Again Iris thinks of her grandmother's whispers, her predictions and promises. It seems that Alile has gained this special privilege and Iris, despite her own lineage, her grandfather being one of the most skilled healers, was left out. Shut out of what could have been. She thinks of her mother, undoubtedly sitting alone in her little home, preparing dinner. Does she feel any guilt for what she has done? For what has she been trying to keep Iris and her siblings away from all these years? For what pushed her to leave this place? For what compels her to press her lips together whenever Iris asks her about the village, her own childhood, even her father?

Her mother has said little about her father to Iris. Iris is the only one who asks about him. Her siblings are more prepared to turn away from the past. They prefer to face the rising sun, but Iris prefers to watch it set. And when her mother opens up a little, tells her a morsel of information about the village or her father, or her sister Grace, Iris feels that warm sun on her face again, Iris closes her eyes and lets the story wash over her.

"Have you learned much from Ade?" She asks Alile this, and keeps her voice neutral.

Alile looks at Iris sideways, out of the corners of her eyes. "He shares many things, but I have to be willing to trust him. That is the only way he can lead me. If I am completely blind."

"Do you trust him, then?"

They stop walking. Alile looks down at her hands which she stretches out in front of her, as though the answer is written on them somewhere. But no, Iris realizes, the answer is not written there; it is not written anywhere, and that is how it can be known.

"Yes." Alile says to her hands, and then they resume their slow pace.

"What about you, Iris? You are a *sing'anga* in the city. Who teaches you?"

Iris pauses. "I am a nurse. Not a *sing'anga*. And I had many teachers. Most of them books. The books taught me a lot."

Alile twists her mouth, undoubtedly trying to imagine learning from an object, symbols on a page. How strange it all suddenly seems. Yet she knows that she could not live without books. Through books she has access to so much, to complete worlds outside of herself. She feels the pride in her, deep down. She is proud of her accomplishments. Just like her mother.

"I learned a lot from books," she repeats. "I have read a lot of books."

Alile nods, in a way that seems to respect this method of learning, imported from a place that clearly has so much more than they do. Encouraged by Alile's reaction, she continues.

"You can know much from the body. Such as the pressure in a patient's blood vessels. The Blood Pressure. We can measure it. When it is too low or too high it can be dangerous. And the heart." Iris raises her right hand to her chest, places it just under her left breast, places her fingers between the ribs there and feels the organ pushing out between the ribs and touching her fingers. "The heart can push too hard, beat too fast, or it can push too slow. When that happens, fluid collects in the lungs, and the patient will have trouble breathing."

"And then?" says Alile. "And then what? What can be done?"

"It depends," says Iris, "it's complicated." She looks over at Alile and Alile is smiling, looking at her.

"You enjoy it." This is not a question. Alile has seen something in Iris, something she has never seen herself.

"And you? You enjoy learning from Ade?"

Alile runs a hand across her head, across the short-cropped hair that follows her scalp so closely. "It is difficult at times. He has me practice a lot in the garden. Once in a while he will leave me with someone. Someone who is ill. He will just leave. And I am expected to listen. If I listen carefully enough, I can hear them. And then I know." She stops herself, as though realizing she has gone too far, said too much. She looks around.

They are alone as they approach Iris's aunt's hut. The village is quiet. The sun is low down and red. It is Iris's favourite time of day. But now she thinks of Bryce, spending his second night on the mountain. She looks over at it. It is awash in sunset red that creeps slowly across the rock. The other side, the side not facing the sun is dark. Almost black. She wonders which side he is on, which blanket covers him now. The red or the black.

Alile takes her hand. "Let's go in and have some food."

She leads her through the fence where Iris's aunt is waiting.

*

Something tickles Henry's arm. This is what wakes him, this tickle on his arm that progresses from his wrist to his elbow in an instant. Feathery but firm, a certain weight to it, pressing on his skin at points in rapid succession. He opens his eyes to see the spider treading up his arm, advancing with a menace that only a spider can possess.

Henry jerks upright and shakes his arm. The thing drops off with a weight. He can hear it land. He is standing now, and stares down at the spider. It does not scurry away. Instead, it waits. It is the size of the larger ones he had seen in the city, a bit smaller than his fist. Almost certainly poisonous. When it was on him, a foot away from his head, he could see its face, or what could be considered its face. The area where its eyes are clustered, and its dagger-like fangs.

What is the safe thing to do? If he moves, will it leap back on him? Will this precipitate a bite? How fast can the thing move? What the hell is the thing doing this high up the mountain, anyway? Before he can make a move, right or wrong, the spider sidles away and disappears underground.

Too easy, he thinks. When he takes a breath in, he becomes aware of how tight his chest had been. These creatures can sense the slightest currents of air. It could probably smell him from metres away. But there was no need for such acute sensory talents for this encounter; he must have been lying on top of its lair, for God's sake. He has been let off with a warning.

The mountain shifts under him. If he remains very still, he can feel the compression and expansion of its breaths. He can feel the heat coming off of it.

It is the mountain's own rising impatience that compels him to move. He slips and stumbles and falls down the remaining slope to the base of Sapitwa. When he stands again he feels light. Lighter than the air up here, like helium that expands and expands into the space it occupies. His vision is dotted with the spinning, moving atoms he shares the space with. Nothing is still. He tilts his head back and looks up the flank of Sapitwa. It reaches high, and from here he cannot see where it ends.

He has not touched it. He brings his gaze back down to the slab in front of him. He reaches out a hand, fingers extended, and closes the gap between them. Sapitwa slides under his fingertips and he feels it shudder. He leaves his hand there on the warm stone. He presses down his whole palm then he strokes it, feels the pits and grooves under his fingertips, the thick and gnarled folds. He slips his fingers into the grooves and grasps hold and then does the same with his other hand. He has a firm grip on the rock now. So firm that he could lift himself, if he were to try. He looks down and nudges a toe into one of the larger crevices about a foot off the ground. He places his whole weight onto this foot and lifts off the ground, pushing up with his toe and holding on with both his hands. He hangs there for a moment, afraid to breathe. He is clinging to the side of this beast, hanging on to its thick hide, willing to go wherever it is willing to take him.

Even here, just a foot off the ground, he feels a surge of power. The air still spins in front of him as he reaches higher up, steps his second foot onto a ledge above his first foot. So easy. Why did he think he needed a different approach? It is as though the mountain is leaning over, making it easier for him, creating folds where there were none before, just for his next hand or foot. He reaches again, grabs and pulls himself higher, steps higher, feels the air move around him, sees the particles of air spinning around him, sees a vortex of particles whirl together upwards, like an inverted tornado, in some sort of organized chaos. He follows this vortex where it seems to be pointing him: up, up, up the flank of the beast. And he steps up. It is as if he is walking, it is that easy. There is such strength in his arms and his legs, they are infused with some new blood, better blood, blood that can do miraculous things. This blood pounds through him with more force than usual, it pulses through each limb; he can see each bolus muscling through his narrowed vessels with each clench of his heart, in each limb, all the way to his fingertips which sink into the folds of the mountain, this mountain that is starting to feel warm and soft, as if he is crawling up a great bosom, as if he could nestle into the cleavage of it, as if it would nuzzle him there, whisper reassurances, keep him safe and fed.

He feels like crying and then he is; great wracking sobs that heave through him. Some kind of terrible loneliness inside him that needs to come out. Once it is released, he will be better. He lets it crawl out of him, this black misery. It slips down the mountainside leaving him lighter, without its burden and he wonders again at the power and strength of this mountain, this place, this miracle.

Clinging to the mountainside, he leans back a little, looks up. Sapitwa still reaches up beyond him, beyond what he can imagine himself ever reaching, no matter how hard he tries. Behind him, beside him, below him is air: not still. No, not still. It spins around him. It collides into him. It pushes him, pulls at him, nudges him, teases him, distracts him with its movement, its empty infinity that envelops him, suffocates him, makes his hands weaken, makes his fingers tire where they grip the breast of Sapitwa, unwilling to part.

Things begin to slip. First, his fingers. They become moist and no matter how hard he tries, they slip out of Sapitwa, slide down her skin. His toes shift in place and he finds another crevice where they might have more room. He stands on his toes, feels the ache in his calves, runs his fingers across Sapitwa but she has smoothed herself out; there are no more grooves or crevices, the rock is impenetrable. Marble skin. Alabaster. And she has tired of him, turned one flawless shoulder to him now. The ledges where he had been resting his feet sink in, the rock becomes featureless.

He slides, still grasping for a moment, and then falls. Drops off her smooth body and down. Down onto a pillow of air that cradles him only briefly before he hits the ground with a crumpling silence.

Chapter 20

Iris's aunt greets Alile and Iris at the door of her hut. They step inside. All traces of her nursing uniform and her long hair are gone now. Iris threw the flower she'd made out of her dress into the fire last night. Flames danced around it. It remained a black heap, a dark spot inside the fire for so long. It was still there, the black flower in the fire, when she was pulled away.

The girl is there. Alile's daughter, Mkele. She looks up at them when they enter and then gets up and runs into her mother's legs. Iris steps away and watches them hug. She wonders who Mkele's father is. Where are all the fathers? Who are all the fathers? All these women without a man. She thinks: when there are too few men, there is trouble. Iris busies herself with the food, sets the eating area, lights the lantern, tries to shift this thought out of her mind.

This is her mother's thought, planted in her mind. Her mother said this: when there are too few men, there is trouble. And yet she took her children away, to the city, to raise all these children alone without a man. When she needed help, she recruited it from the women in their new neighbourhood. The men she kept away. The men she used for money. No man ever set foot in their new home in the city.

The closest they got was a knock on the door. Her brother was the only one, and he didn't count as until recently, he had just been a child.

Now he is a man. Her brother has grown into a big, tall man. He works in a bar, ogling women, pushing sweaty beers across the counter, grinning his grin. Her brother with his broken arm. *Your brother has a broken arm, I have a broken heart.* This is another thing her mother said. More reasons to stay away from the village. The village is where hearts and arms are broken. And lives. Her father's life was broken here, too.

Iris stands up from where she has been spooning out the relish onto plates. She blinks and looks around. She is the closest she has been to where her father lost his life. Suddenly she wants to see the spot where he was killed. She wants to see the ground where he lay, where his broken body breathed its last breaths. Where the white man stood staring, hands on his hips, as he died in front of him. She wants to see this place.

Her aunt and Alile are chatting amiably, waiting for the meal to be served and she is standing there with a dripping spoon. She can't go tonight. But tomorrow. Tomorrow she will go to this place. She will go where she might be able to feel him. She has not felt her father in so many years.

She kneels back down and continues spooning the relish, and then she passes around the *nsima.* Finally, she sits down on the mat, takes her plate, and begins eating.

Iris leaves soon after breakfast the next morning. She tells her aunt and Alile, "I'm going for a walk," and sets off with her head down, ignoring the feeling of the women following her with their eyes. She walks out through the village, finds the path through the field. She walks along the narrow footpath, enjoying being alone. This is one thing she has learned: how to like being alone. She is aware of the paradox: the bigger the community, the more alone one is. It is nearly impossible to be alone in the village; everything is centred around community living here. Survival depends on it. One cannot last long being alone in this environment and she thinks again of Bryce alone on the mountain. If anyone can, he can, she thinks. He bumps and jostles with his environment and with the people around him, but remains unaffected. He carries about him a sense of control and in this, in this need to remain in control, he will never truly be affected by anyone else. He cannot. It would destroy him. She feels a wave of tenderness and pity, she feels her heart rush out to him, wherever he is, up high on Mulanje. Walking here, on this plain, she feels as though she can touch him and she tries to do this, tries to stretch out a piece of herself, thin and insubstantial as it is, out to him across the plain and up the mountainside where he lies somewhere weak and tired and alone.

This is where she and Bryce differ: she feels better when she has done this. When she has pushed out a part of herself into the world, when she has made herself vulnerable. The way he communicated: the cold, silent agreements, the immovable wall that existed between them, it nearly destroyed her in its sterility. But she found herself moving into it more naturally than she had expected she could, and this terrified her. Was she this capable of closing herself off, of losing her spirit altogether?

She watches her skirt swish swish swish with each step. It makes the same sound as walking through the grass. The colour of the plain, the sound of her skirt, the sound of the wind in the grass, the feel of the sun on her skin. All of this—she shares it with countless generations of ancestors and as she walks she moves into them, into the memory of them here on this plain, moving in this direction, feeling the sun in this very place in the sky, leaving this very brightness as spots in her eyes, burning a warmth in this very spot on her shoulders.

She doesn't see the road when she reaches it; she sees burning red slice through the yellow savannah and she moves into the red and the sun feels even more hot and bright and she moves across it until she sees a darkness within the bright stretch of ground in front of her. She sees the stain on the road. Her ancestors remember. They remember all the living and all the dead and they feel him here, where he moved from one life to the next and the dust swirls up around her, creates a spinning cloud around her, until she almost disappears in it. And she stands in the middle of it and feels him as the man he was before he died.

She hears a sound. A very quiet sound, like the wind, but more persistent and growing in pitch and volume. The cloud around her moves away in one great sweep and she sees it coming up the crest, floating for an instant above the mirror that shimmers on the road, before it is on her, almost on top of her: the large, dark, noisy, hot hood of the car. It screeches and slides and skids for a few feet and finally stops, half off the road and within a few feet of her where she stands on the other side of the road.

She hears the grinding squawk of a door open. And there is a large white man, standing behind the door with his hands on his hips, then walking around the door past the front of the car and toward her.

"Iris?"

It is Dr. Ellison striding toward her, foreign in size and gait and voice and mannerisms.

"Iris! I nearly hit you! What were you doing standing in the middle of the road? You were covered in dust, I could barely see you. It is you, isn't it?"

He comes closer and stands over her.

"You're different," he pronounces. He peers down at her. "Are you okay?"

"There were chickens." She points to the road in front of her, between her and Dr. Ellison's car. "There were chickens on the road and the man was trying to avoid the chickens when he hit my father."

Dr. Ellison is silent for a moment, probably taking stock of the situation, taking stock of her. Then he says: "I'm sorry."

Iris turns away. "Yes." She looks out at the field past the car, looks at the grass flattened by two of the car wheels. She looks for the footpath back to the village but can't see it from here.

"How's Bryce? Back in the village?" Dr. Ellison takes a step toward where the footpath is hidden.

"He is on the mountain."

She waits for the reaction, for the concern to cloud his face. But there is no darkening on his face, there is no worry. He has turned toward Mulanje and gazes upon it. Respectfully, she must admit. The mountain, from this vantage point and with all the morning sun on it, looks cheerful and bright. Reassuring. Perhaps she is overreacting. Perhaps this climb is recreational, just as it was when he went with Ellison a few short weeks ago.

Now Dr. Ellison nods. "He enjoyed our trip there a month ago. He really wanted to attempt Sapitwa. Maybe that's what's drawn him back."

"Yes," Iris says. She holds back her other thoughts. Dr. Ellison doesn't want to hear of dark spirits, of lost souls. "He is a strong man." She is not sure why this thought came out through her mouth, and clamps her lips closed.

Dr. Ellison sighs. "Too strong. Strong-headed." He turns away from Mulanje and mutters: "Not the best place to be strong." He looks down at her. "Sometimes a softness, a flexibility, is a good thing. Even bone bends under pressure. Did you know that, Iris? That bones bend?" He smiles and Iris feels a warmth from him that comes as a surprise. This rough, bushwhacking white man. So there is a softness even to him. She smiles back at him.

"How is the boy with the broken leg?" She asks this to break his gaze. She has trouble with this: holding gazes, sharing smiles, all this warmth passing between two people. "Is he recovering well? How is his leg?"

"He's doing well. I think he'll need to stay a little longer. He won't get the rest here that he will in hospital. I'll keep him until his cast is off. About four weeks."

Iris thinks of the boy there in the ward with all those closed-eyed strangers.

Dr. Ellison adds: "He'll do fine. He's already making friends. He may even want to stay on. His father has found some family in town."

Iris feels like crying and stifles what is rising behind her eyes. She looks down at her dress. The skirt hides her feet which she knows are bare and dirty. She feels Dr. Ellison sweeping his gaze over her appearance: her clothing, her hair.

"You look like you've settled in nicely here."

She is not sure if he is being kind or cruel. She can't tell these things anymore. She can't read people. Only books. And she misses them, she realizes. She misses the books. In

Blantyre, she made a habit of borrowing them, one at a time, from the library.

"It's my home."

Dr. Ellison looks at her. She can see he is surprised.

"I didn't know that."

When she says nothing, he takes a big breath in, fills that enormous rib cage with air. He puffs up even larger than usual. And then he lets it all out. She feels the wind of it on her face. He has no scent, not to his breath or his body.

"Well, I guess we'll leave Bryce to his mountain, for now."

Iris is quiet beside him. How much of her concern is driven by mere belief, a fear of the mysterious? She had thought that she had been away too long for this. But it is there still inside her—this irrational fear.

"So it looks like I'm on my own for the clinic." It is in his voice—the ruffle to his feathers. "And you, Iris? Are you coming? I could sure use your help. There's a load of work waiting."

She looks in the direction of the village as she speaks. "I would like to stay. I will wait for Dr. Bryce. I'll make sure he's okay. Then I can take a bus back with him." She looks up at him and sees it there on his large face—the only reason he does not insist she accompany him. He thinks she is in love with Dr. Bryce. She can see that in his smile, that secretive little smile. Let him think it, she decides. Let someone somewhere think she is in love.

*

He is lying on something. It presses up into his abdomen and smells thick and organic like singed hair. When he rolls over, he sees that what has been pressing into him is a heap of bones—the long bones of arms, legs, fingers, ribs, the smooth flat bowl of the pelvis, the squat cylinders of vertebrae. Shapes barely recognizable, deformed by time, yet he can still see the grooves and condyles where they used to fit together, each yoked to the next but now disjointed, separate, meaningless in their fleshless clutter.

Inches away, he studies them, sees everything. They are not solid—even the thick outer ring of the cortex is fenestrated and full of air. Something about this bone, somehow he can see all its microscopic secrets: the delicate architecture, the spaces where the cells used to be housed in their individual lacunae, their tiny offices of ossification. Peering through the yawning cavities and between calcified arches, he can see how bone is built like men build houses: tall, arched doorways, open chambers, floors and ceilings. Built to bear the earth pushing up against it, built to withstand the forces that pull on it. Each calcific spire in this skeleton is a monument to all the burdens weathered, all the stress absorbed and transferred and shared.

But it is the emptiness that awes him; the space cradled between the spires. It is equal to what was built around it; without it, the stress could not have been borne. And this is the miracle: it still remains, it will never change. The ceilings and walls may degrade and erode, but the space cannot. It has always been here. It is still here.

He presses up off the ground but is stunned by vertigo and pain and his arms fold in. The ground tumbles up toward him and the hard dust of it slams into his face, his eyelashes sweep sand aside while he scans the tilted horizon.

There—straight ahead, along the ground that angles strangely, beside the heap of human rubble—the skull. It is pressed sideways to the ground just like him, two eye sockets swollen with space, bulging with the unfulfilled desires of a child.

His breath comes out hot and dry.

It was a child.

He shuffles and drags himself closer.

His finger across the blackened parts comes away dark with soot. Was this the mechanism of the death or was it an incomplete cremation, after death had already come and gone?

Is it possible for a cremation to be complete? For something—someone—to be completely transformed from solid to a flutter of light to heat and then gone into the air in a windless flight? There are always remainders, reminders. Like the memories that are still here occupying his every hour, minutes that creep across the face of a clock but leave nothing in their wake except the emptiness of time passed.

But now time is backing up, filling in.

Those gaping sockets are filling with flesh: abundant, liquid, living, vitreous, rich with blood and lymphatics and all the history that was behind him is now in front of him as the skull fills in and is blanketed with fat and skin and there are the eyes those eyes he knows so well.

Emma lies there sucking in the dusty earth and he gently lifts her head and places it on his cradled arm. His other arm is around her small thin shoulder that is as pale as the sun-bleached bone within it, and this pose is as natural as breath. Her small body, hot with sun or fever or both, tightens with each gasp and he knows that it can't be undone any more than this, this is as far as history is willing to unwind so he clenches down with her paroxysms, breathes her breaths, feels her fear. A tear cuts a clean path through the dust on her face and he hugs her closer, pulls her hollow bones into his.

Chapter 21

Dr. Bryce has been found. High up on the mountain, at the base of Sapitwa, fallen and lost. This is how he is described to her: fallen and lost. And broken. Another broken man. It is Ade, her grandfather and Alile who attend to him first. Iris waits outside Ade's *khumbi*. She hears nothing coming from inside. Is he even alive? But then, just as she stands with her hands up around her head, she hears him. It is a soft groan, or a sigh. And all the terrible feelings slide off her instantly and she goes back to waiting quietly outside the *khumbi*. She sits down on the step and waits.

She overhears a hushed discussion between Ade and her grandfather. The two men have already stepped out of the *khumbi* and circled around it to the back to talk. They are talking about what is wrong with Dr. Bryce. Ade thinks it is just broken bones from the fall. Her grandfather feels it is much more than that. Her grandfather wishes to perform a ritual that is much more intensive, even dangerous, but it is the only way to cure Bryce. Ade thinks such an intervention will be unsuccessful in a *mzungu*. They must modify their treatment, give the *mzungu* what he expects.

Even in the hushed tones, Iris can hear the rising anger. A disagreement between two *sing'anga*, between the headman and an elder: this is a very bad sign. Alile steps out of the hut during this conflict. She looks at Iris with wide eyes.

"How is he?"

"He is very ill. I hear nothing." She looks inside the hut with her mouth flat. The women stand there and listen to the rising voices of the two *sing'anga*. Iris has never heard her grandfather become angry. She didn't know what his voice could do. Now she knows: it becomes altered, strangled with the effort of trying to control it.

Iris looks at the entrance to Ade's *khumbi*. A dark mouth. She puts her index finger between her teeth and bites. The pain from her teeth pressing into the skin, pressing up against her bone, keeps her here, helps her to think. She remembers seeing an x-ray of her hand, once. It was captured while she was helping to hold down a patient who was sick with meningitis, who could not stay still for the chest x-ray. She held his shoulder and there, pale on the blue-black film, was her hand. Even her skeleton was short and stout, each bone in her finger sturdy and irrevocable. The tips flared in a strange way. But there was an elegance to her structure, deep under all the tissue. An elegance and leanness that was surprising to her, but not unexpected. She knows there are secrets about her, secrets that could surprise and please.

She takes her finger out of her mouth and studies the teeth marks: two thin lines. She rubs over them and it feels good, rubbing away the bite. She looks at the door to the hut. She says to Alile: "I will go see him." And steps through the doorway, past the curtain into the darkness.

At first she can't see anything. Both her grandfather and Ade have no windows on their huts. There is always this blindness when she enters. A time when she is lost, if only briefly. And it seems, once she regains her bearings, that she is already changed somehow, more ready for whatever will occur in this place.

She can smell him. There is the sharp odour of body fluids. He has had diarrhea, and vomiting. She wonders how much fluid they have managed to put back into him. He must be dangerously dehydrated. She hears him shift in the darkness and wonders if he can see her. Iris moves toward the sound and she is beginning to see things. She can see the herbs and bottles hanging from the ceiling and now, on the opposite end, she can see a dark form on the floor: Bryce.

He lies on his right side, facing her. There is the jut of his shoulder and hip. And the looseness of his limbs spilling out from his torso, completely lacking in tone. His right hand is stretched out in front of him, turned up as if to receive something.

His eyes are closed.

His breathing is fast—in and out through his nose and partially opened mouth. A sourness travels on these breaths—a sourness tinged with death. She can smell it from here—Bryce's death. Maybe this is what frightens her: the presence of death in a living body. Wave after wave of death coming from him in tides that rise higher and higher and pass over her head with a suffocating silence. She is overwhelmed by his almost-presence. No wonder the ancestors are silent.

Mother of God.

She hears her own raspy whisper move around the hut. Why does she say this now? It is something her mother would say, and it meant to Iris that her mother had completely disengaged from the village. Her mother began praying to a different god a long time ago, as long as Iris can remember, long before Iris's arrival in this world. So why, then, is she surprised? She is this person: a part of her mother, her upbringing, raised in a city where this is usual. Of course this would be the first thing to rise out from between her lips when the time came.

She moves toward him and kneels down. He has opened his eyes in response to her whispered words. They are swollen and they open in slits. She can see the shining liquid between his lids—his consciousness gleaming from those narrow openings. His whole face is swollen and misshapen. She wouldn't know it is him but for the telltale colour of his hair and his beard. Even in here, in the near-darkness of the hut, she can see its fiery colour. It glints red and gold. Even here.

She reaches out and touches his hand, the one that already stretches out from him on the floor. It is hot and dry. It does not move when she touches it. She sees that the wrist is swollen and is peculiarly angled. It must be broken. The leg that he lies on is also grossly swollen, the entire length of it distended, twice the width of the other. More broken bones. She wonders how much he has bled from these fractures. She wonders how they managed to move him here, all the way down the mountain.

She moves her fingers to his other hand, the one that is not swollen. She slides her fingers over his wrist, just below the thumb, to the radial pulse. Her own pounding pulse floods her fingers and for a while that is all she can feel: the rapid pounding of her own pulse pushing out her fingertips, pushing into Bryce's heartbeat, filling the void. But after a few moments she feels it: Bryce's pulse. It flutters under her fingers like the feeble, panicked wing-beat of a moth trapped under her hand. She draws her hand back because she doesn't wish to trap it; she never intended to trap him. This was never her intention.

She stares at the gold hair on his arm. And gold flecks along the lengths of his legs. He is naked. She can see the shade of his umbilicus and a thin strip of golden hair leading down to a triangle of darkness that is covered by his leg. She cannot tell if this hair, too, glints red-gold in the light but she imagines it must.

Iris runs her fingertips across the hair on his arm. It is smooth and soft. The skin beneath the hair is hot. She does it again. She hears something. Soft sounds. Something whispered. She looks at Bryce's mouth that remains partially opened and she sees his tongue touch up against his teeth, twice. In time with the sounds. Ai. Iss. Ai. Riss.

Iris.

She keeps stroking his arm.

"Yes," she whispers. "Yes."

He looks at her. Bryce shines out at her from behind those swollen lids.

"God." Says Iris. "Mother of God."

He closes his eyes.

The sun is violently bright in her eyes when she leaves the hut. It saps her energy. It is all too much. The responsibility of Bryce's well-being. A man like Bryce. A man like that. Relying on her. She sees Ade over in his garden, rummaging through the herbs. Why can't she relinquish responsibility to him? Or her grandfather? They, and their predecessors, have maintained the health of this community for generations upon generations.

Iris wills this oppressive weight over to Ade. She imagines it lifting off her, floating over to him, settling on his shoulders. Those broad, capable shoulders. And, for a moment, she feels better. But then she recalls the argument between Ade and her grandfather. The discussion about his illness. His broken bones. His fire. His nausea and vomiting. But there was no mention of malaria. Of course not. They know of it. Everyone knows of it, but this is not the way illness is approached here. Back in the *khumbi*, it occurred to Iris that Bryce had malaria. She saw the mosquito bites all over him. She smelled evidence of the vomiting, the diarrhea. In addition to his multiple fractures, he contracted malaria on the mountain. She is sure of it. As sure as she can be here, in this village, without a laboratory to check a blood smear, without a microscope to view the organisms.

She watches Ade pluck leaves from the garden. She sees the bundle he clutches in his hand. Perhaps this is what he is gathering: natural antimalarials. But perhaps not. She thinks of her sister, Grace. Her final memories are of her lying in a heap in the corner of the hut, waves of black death sweeping over her, sweeping over all of them as it took her. Just like Bryce. It will take him, too. They could not save Grace. Ade and her grandfather and the other village *sing'anga*. They could not save Grace. And when Iris thinks of it, when she allows herself to think of it, she knows that her sister died of malaria. She has thought over and over again as she learned about malaria in a textbook, and then as she treated it in the hospital, that her sister could have been saved. If she had the knowledge then that she has now.

Knowledge. She watches Ade move from plant to plant, his eyes mostly closed as he runs his fingers over the leaves, plucking this piece and that. Does Ade have knowledge?

Does her grandfather? No. They do not. Knowledge is something written and applied time after time, over and over again. Knowledge is something firm and immovable, like a stone. Knowledge is something discovered. Knowledge is something shared. No, Ade and her grandfather do not have this. What they have is belief. A belief so strong and so deep, a belief that plunges into the darkest reaches of consciousness, a belief that plumbs this consciousness, and comes out with a knowing. But this knowing is so specific to an instance, so dependent on the spirit and the circumstance of the moment, that it cannot be shared. It cannot be written. It would be useless in any other context. All that can be taught is the belief itself, not the knowing. This is what Alile is trying to learn. This is what Iris has been cut off from. She will never have this belief. This belief is gone.

And this is why all she feels as she watches Ade gather his medicine is doubt. And this is why, as she sits on the step of his *khumbi* and watches him, and thinks about Dr. Bryce inside his *khumbi*, all she can do is cover her face with her hands and close her eyes.

*

He is on the back of a beast, rides it like a bull. It bucks and heaves and snorts and whips him round. To breathe is to hurt. With each gulp of air, coals glow red deep inside.

Mother of God.

Mary Mother of God. A soft smell, candles or incense, polished wood of the back of a pew. The non-pious gleam of it, made shiny by the touch of so many sinners' hands.

Sweat makes his hand slip. He waits to fall, he wants to fall, to feel impact, to pack it in, to give in, to give up, but somehow he still stands, twisted and dizzy and nauseous. Blinking against the glare from the hateful curve of the pew.

Her casket is open. Leaning in from the wall behind it Mary looks down on him with smooth stone eyes, her hands clasped beneath the immovable folds of her marble robes.

He paws at his own eyes—fixed, staring pupils dug out wide to catch what little light there is, capturing mostly a shapeless grey space.

There is a night sky above him, and constellations cluster in the dark. With each blink they move: gather then spread, spiral in then disperse. He tries to follow just one, to see where one star goes but it is like trying to follow one drop of water in a river. Sometimes the stars coalesce so densely, cluster so brightly that they are eyes, then a face. The face is recognizable only in how it looks at him—he knows he has gazed down the same way on others. Then the clot of stars begins to bleed and he forgets about the face. He blinks and squints and looks for the darkness that the stars traverse, an absence so complete it must contain something. He searches for what hides in between those pins of light.

Chapter 22

The road opens up before her. It is an unremarkable road, unstained. Merely dusty from the dry, reddish soil. Iris stands in the middle of it and looks down along the length of it. It is a pale red ribbon that unfolds in yellow grasslands. These are the colours of her home: red earth, yellow grass. She memorizes this so it can sustain her while she is gone. She has made the decision to leave the village, to return to Blantyre. Just for a little while. But even this brief departure, just the idea of these few days away, is enough to make her crumple to the ground with weakness and fear. It is as though she is leaving a sphere of protection, although she knows this cannot be true. What, after all, would be protecting her? She is unattached, free to float from one existence to another. There is nothing tying her here or there. She can go wherever she chooses. So she has chosen to go to Blantyre. She will go back to Blantyre to save Dr. Bryce. This is her task, for now.

When a truck comes round the bend, it stops to her wave with a jarring screech of unpadded brakes. She negotiates a price with the driver and he waits for her to climb into the back where two families sit and watch her, bored.

Iris looks out the back of the truck as wind fills her ears, whips tears from her eyes so that she can barely see the savannah. All she can make out is a blurry transition from ground to sky. She can't see the mountain at all.

*

What lies in between, what he seeks, is becoming harder to find because there are distractions all around him. The needle-like slivers of starlight are lengthening. Now they stretch into flat fans of light that sweep over him in vague and changing patterns. And there are more faces, movement, voices.

He needs silence and darkness—the perfect conditions to listen, and watch. And search. But what he is seeking slips between the stars, the light, the noise. It hides among the clamouring movements, the throbbing sounds and the flickering objects that pretend to fill the space. Something familiar slowly fills itself outward until it consumes his every thought, defines his very presence.

He has lost it. What? What has he lost? For a moment it still exists as a flimsy flutter of an idea in the armour of his mind, and then even that is forgotten.

*

Once in a while, a touch. A cool cloth or fingers on his skin. It is a miracle, being touched. His skin knows things that his eyes and ears could never know. Touch brings a joy he could never otherwise imagine. Better even, than a voice. They say it is smell that is the most powerful sense. That smell ignites the brainstem, the most primitive part of oneself. That smell awakens deep, old, long-forgotten memories. No. It is touch. It is touch that brings him back to those ancient places, back to safety, back to where he can be gently held. It is touch that saves him, over and over again.

And there is a woman's voice. Somewhere nearby. He turns his head, slowly, with much effort, to the side where he can hear the voice and she moves into sight. Alile. She hovers over him, wearing a grave expression.

Something firm and deliberate—her fingers—press on his leg. As she works, the pain swells and moves closer to him like a returning tide, each wave larger and closer than the last. She disappears from sight for a minute or an hour. He absorbs wave after wave of pain. She returns with a bowl, places it between his lips and tips the liquid in. It slides down his throat and soon he follows it down and into the deepest parts of himself. He closes his eyes and feels her touch again, now gentle, as gentle as a breath on his skin.

*

When Iris steps off the bus, she walks a few feet and then stands in the midst of the crowd of travellers, knowing she is in the way but unable to go farther. She has a purpose; she knows why she is here and what she must do, and yet the next step seems so unclear.

It is dark. The journey, a hundred kilometres or so, has taken almost two full days. She can't go to the hospital, now that it is night, although it is possible that Dr. Ellison may be there, attending an emergency surgery. It is possible that if she wandered the dark halls for long enough, she would find him, or someone else. Or the hospital could be quiet. Nights are often quiet, tended only by a few nurses and the night watchman. And, she admits, the nurses rarely call in the doctors, even if it is warranted, even if one of their patients is in trouble.

This terrible truth overwhelms her now. She has felt love, recently. No one in particular. Just a feeling of it inside of her when she moved within the village community. A warmth within her, a knowing that she and they will be fine because she is with them, and they are with her. And now she feels the isolation of her hospital work like a distant ship on a cold ocean. Maybe it was the sheer quantity of death and suffering, all gathered together under one roof. Maybe that was what made them give up. But that was not it. It was something else.

When does a wilful, happy child become the hopeless adult? It happened to Iris when her father was killed. And maybe this is when it happens to them all: fathers, mothers, sisters, brothers lost before they have a chance to grow into the people they were meant to be.

Iris moves over to a curb and sits down. She spreads her hands out wide in front of her and remembers the x-ray. She remembers this rare glimpse of herself as she is without flesh, without muscle or skin or vessels or a beating heart. As she will be when she returns to the earth, when her flesh inevitably melts away. She runs her fingers over the skin of her forearm and thinks of what her grandfather would say. He dislikes inward ruminations almost as much as speaking or writing. The path a mind will take: increasingly narrow as it goes until it is closed off on all sides, until there is no escape from it.

She looks up at the night sky. Here in the city, with the sulphur-yellow of street lights shining down on her, she can barely see it. It exists as a shapeless darkness beyond the brightness of the lights. It lacks the depth and meaning and orientation that it provides in the village. She wishes she could listen to her ancestors. But they were silent to her even in the village, even when she was kneeling on their very bones.

She stands up and begins to walk down to the road. She walks without thinking, in no particular direction. She holds on to a belief that she will know what to do when she gets there.

*

Most of the time when he sinks down into a dream he is running. Running down a hospital corridor or a trail in the forest or the hallway of the house he once shared with Sarah and Emma. But this was not how it happened. The loss was slow and vague and he barely moved through all of it. He sat in a chair by her bedside for hours, days at a time, seeing only the white of the sheets and the translucent pallor of her skin, the thin web of vein within it. It was only his mind that was racing, running through all the knowledge, stacks and stacks of it in disorganized bundles and he sifting through it, trying to find the one thing, the one missing piece of information that could have saved her.

Everyone said there was nothing to know. Or everything there was to know was used up or useless. All there was to know was that whatever they tried only made it worse. All there was to know was that she was suffering, gulps and gasps of air, eyes squeezed shut against the pain.

And then all there was to know was that he was no longer a father.

"Emma."

When he told Kumwembe that he was not a fighter he was lying. He has been fighting all along, fighting everything in his path, clearing the way in front of him with long, strong sweeps of a machete, beating down all the pirates of the world, all the things that don't behave cooperatively and predictably, that don't respond as they should. He has been trying to beat the rogue cells out of them, beat the life into them and that is not how to be a doctor. That is not how to live. That should not be why she died, or how she might have been saved.

"Emma." There must be a wild look to his eyes because Alile's gaze is extra calm. He needs her to understand.

"Emma." He says again. But how can he explain this to her? He closes his eyes and sees her face and knows that is all he will ever see.

*

The room brightens then dims, which means someone has entered. Over by the doorway is the small and slender frame of a girl, her right side a thin glow of outdoor light. The lit side of a moon. She orbits him in a slow ellipse then comes to a stop beside him. The girl—he knows her, what is her name—stands with her arms crossed and studies him; her gaze lingers on his naked skin. When she crouches down and reaches over him, the smell of her is smoky and damp like an extinguished cook fire. She stands abruptly then darts to the other side of the hut and when Alile enters, the girl slips behind her toward the door. In her hand is something pale, and she clutches it tight, and this is the last thing he sees of her before she is gone into the outside. Into the light.

*

Alile bows her head over him. The scant light is enough for him to see her face and her features. Although it is dim, he can see how light her eyes are when she turns them toward his face. They are remarkable eyes. They are the gold-flecked oval eyes of a feline, and possessing the flickering thoughts of a thousand generations. She is looking at him, directly at his face, absorbing his expressions and processing them. He knows his expressions are completely transparent now; he knows that the wonder, the curiosity and the faith all flow steadily under his skin, moving through his muscles in wave after uncontrollable wave.

Alile lays her hand flat across his thigh and leaves it there for a moment, stares at her fingers on his leg. She takes a deep breath in through widened nostrils and then, with a long exhale, removes her hand. She backs away from him and stands up. He turns his head to watch her as she moves away from him, as she turns her back to him, as she moves the bottles and gourds hanging from the ceiling, sorting through them and they clink and clang together in a strange music. Henry closes his eyes and listens to this, the music of the bottles and gourds moving against each other. When he opens his eyes, she is gone.

*

When Iris passes a familiar row of wild bougainvillaea bushes that cascade silently over a long brick wall, when she smells the blossoms and looks down the street she is on, she realizes she has led herself home. Her home, and her mother sleeping in it, are just a few blocks away. She continues walking. Without thinking, she has come home, but it makes sense. Where else would she go?

She walks the final two blocks until she reaches her street corner. She turns down an alley, into a row of single-storey concrete buildings, and finds her own familiar doorway. She looks at it for a long time. She doesn't have the key. The key held no significance in the village. When she had removed her nurses uniform, the key had been in her pocket. She'd dropped it on the floor of her aunt's hut. She'd kicked it into the corner where it probably still lies, covered in dust and as useless as a stone.

Iris knocks quietly on the door. She listens. When she hears shuffling movement inside, she wipes her hand over her face, as though she can wipe away all that has passed over these last few days, all the questions and answers and more questions.

Her mother must somehow know it is her because, without even calling out and asking who it is, she slides the lock and opens the door. She doesn't even open the door a crack; she opens it wide and smiles almost as wide when she sees Iris standing there. Iris can see all the gaps, the holes where teeth are missing in her mother's mouth. And this broken, imperfect smile brings a feeling of love to Iris that she didn't know she was missing. Iris gives her mother a long, tight hug. She breathes in her mother's smell. She kisses her on the cheek. The skin on her face seems even more papery dry and thin than before she left Blantyre and Iris's relief is replaced by guilt. She puts her arm around her mother's shoulders, feels her sharp bones move under her hand, and the two of them walk into the house. Iris pulls the door closed behind them. She turns the lock.

They walk over to her mother's sleeping mat and Iris helps her sit down on it. Her mother pulls her knees up to her chest, wraps her arms around her legs and looks up at Iris like a young girl waiting for a story. Iris sits down beside her, feeling too much like the adult, weighted down with responsibility. Somehow her mother seems lighter, free from all this. Free even, from the past. Perhaps this is a sign of just how quickly her mother is approaching the spirit world. This sort of peace is usually only available to the very young, or those closest to death. Iris puts her arms around her mother again.

"I have been to the village, Mama."

Her mother nods.

"I stayed with Auntie. And Grandfather. They are well."

"There is a woman. Alile." She waits to feel her mother stiffen, to react somehow, but she does not. She leans against Iris and listens.

"She has your eyes," says Iris. "Mama, Alile has your eyes."

Iris looks over at her mother and sees that her mother has closed her eyes. She leans into Iris like a child. She seems to be getting smaller, lighter, younger by the minute.

"And she is very skilled. She is learning to be a *sing'anga*. She is learning from Ade. Mama, you would be very proud."

Iris looks at her mother again and sees that there is a very small smile there and now Iris feels it rising inside her: the questions, the anger. She sits up and lets her arms fall off her mother.

Iris asks: "Is she why we left?"

Her mother looks down.

"Did father know?"

Her mother looks at Iris, turns those eyes on her, the eyes she shares with all her children except Iris and Iris feels her allegiance with her father grow steadily.

"Who was he?"

She stares hard at her mother, impatient with her frailty and her weaknesses.

"You must tell me, Mama. You can't keep it from me. I have the right to know." She can't stand even the warmth coming off her mother's skin and warming her own skin, an inch away. She stands up.

"It doesn't matter." And the way she says it, so quietly without any need to convince, calms Iris. It must be her mother's proximity to the spirit world that gave her the power, in one brief statement, to make Iris realize what she says is true.

Her mother points up to the wall above her mat where a crucifix has been hung. Seeing Him there, hanging His head over her mother's mat makes her want to cry. "He will tell you, if you ask Him, that it doesn't matter." Her mother says. "He forgives us, Iris." Iris folds down on herself. She hugs her knees to her chest just like her mother and keels to one side, then the other.

"No." Says Iris. "It doesn't matter anymore. But what do I do now?"

She looks over at her mother, feels the pinprick of tears. "Mama, what do I do now?"

Her mother lays down on her mat, pulls a light cloth over herself. She closes her eyes and says: "Look at you, with all these choices."

*

Henry has memorized the hut, counted all the bottles and gourds and collections of plants drying upside down in bunches. He knows the pattern in which they are hung. There is an artistry in how they have been arranged, and he is aware that there is an order to this, an order that serves many functions. He knows which containers hold his particular medications, the ones from which they retrieve the dried plants, and then the bowl in which they grind them, and the stone urn that holds the water that they add to the plant matter in order to make a paste to apply to his wounds, or liquid to pour down his throat.

When Alile begins her daily ministrations, he seeks out her eyes first. He waits for her gaze to come to his, and counts the minutes it takes for this to happen. It is taking less time. With each visit, she moves to him more quickly with her eyes. And her expression is changing. It is changing from the reserved and benevolent attention from a healer to her patient, to the engaged and thoughtful look of a person seeking out another person. There is evidence, on her face, that she has thought of him when she was away.

But when their eyes finally meet, her face changes, and that softness goes away. She busies herself with her tasks. She studies the gourds. She spends long minutes trailing her fingers across the hanging bottles, causing them to bump one another, making their gentle music, her look unfocused and remote.

When she is ready, she will begin to collect materials from several different containers. She will rub leaves in her hand. She will smell them. She will look away, and listen. Then she will drop the particular plant in a bowl, or return it to its storage vessel and reach for another. This goes on for a long time and through all this he remains respectfully silent. He watches her arms reach up to a bottle, the muscles reshaping with the effort. He watches her fingers massage a leaf. There is the twitch of her jaw muscle when she is considering a choice, and he waits for the barely perceptible shake of her head when she decides against something.

He lingers on the nape of her neck, the shadowy groove that runs from her scalp to the base of her cervical spine. He has memorized the size and shape of the gentle hills of her spine that descend down her back, and the dips between each of them. He can count four before they continue beneath her blouse.

And her scent—a mixture of smoke and air and fresh broken green leaves and the more personal smells of damp, musky sweat and sweetly soured skin. If she enters when his eyes are closed, he can know with certainty that it is Alile standing at the door, looking toward his corner of the room, waiting for her eyes to adjust to the new darkness. It is those moments, the time when she has entered a darkness that he has adapted to but she has not, that he feels everything slow down. As he watches her face during the only time of uncertainty for her, when he can see and she cannot, he observes a certain vulnerability that is never there again. He loves those moments. It is the only time when he feels like he could do something for her, protect her from a certain danger, protect her from this darkness that he has adapted to. He has learned to see in the dark.

So today when she enters, and he watches from the corner, he uses this time to linger on parts of her that he ordinarily could not. Her eyes, of course, and cheekbones. Her lips. Her clavicles that are so well-defined, the deep notch between them. The smooth curves of her shoulders, the graceful position of her arms and hands, how they curve down so her hands meet below her navel like a dancer where they press her skirt against her body and he can see the subtle roundness of her stomach beneath the fabric.

Now she looks at him directly, and something changes. The vulnerability stays. And something else appears in her face, beneath the skin: something soft, a tenderness that he has never seen. He holds his breath for longer than was possible a moment before and his heart thuds with an expectation and with a need for more—more oxygen, more of this. This new something he sees in her face, in her eyes. My God, what is this?

He is breathing more raggedly now. He can't stop this breathing, it is beyond him. She has always been beyond him and he wonders how long he has been waiting her to be within reach. How long has it been? He can only count two nights, but it could be more.

Alile moves across the hut. She kneels beside him and looks down at him. He can see her eyes travel over his hair, his brow, his lips where they must be hidden in his beard, and then back to his eyes.

He reaches out with his left hand, his uninjured hand, and stretches his arm across his body over toward where she kneels beside him. He just wants to touch her, that's all. Just to touch her with his own fingertips, to feel her skin like she has felt his. She is as familiar with his skin as she could be with a body that is not her own. But the same cannot be said for him.

She stares at his hand that still reaches across his chest and over toward her. She reaches out and touches it. Their fingers slide across one another. She slips her hand around his, her fingers cupping over his, and she gently presses his hand down, moves it back over to his side, presses it down onto the mat beside him. Then she removes her hand and stands up. She moves over to the gourds and begins her usual ritual. She has turned her back to him and he can no longer see her eyes where her feelings were expressed, clear as the night sky in this place, just a few minutes before. He watches

Alile move among the bottles and then closes his eyes and listens to the music of the gourds.

Chapter 23

The hospital has not redeemed itself in her absence. It stands no taller, it feels no more reassuring. And what falls on the people who enter, what they must carry on their shoulders—it weighs on them as much. They stagger under it.

She follows her usual path to the medical ward before remembering she must go to the surgical suites. She redirects herself and walks up the gentle, uneven slope of the corridor. She pushes open the swinging door to one of the operating theatres and slips inside. There are quick glances from the scrub nurse and the anaesthetist; both raise an eyebrow at her presence and her attire, but say nothing. She has put on a mask and surgical cap as per protocol but she still wears her borrowed blouse and *chitenje* wrap.

Dr. Ellison, scalp shiny pink under the surgical lamp, peers down at his patient, or rather his patient's leg. He wields the saw deftly. Even with her surgical mask on, Iris can smell the wound—the raw, organic smell of flesh and bone being cut and cauterized. The lower half of the patient's leg is now on the table below him like it has been misplaced and must simply be reattached. But it will go in the bin with the others and will be disposed of in the usual way. The idea of parts of bodies being discarded, when the remainder of the body still lives, has always disturbed Iris. When she trained as a student nurse she woke with dreams of these misplaced parts, of the owners returning to claim them, trying to find their own amongst the pile. She tries not to think of the patient, what he will see, what he will feel when he wakes, groggy and nauseous from his morphine dream. She breathes into her mask and feels her trapped breath condense wetly on her chin and lips.

When the limb has been burnt beyond bleeding, when all nerves and vessels and flaps of tissue have been dealt with, when the skin has been sewn over the limb and closed off neatly like a purse, Dr. Ellison hands his last tool to the scrub nurse. He swabs the stump with a wet gauze pad and does not look up when he speaks.

"Iris."

"Hello, Dr. Ellison."

"To what do we owe the pleasure of your visit?"

She pauses. "Perhaps we should discuss it in private." The nurse and anaesthetist watch her with more interest, give her more consideration.

"I'll be done shortly." He lifts the amputated limb and wraps it with a long roll of dry gauze, covering the stump with a layer of cotton. Iris leaves the room and waits for him outside the surgical suite. Once outside, she pulls off the mask, feels the cool air on her wet face and wills away her nausea.

They share a tea in the canteen. Iris sits opposite Dr. Ellison and feels the vapour of her tea touch and then condense on her chin and lips as her breath did under the surgical mask. She can't seem to warm up.

"So he's got malaria," Dr. Ellison ticks a finger as he counts ailments, "dehydration, fractures—an arm and a leg. Semi-conscious. Perhaps a head injury from the fall." He lays a long stare on Iris until she starts to feel guilty again, as though she sent him up the mountain. She did not want to feel the weight of responsibility heaped on her by someone else; this is why she came here, to free herself of that feeling.

Dr. Ellison looks down at his teacup. He wraps his thick fingers around it and the cup disappears behind them so all she can see is the steam rising off it in a lazy spiral.

"Strange." He looks up at her again. "Isn't it strange, Iris?"

"Well, it was a bad fall. And malaria, well … anyone can get that."

"I mean strange that a smart man like Bryce would get himself into such a pickle." He fixes on her another long gaze. "Almost as if he wanted it. Either that, or it was simply out of his control."

Iris says nothing to this. She steals a glance at the doctor's face. More thoughtful than usual. He has surprised her before with his warmth. Maybe he will surprise her with his consideration, too. She chooses her words carefully.

"The mountain is a dangerous place. Some … visitors … don't realize what can happen there."

She notices his half smile now and stops herself.

"Mother nature can be a real bitch. 'Scuse my language, Iris, but you know what I mean." He looks out the window to the courtyard where laundry is being hung. "There are some things you just can't control." He tips his cup up to his mouth and drains it. He stands up. "I've a few things to wrap up. It's early still. We'll leave first thing after lunch." She watches the doctor leave the canteen, how all the rest of the patrons avert their eyes, how they don't rest their gazes on him for too long as though he, like Mulanje Mountain, carries about him some power that he could wield one way or another, depending on his mood.

After her cup of tea has been emptied into her stomach where it seems to swish and stir and keep her insides unsettled, Iris leaves the cafeteria. She finds herself again returning to the medical ward where she and Dr. Bryce spent all their working hours until recently. They have only been in the village for a few days, yet somehow it feels like an eternity, as if they have lived entire lives, had births, deaths, and rebirths. She feels as though Dr. Bryce is in between lives right now, perched as he is between worlds: the spirit and the tangible. The more time spent in the village, the less she knows, it seems. Maybe it is the effect of her grandfather: how quickly he reveals how little she knows, or how little there is to know.

She stops in the corridor now. Ahead lie the yellow wards of Dr. Bryce's efforts. Behind her, the grey. She moves into the yellow and she is struck again by how odd the colour is, effortfully bright and cheerful.

She turns and leaves the yellow. Back to the grey. Back to her mother for one more visit before she returns to the village with Dr. Ellison, bringing another piece of this place with her to the village. For a brief instant, she wonders whether she should, but this thought passes and she is left with a firm resolve that this is the only way. The doctor needs to be saved and this is the only way.

*

Iris sits beside Dr. Ellison in his car. Dr. Bryce's rucksack leans against her legs and she twines her fingers through the loops. She found it in her aunt's hut. She emptied it of the few items he'd packed: a change of clothes, a book, his stethoscope. She'd glanced at the title and the back of the book before placing it down with his clothes. Something about spies during the Second World War. Something about the Cold War. It didn't interest her at all. She supposed she shouldn't find this too disappointing—she would have expected that she and Dr. Bryce had quite different tastes in literature.

Together, she and Dr. Ellison have filled it with the essentials. All the lifesaving equipment gathered into this one bag. Some small vials of liquid—surprisingly little is required—to kill the malaria. Other vials to kill the pain and the nausea. Bags of IV fluid. And some plastic tubing to feed it all into a vein. All these years she has numbly pushed such tubing into various veins in various arms, thinking little of it other than the nuisance of having to do the same procedure over and over again, yet now: now it seems a strange technology. Not a miracle, not magical, and no need for belief. One just needs to know the illness, and the treatment follows naturally along a flow chart crafted by others much more clever than herself. She just needs to read along and carry out the instructions—tube by tube, vial by vial. This feels reassuring to her right now: that it has worked in others. There is a satisfaction in the complete absence of mystery.

As the car bumps along the raw road, she leans her head back against the seat and closes her eyes and thinks about Dr. Bryce. Lying there in the corner, he reminded her of Grace, how she looked in the days before she died. The same slump of the body, the same odour filling the hut. She remembers her mother trying to spoon medicine into Grace's mouth, how it ran down her cheek, how she stared out at Iris, how there was nothing in her sister's eyes. Nothing. It was as though her sister had already departed, but through some cruel deviousness had left her heart still pumping and her lungs still taking air.

Iris remembers clearly her mother's friendship with one of the clergy from the local Christian church. The woman was invited into their hut on many occasions and her mother often went to visit her, over at the church, several miles away. Iris and her brother and sisters were taken there to receive a blessing. A baptism. They were initiated into Christianity as infants, before they could make such choices. They were given Western names. And, over the years, her mother did not perform many of the rituals recommended to her by the village elders and *sing'anga*. When something went wrong, amends were not made to correct the errors. Instead, her mother went to the church where she knelt on a wooden beam and spoke to a different God. And when her mother committed the biggest betrayal of her life, when she went to another man, she did not perform the rituals that might have saved her family from the inevitable ruin. This far-off church God did not listen, or did not hear her, or chose not to help her. The destruction that followed, Iris now wonders, could it have been prevented? Is her mother beyond saving now? If her mother returned to the village and performed the necessary rites and rituals, would she be forgiven? Could things be made right again?

No.

This, Iris knows to be as clean and clear a truth as there ever was. It is impossible. Her mother has proven this. And she, Iris, must eventually choose. A person cannot live in two worlds. She looks down at the rucksack between her knees, at her fingers woven into its fabric and wonders if her choice has already been made.

Chapter 24

Henry spends most of his time waiting for Alile. He waits for her to enter his world and when she does, he forgets what passed immediately before her arrival. When she is with him, he is a loose bundle of sensations. And today when Alile enters the hut, he closes his eyes. He listens to the activity of the surrounding village, muffled and remote, enjoys the cooler air on his skin, smells the thick, organic fragrance of the drying herbs and medicinal bottles, feels the presence of the bottles—dense, still, full of strange possibilities.

And then he feels her fingertips, touching lightly on his temple then sliding downward to cup his cheek. He opens his eyes and sees her, so close. Her solemn look. He reaches up for her hand, slides his fingers down the length of it, and she lets him.

This is some sort of love or kindness that is new to him. He has never experienced it before, not from a friend or a lover. A sad sort of kindness that binds two people, that knits them together. For now.

*

When Iris and Dr. Ellison arrive in the village, the sun is still high. She has lost almost three days travelling into and out of the city now. They walk silently through the field in single file—first Iris, then Ellison. They said little to each other on the drive. Ellison's mood has been grim since she told him the news. He has been concentrating on this news as he does on a patient when he is working in the surgical suite—saying little, looking stern.

When the path opens up and the village surrounds them with all its colour and vivacious energy, they march right through it. Ellison moves in front of her and walks through the village as if the life around them is no more than a stage prop. If she didn't know better, she would be embarrassed by it. His ability to ignore the smiles and nods, the efforts being madc all around him to make him feel welcome. He walks on to Ade's hut, nods briefly when she gestures toward it, when she indicates that this is where Dr. Bryce is being housed. He allows Iris to go in first, then he follows.

Here, just inside the hut, they both stop. The blindness stops everyone in their tracks. Dr. Ellison stands at the threshold and sniffs the air—Iris can hear him taking noisy deep breaths. She wonders what he smells. To her, the air is clean. Damp, yes, but no odour. The smell of death is gone and for a moment she fears that Dr. Bryce is gone with it, but then she hears a shifting in the corner. It is taking her longer than usual to regain her bearings. She feels her skin prickle. Fear? A warning?

"Iris." The sound of her name being pronounced makes her jump. She looks to where it came from and then she sees the shape that must be Bryce. He is sitting, propped up on some blankets. She sees more of him, now. He is looking at them with a crooked smile.

She slides the rucksack off her shoulders, onto the ground, and feels coolness where sweat has gathered under the straps of the bag. She follows Dr. Ellison and moves over to Bryce and they both stand there, looking down at him. He looks better. Much better. He looks surprisingly well.

"Bryce." There is relief in Dr. Ellison's voice. "I must say I was expecting much worse. Iris told me … " He glances at her, then decides not to elaborate. He leaves the sentence unfinished.

Dr. Bryce looks at her. "How are you, Iris?" It is said as though it is she who needs looking after.

He still has that smile on his face, as though he knows something. Something he will keep from her.

"We brought you something." She lifts the pack a few inches off the ground and deposits it again.

"Oh?" He sounds only mildly interested.

"Antimalarials," she says, "I think you have malaria."

"Malaria." He says this slowly, as though he hasn't thought of it. How could it not have occurred to him?

"You have had a fever, and you have been vomiting. Diarrhea."

"Yes." He says. "And horrible stomach pains." He brings his left hand to press into his stomach as if to test it, to see if it still hurts.

Iris lifts the bag again. Puts it down. She bends over it and opens the top, begins to pull out the intravenous line. She rummages for the vials of medication. She finds one and holds it up, turns it so he can see the label: Chloroquine. "You need this." She says this firmly.

Bryce regards it strangely. He looks at the string of IV line as though it is a snake that has made its way into the hut. He hesitates. Iris is incredulous. Why does he hesitate?

"I'm getting better, Iris. Alile..." For some reason he stops. Looks down at his broken hand and then looks toward the doorway.

Iris waits. She suppresses a rising wave of anger in her. After all this, she thinks. For God's sake. After all this.

Dr. Ellison has been silent beside her, taking stock of the situation. He will come to a conclusion and will be immovable once he arrives at it. But Iris cannot wait for Dr. Ellison to say something. She saw Dr. Bryce's death, smelled it, felt it so near, lurking in the corner of the hut with him, just a few days ago. Just like with Grace. It hunkered down and waited. It can be patient, she knows this. It will return. Something needs to be said. Something needs to be done.

"You don't want this. You don't want proper treatment." The anger makes her voice tremble. She drops the vial of Chloroquine back into the rucksack. The IV tubing lies in a tangle on the floor. She kneels down to gather it. Why does she feel on the fringes all the time? Like life is moving on and she is always arriving late to the scene. She is never prepared. She is always the last to know.

Dr. Ellison finally shifts beside her. He starts to make a noise as though he is about to speak and then he does. He says: "Before we make any big decisions, let's have a look." He kneels down, pulls out his stethoscope and listens to things, feels Bryce's pulse, prods his belly. Taps at his knees and elbows. Looks in his mouth. Looks at his eyes, the creases of his hands. "Jaundice," Dr. Ellison mutters. He lays his hands on the broken leg, squeezes gently, rolls it back and forth. He palpates the damaged hand, which does look better to Iris, less swollen. Dr. Ellison sticks a thermometer in Bryce's ear and when it beeps he reads it: "39." A fever. She hears, in Dr. Ellison's silence, his concern.

Through all this, Bryce has been looking up at the ceiling as though stargazing. Looking for falling stars. Even in this dim light, she can see that his skin has turned yellow. Sour yellow like bile. And his eyes are strange—the pupils have shrunk to nothing—pinpoints in the pallor of his iris. The whites of his eyes have gone yellow, too. The bile has seeped through him, stained him everywhere.

She feels a desperation that has nothing to do with how sick Bryce is now. It has to do with Grace. And she feels Grace, or the memory of Grace in the corner, well up inside her. How can this man decline something that could change the possibility of an outcome like Grace's, could stave off death? This man who has wielded this power, saved others with it time and time again? The desperation turns to anger. She reaches for the rucksack again, where the plastic tubing hangs messily from it. She fumbles for the vial inside. "This will prevent it from worsening. Let me just … " She reaches for his arm.

Dr. Bryce turns his head to watch her hold his arm. He watches her try to find a vein for a long time. And then he squeezes his fist, forces the veins to fill. It is as much of an acquiescence as she could hope for.

She opens up the rucksack again and reaches in to it, pulls out the lengths of intravenous line, pulls out the needles, the tape, the gauze, the bottles of medication. She thinks about her sister Grace as she does this, she imagines she is holding her sister's arm to find a vein. She imagines she is wrapping the elastic tensor band over her sister's forearm and squeezing it tight, whispering "Shush, it's okay" to Grace as she presses the needle to the skin, and as it punctures the skin and enters the vein. She imagines it is her sister's blood—dark, red—that flashes back into the tube, it is her sister's blood that is chased back into the vein when the IV fluid starts flowing. But it is Bryce whose body is lying on the floor when she steps away. It is Bryce who receives the medication. It is Bryce whose life will be saved.

Chapter 25

When Iris and Dr. Ellison step out of the hut and into the sun, Alile is standing in the yard. Iris wonders if she has been there all along. They did not ask permission. He is her patient, after all. This would never be allowed in the hospital; one doctor would never move in on another doctor's patient without permission. And this shames her now: the audacity by which they just took over care. Iris is about to apologize when Alile speaks.

"Thank you."

Iris nods. She feels Dr. Ellison hang back.

"They wouldn't do anything for him." Alile says. "They were willing to treat his bones but nothing more." She turns to Iris, her eyes big and beautiful and youthful. So inexperienced. Nothing like the eyes of a *sing'anga*. "He needed so much more and I couldn't do it alone. I couldn't do anything, really. I just stayed with him." She glances over at Ellison and then leans in closer to Iris. "*Nthenda ya majini ndi mutu basi.*"

"I understand." Iris says. Spirit illness is a head ailment, Alile said to her, studying her for evidence of understanding, of confirmation of what needed to be done.

Iris moves forward and hugs her sister. It is the first time she has felt her skin against her own. She feels like a sister in her arms, her arms feels strong like her own. They have strength, both of them. This is what they have in common. But the strength does not come from their common bloodline. It comes from their fathers. A different type of strength from two different men. From their mother they have inherited something else, something harder to describe but equally important, perhaps more important: an intuition of sorts, the ability to feel things.

Iris releases her sister, moves back a little. She holds her shoulders and looks at her wet face. She will tell her another day. When she is more ready to hear it.

Alile leaves them. She steps back into the hut where Dr. Bryce lies, silently receiving his medication.

Dr. Ellison is regarding the hut, and seems to be listening to something in the quiet of this yard. His own thoughts. His preoccupied looks always make Iris uncomfortable. She can feel the scales tipping in his mind, over to a conclusion. Someone is always being judged. Circumstances weighed and considered. And what judgements has he passed on this village? Dr. Bryce has improved. Whatever remedies they spun out of the plants, the air, the earth. Whatever it was they did seemed to help, a little. Iris presses her fingers to her eyes. She wishes she doubted less. She wishes she believed more. Even Bryce has more of it: this belief.

Dr. Ellison puts his hands on his hips. "He's quite weak. I don't think we should try to move him today. See how he does with some fluid and antimalarials in him. We'll try to leave tomorrow."

Iris nods. She can't imagine transporting Dr. Bryce to the car now, as big and strong as Dr. Ellison undoubtedly is.

"You'll be okay here?"

Iris leans over and slips off her shoes, feels the warm earth under her feet. "Yes." She turns to him. "And you? Where will you go?"

"I have a friend near the mountain. Runs a hostel. I'll stay there."

She nods again. She doesn't know whether to be relieved or hurt that he doesn't wish to stay here. He does not wish to become a guest in the village. She realizes later that she didn't even ask but it wasn't her place, really. This isn't her home.

*

When Iris and Ellison leave, Alile enters. She moves swiftly to him and kneels at his side. She reaches out and gently touches the intravenous line which burrows under his skin. She follows the line with her eyes as it tracks up to the bag of fluid that they have hung from the ceiling in place of a bottle. He wonders if this has somehow disturbed the equilibrium of the healing room, if one bottle moved throws off the intricately balanced system. Her eyes come back to rest on him, on his face. She touches his forehead—light, feathery touches, then rests her hand on his arm.

"I'm sorry, Alile."

She looks at him, shakes her head.

*

After Dr. Ellison's departure from the village, Iris does not immediately return to Ade's hut. She leaves Bryce there for a few hours, allows him to receive his medicine, and to indulge in his attraction to the *sing'anga*'s dried herbs, bark, roots and potions. She wonders if it is the malaria, gone to his head.

She knows of such a thing, has seen it on the ward: cerebral malaria. How else would a sensible man hesitate when offered a lifesaving remedy?

Iris goes to her grandfather. He is there, waiting for her on his step, hands on his knees, sitting like a statue. She sits beside him. After shouldering so much burden, she is happy to drop it all. She leaves it at the doorstep of her grandfather's hut. With her grandfather, she finally feels young again. With him, it is safe to be confused, it is safe to give up, to stop trying. She is not sure how much of her he can see through his cloudy eyes, but he can hear her, and he can feel her. He is always waiting for her when she needs him the most. He speaks little and listens well. He nods thoughtfully at the right moments. He asks the right questions.

"I went to Dr. Bryce today. I administered some treatment."

Her grandfather nods.

"Ade and Alile have helped him," she admits. "He looked better, but still very ill."

Her grandfather shakes his head. He swats at a fly with a stick and shakes his head again. "They have treated the broken bones but have done nothing about the other things that ail him."

Iris thinks about malaria, wonders if this is what her grandfather is referring to.

"They can't do anything about that." He continues. "Ade was right. It would be too difficult. Too risky."

Iris wonders how her grandfather seems to have a finger on the pulse of the entire community. He spends long hours in a room in his hut with his shells and often comes out looking more troubled and thoughtful. She wonders how he would have knowledge about Bryce without ever visiting him, and then she remembers the shell he had given him upon arrival in the village.

"Does he still have your shell?"

Her grandfather turns his clouded eyes on her. Now both are affected by cataract and each day they seem more opaque. Finally, he says: "A shell, yes. Or a bone." He says it importantly; in a way that accentuates the significance of her question, and his answer. And she wants this: to be pulled into the current of this magic alongside her grandfather, but still she stands aside it. She has lost the willingness to release reason—she grips it like a child holding tight to a helium balloon. And if she were to let it go, would it be lost forever? A shrinking pinpoint on the great blue expanse?

She says, "A bone. But I don't see how it… " Here she pauses, trying to explain where she stops short, what she is having trouble with.

Her grandfather stands up abruptly, throws the stick he is holding to the ground. "See?" Even his voice trembles. "Why must you see? *Kumva*! Listen!" The cataract clouds are white blooms over his pupils. He must be completely blind. And he stares at her with those clouded eyes, shakes with his disappointment in her, in who she has become, and who she must have left behind.

Chapter 26

There has been a death. And there will be a funeral rite. He was an important man, a brother of the headman of a neighbouring village, and the headman has called upon the *Nyau* men to visit as a medium, an in-between, overseeing the passage of this man safely to the world of the ancestors.

Iris joins the women in the common kitchen area. The wailing of the women has already begun, it carries from the dead man's hut and continues on. Although the family grieves, the mood in the village is a strange mix of raw grief and anxious excitement, no doubt driven by the anticipation of the visit by the secretive *Nyau*. The women, when Iris arrives, are chatty. They smile and nod to Iris as she enters the group. They find her a task and someone takes the time to give her brief instructions. She is to grind the maize that will be used to make *nsima*. Although all over the village there are bags of mill-ground maize for this daily staple, when there is a ritual the flour must be ground by hand. Iris stands beside an urn, her hands on the pole that will be used to grind the maize, and looks around. Standing here, on this land, with this pole in her hands and as she rotates the pole and begins to grind the grains, as she creates the vibration that she can feel in her feet, Iris knows her ancestors can feel it too. She can feel their approval, she can feel their hunger. She knows that she is meeting the needs of the village, and the needs of those who came before them, who gave them life, who wait for acts like these to confirm that they have not been forgotten.

Iris leans into the pole, puts more of her body into the grinding, feels the tight ache in her muscles, feels the sweat collect between her breasts and on her forehead. She closes her eyes, moves her body and begins to sing. She joins the women in the song that gathers around her and in her and helps her grind the maize.

Maybe it is her grandfather's anger that makes her start thinking this way. Or maybe it is what Alile said after they treated Bryce in the *khumbi. Imalowa m'mutu.* The spirit enters the head. Iris doesn't believe it, but still she thinks it. Maybe it is the old Iris, the one her grandfather is mourning, who reaches up from deep inside her to plant the seed in the shallow soil of her mind. All her adult life, she hasn't given much attention to *matsenga*. When she heard it uttered by patients, or patients' families, she usually rolled her eyes. Even the mention of it was a source of embarrassment, a superstition she wanted to hide from the world, the foreign doctors, from herself.

But the sight of Dr. Bryce in that hut, ill as he was, and saying those things. Wanting to stay! Refusing treatment! It was unimaginable, irrational. It was the talk of a man possessed. And then, as simple as that, the idea of sorcery made a home in her mind. And it grew there, getting fatter and uglier—a greasy, gawky adolescent thought that kept maturing. It grew until it was an overbearing adult thought that wielded blame, flashed it like a sharp knife. Self-blame. She began to think about how *mfiti* and *matsenga* sometimes work this way, striking not the guilty person, but those in the vicinity. This is how her mother was attacked. And here Iris is, back in the village—why shouldn't the attacks begin? Why shouldn't Bryce be the first casualty? She has been around long enough to know that things can change, depending on what chair you sit in, what direction you face, which god receives your prayers. Or doesn't.

She almost can't go to the ceremony after the funeral; she has become this afraid of seeing Bryce there—the unfortunate possessed. The one to whom the dances, the jubilant, terrifying cries will be directed. By the time she is close enough to see the large crowd gathered in the centre of the village, she is shaking. Bryce isn't there, but still she feels a threat.

The *Gule Wamkulu* is underway, and the drumbeats are frantic. The crowd sings, cheers, claps and yells, and the *Nyau* dancer in the centre clearing stomps, kicks dust, and gesticulates. He is telling a story, he is teaching a lesson. With his mask on, and the spiralling horn that jabs skyward from his mane, and the erratic swings of his costume, she can't tell where his intentions are directed as he threatens, gyrates, teases, condemns. She circles wide around the crowd and searches each face for something: anger, or the guilt of revenge. And she almost finds it, over and over again in each face: something menacing as they watch the antics of the masked dancer. Ade watches her studying his people. He sees her fear. She walks around the circumference of the small fires over which the drummers are warming the skins of their instruments, feels the heat on her legs, the smoke in her eyes. Ade nods when she arrives in front of him. He waits for her question.

"Is it *matsenga*?" She asks. "Has he been taken by it?"

To these questions, and to her twisted, anguished face, Ade laughs—yellow teeth, black spaces. His laughter is deep-chested, honest. Mean. "He is his own witch. Our spirits, our ancestors had nothing to say to him. But perhaps his own did." He gazes up to the sky, as if trying to determine the path of their flight, or perhaps to witness their escape. White or winged or shapeless on the black of the night, fleeing westward. Homeward bound, now that the job has been done.

Iris leaves the ceremony with the need to see Bryce. Her fear has not been abated by Ade's mocking laughter. In the cool darkness outside the circle of firelight, she starts to feel more calm. With a cool, thinking head, she reasons that Ade's explanation could be accurate. Why not his own demons? Why else would he wish to stay but to escape them, to avoid returning to where they rage unchecked in a low, grey building in Blantyre?

There is a lantern on in the hut; she can see the yellow-orange glow through the curtain in the doorway. She steps up to the door and moves the curtain aside. She goes no further. She sees Alile, moving over Bryce. Her hand cups his face. Her body covers his. He looks up at her with a gaze she has never felt cast on her own face. It is the gaze of love, or lust. Iris is unfamiliar with these looks; she is unable to distinguish between the two.

Iris steps back and drops the curtain. She moves away from the hut and then turns and runs out of the yard. Once on the path, she walks swiftly, fast enough that her breath comes more and more quickly, until she can't catch it at all.

Of course, she thinks, as her face becomes wet and she swipes at it, smears the tears all over. She hiccups and tries for some deeper breaths. Of course it's not *matsenga*, or vengeful spirits or ancestors of any sort and she feels so stupid, so *stupid* for ever thinking these things. It is nothing of spirit at all. It is simple, ubiquitous malaria that has made him ill. And it is even simpler, and even more ubiquitous *otentha* that is keeping him here. Heat. Lust. He is a man and she is a woman. Of course.

She stumbles onward, passes villagers who look at her strangely, give her a wide berth.

Dear Alile. Fallen under the influence of Bryce. Alile who has been given everything and now Bryce, as flawed as he is. As difficult and confused and flawed. Despite all this, and maybe because of it, he was beautiful to her. And she wanted to keep his damaged soul all to herself.

These thoughts that tumble through her make her dizzy. They sicken her with their green taint of envy—the trait of someone with a dark heart. *Ku-dukidwa*—jealousy—it brings her closer to becoming *mtima woipa*—not a real person, already on the muddy path to becoming *mfiti*. A witch. Is this what they think of her? She remembers her grandfather's angry white eyes.

She walks toward her grandfather's *khumbi*. But for the first time, he is not there waiting for her. The *khumbi* is empty and cold and dark. She leaves the *khumbi* and moves back into the crowd, allows herself to be carried by it to the ritual dance and then she moves past it, toward the wood.

She goes to the thicket because she needs a cooler space and so she steps through the gate and enters her grandmother's *kachisi*. The offering pots are there and again she feels shame for entering this sacred grove empty-handed. Most of her memories of this place, Mapiri village, are of times spent with her grandmother. Until a girl is old enough to join her mother in household tasks like fetching water and sticks for the fire, or cooking, she remains almost solely in the guardianship of her grandmother and they were so similar, the two of them. In so many ways they were like sisters.

She wonders what her grandmother would think of her now, if she would be as disappointed in her as her grandfather, or if she would somehow understand that the life she leads—celibate, mostly alone—came about by happenstance, not by choice.

As she kneels down in front of the *kachisi*, she feels the heat again, now centred in the area of her genitals. The irony stings: that her mother's promiscuity and infidelities are more natural here than her own chastity. Yet her mother worshipped a God that condemned her for it.

Alile was lying on Dr. Bryce and his hands were on her waist, drifting toward her buttocks. Iris presses her hands between her legs and feels the heat of her labia swollen against her palm. If she had been initiated, she would have labia stretched long for the act of sex. If she had been initiated, she would be a woman now. She lies down on the ground, smells the sour *ku-konda mowa* from the offering pots, listens for rustling in the leaves, waits for another visit from her grandmother, her *mzimu*. If she had followed the path her grandmother had chosen for her—to become a diviner, a spirit medium—she would never marry. But even then she would have nocturnal visits from a *kamundi*—a shrine official who represents the spirit. A spirit that would enter her in the form of a python. Even then she would not have to remain cold and lifeless. She closes her eyes to the darkness here and listens carefully for the arrival of the *mzimu*.

When she wakes it is still dark, and her shoulder and hip are cold from being pressed against the ground. She feels a wetness between her legs and reaches down there. When she pulls out her hand and holds it up to the moonlight she can see that it is dark, almost black. Menstrual blood. Proof that her earlier heat was not for lust and that her womb will not be carrying a child.

Scattering seeds. This is all any of them wish to do, is it not? Alile her garden. Men their women. She looks up through the web of branches and wonders how she will scatter her own. No one is meant to be barren forever. She wipes her hand on a leaf and then begins to make her way back to the village where she can hear the drumbeats. The funeral rite is still ongoing. She hasn't missed anything and hasn't been missed.

As she approaches the fire—now bigger and brighter—she feels the drumbeat enter her. The *Nyau* are gone, have passed through like a wind. The dead one has been escorted, is now safely established in his new domicile and precautions have been taken so that he cannot find his way back to this world. And the people of the village, left behind, mourn death and celebrate life.

Someone adds more wood to the fire and it sprays upward in a fountain of sparks, chased by tongues of flame. Bodies move and dance around her, frenetic claps urge them on. Iris stands still and watches the drummers for a long time, their arms moving so fast, so fast that they are gone and all that is left are two bright wings. The wings blur in front of them, the wings create the drumbeat, the wings pulse faster and faster. Everyone must keep moving and so Iris begins to move, first slowly and then faster and faster until she is moving as fast as the drummers' wings. She spins and spins and spins until she is something spinning out of nothing. Stars fly from her fingertips, streak through the sky, scatter like dust across the womb of space.

There are hands on her. The hands direct her as she spins, move her away from the fire. She can't stop, though. She keeps spinning around and around and then, as the hands hold her firmly over her hips, she stops long enough to feel the water. It runs over and down her and she stumbles and falls and then she is submerged, covered in water, takes water in through her nose and mouth. Then she is still for a long time. When she opens her eyes again, she is lying on her back and she sees a face above her. It hovers there and it is her father. Her father is looking tenderly down at her and she cries "Papa! Papa!" The face moves away and then all she can see is the night sky, bright with the seeds of her dance.

*

Henry could hear the ritual. He listened to the throb of the drums, long after Alile left him alone in the hut. He lay in the dark and felt the drumbeat come up from the ground, move through him, force the blood through his vessels. He felt his heart clench strangely, in time with the beat, not quite a regular rhythm. He heard cries. Terrible agonies or beautiful ecstasies out from the throat. Sounds he knew were his, and theirs. Sounds of the land itself, as though it were tearing open beneath the village and releasing things that lived there, things that could not be forgotten. Parts of himself. Parts he wished he could remember. Parts he would rather forget.

Lying there alone in the hut, his eyes stung from the heat and the smoke, he saw the animals, throats cut, bodies limp and still. He smelled their blood, watched it sink into the sand. He saw the dancers. Bodies that moved and writhed. People that sang and danced in an ancient way and as he watched them, he felt a terrible grief. He fell asleep with this grief gripping him tight.

*

When Alile enters the hut the next morning, Henry cannot look at her. Some time in the night, guilt overcame the grief. He declines the medicine she holds up to his lips, accepts the pain as a sort of penance. He holds her hands and cries, sees that her eyes are dry. But he released the worst of it the night before and so, apparently, had she. When Iris and Ellison step into the hut a short while later, he is ready. Alile is already gone, and he pushes himself up, reaches up for their hands, accepts their help.

The light outside the hut invades him; a searing pain. He can't take another step; it is as though he is tied somehow to the interior of the hut, a premature infant leaving the womb too soon. He slumps against the hut and requests a few minutes alone. He needs time to just be there in that sun, under that sky that casts down on him a condemning heat. He can't rush this. Iris and Ellison help him onto the step where he can lean against the hut and rest. As he sits there alone, contending with the sun and the sky and the yard that reflects it all back on him, a child appears.

It is Alile's daughter, Mkele. She steps out from behind the garden and into the blinding light so he can see her, as though she is revealing the hiding place where she has been observing him all along.

Since he returned from the mountain, she flitted in and out of his sight, in and out of his dreams during that period when lucid moments were difficult to pry apart from the delirium. If she did enter the hut, she was always alone, silent and distant. She rarely approached him, staying close to the door for a quick escape if this became necessary.

She stays put near the garden but continues to watch him. Henry waves to her. She remains silent and still.

Henry reaches into his pocket and finds the shell there. It is warm and soft as Alile's hand. He wraps his fingers around it and pulls it out into the sunlight. It is the same object, no different from when Iris's grandfather placed it in his hands. But he knows this cannot be true. It, like him, is changed. He looks up and sees that Mkele is still standing there. Her interest seems to be piqued by the shell in his hand. He feels a rush of warmth for the girl. He reaches up with his hand and waves her over to him. This time, she comes. She pads across the dirt in her bare feet, clutching the skirt of her blue dress with both her hands. She stops a foot away and looks at the shell. Henry watches her study it. He sees the lines of her neck sloping into her shoulders. The straight nose. The small chin. The long limbs. She is mostly Alile, but Henry knows that someone else, another man, lurks within her, buried in her genes, peeking out in various ways, influencing the shape of her cheekbones, her posture, the way she thinks about the world. Henry wonders who he is, what man shared an intimacy with Alile to create this girl. He has no right to think about this man. He has no right to feel what he does right now: a swell of protectiveness for this girl.

She looks up at him, studies his face. Like a cat, her eyes hold no expression. She looks down at the shell that he still holds in his hand and she reaches for it. She picks it up out of his palm and cradles it with both hands. Henry wonders how it feels in her hands, whether it is warm or cold, hard or soft, heavy or light. She looks once more at Henry's face and then turns on her heels and runs away from him. Quick and silent, she runs and is gone.

Part III

I'll meet you there

Chapter 27

The man is thin. This is the first thing Jakob notices about the doctor. His beard is overgrown, like a wild-man's. A bush man. As with many things in the hospital, the doctor's absence had been noticed but not discussed. Jakob had assumed he had gone as they all do eventually.

He studies him lying there, sleeping on the bed. So where is his anger now? In his muscles strung tight like bowstrings? Without any fat under the doctor's skin, Jakob can see where his muscles attach to his arm and leg bones. They are so taut they must still harbour a lot of anger. Even in sleep. He breathes deeply, like a man who is catching up on breaths he should have taken years ago.

He heard that he climbed Mulanje Mountain and its peak Sapitwa, all alone. Jakob imagines the doctor standing up there near the clouds and shaking his fist at Sapitwa. That is what he must have done for the mountain to pay him back with such a liberal dose of punishment.

Jakob steps a little closer and puts his hand on the doctor's leg; there is a thin sheet between the warmth of his palm and the doctor's skin. He still breathes the deep breath of sleep.

"What a fucking mess."

Jakob says it loud enough for a few patients nearby to stir in their cots and watch him.

Dr. Bryce opens his eyes. The whites are yellow. But they are calm, placid even. No anger in them. And so Jakob doesn't say what he had planned to say next. Instead, he blurts out:

"My mother is dying."

Because now Dr. Bryce looks like a healer.

*

Maria giggles and Jakob shushes her. He puts his hand over her mouth, hovers it there not quite touching but feeling her breath warm his fingers. Her breath changes a little, it becomes shallower and quickens. Taking his hand away, he leans over and puts his mouth over her lips; they are soft and compliant and open a little so he licks them and thrusts his tongue between them. Then he moves away, looks at her big eyes in the thin light coming in under the door of the storage closet. She sighs. He moves in again, this time burying his face in her neck which he kisses and he breathes in her soapy scent. His heart hammering against his breastbone, he places his hand over one of her large, soft breasts. Her nipple pushes out against the fabric and he brushes his thumb over it—just once. He moves away. He has learned that restraint reaps enormous rewards.

He holds her hands for a moment, then squeezes them once and stands up, pulls her up with him. They stand close; she is the same height as he is and when they hug it feels perfect to him. She is soft where he is all angled corners. She sighs again.

"We should get back to work." She sounds reluctant. Jakob knows she will meet him here again later today.

"Yes." He likes that they speak English to each other. He admires how well she pronounces her words.

It had come from a dare. Solomon, still poking fun at him for stealing biscuits to give to the nurses, had dared him to take it further. He had dared him to kiss one of the nurses. Jakob had chosen Maria because she was the one who helped him get his job. She was the youngest (he now knows she is just two years older than him) and the softest and the kindest. And now Jakob wishes this hadn't come from a dare. He hopes that Maria never learns of his bet with Solomon, who had to pay him 2 *kwacha* for the kiss. They shared their first kiss behind the hospital where Jakob knew the men could spy on them and be sure it really happened. It was brief and dry and awkward and Maria had laughed in the middle. He felt her teeth against his lips when she laughed, and her lips had been soft and he was left wanting to taste her tongue. They had been leaning against the back wall of the hospital and he'd had to slide down to a squat to hide his excitement. She tucked down next to him and he held her hand for a few moments before she stood up, straightened her dress and slipped back inside the hospital and then Solomon and a few other orderlies came over and slapped his back and passed him a cigarette and he wished they would just leave in case Maria came back. She didn't.

But she did smile at him when he saw her on the ward later that day, and she agreed to meet him here, in the storage closet the next morning. Now it is the best part of his day: meeting Maria here in the darkness of this room where no one can spy on them or tease him or push him to do even more. He would like to, but he doesn't want to ruin it. Now that he is a man, he knows how important it is to have patience, and to be willing to wait for things. He knows he is not as hasty as he once was; he doesn't do anything without thinking long and hard about it first. Maria has told him, in fact, that she noticed that about him, that he was different from the others in that way. His patience. His calm.

He hugs her one more time and then takes her hand and leads her to the closet door. He unlocks it. She leaves first and in a few more minutes, he will follow.

*

"My husband"—the woman spits out 'husband' as though it is a dirty word—"found other women. Again and again, he found them and bedded them and tossed them away." She pauses here to take a sip of the water she had asked Jakob to bring. "To tell you the truth I didn't care. Let him have them. Let their bodies be used up. I have my home and my garden. I have my body."

At this, Jakob takes another look at the woman perched on the edge of her bed as though she is trying to minimize the parts of her that touch the mattress. She is in a private room. She sits on a larger bed in her own room with her own window and her own attached bathroom. It is a room reserved for dignitaries and the like, although it usually sits empty. People with money usually fly down to South Africa, or attend a private hospital instead. Jakob isn't sure why this woman who sits so elegantly in her plush bathrobe is here, is occupying this room. If she has money enough to have this room, then she must have money enough to avoid the place altogether.

The woman drains the cup and places it carefully on the bedside table and then, very suddenly, she begins to cry. Her hands move over her face and she heaves large sobs until her hands are wet and her makeup is running in black rivers down her cheeks. Jakob reaches for a tissue in the box on the table beside her and hands it to her; she balls it up in her hands. He doesn't say anything. He is not used to this. Most patients lie quietly in their beds, stare at the ceiling or out the window if they are close enough. Their sadness is felt, not seen. And they don't wear makeup.

"I had my body. Or I thought so, but he used it up, too." Her voice trembles and she uses the balled-up tissue to wipe one streaky cheek. "He gave me a dirty disease from all his dirty women." She looks up at Jakob, as if seeing him for the first time. "How old are you?"

"Eighteen," he answers untruthfully.

"You look like a child. Still innocent." She sighs and looks at her hands. Her fingers are long and skinny and are cluttered with fat rings that jingle when she moves her hands. "Look at me." She opens her soft bathrobe and reveals a sunken chest with breasts that are narrow and droop down into the long dull points of her nipples. Under her breasts he can count her ribs. "I'm so skinny now. And this rash." She lifts up one end of her robe and shows him a bony ankle where a reddened area thickens the skin. "It's so ugly." She drops the robe. He wonders how old she is. Her voice—high and girlish—is the only thing that seems young about her. A coarse cough rattles in her narrow chest.

"The doctors are good here, aren't they? Not like ours." She squints at him again.

"Yes'm," he replies truthfully.

"They gave me these." She reaches to the bedside table again and picks up an orange plastic bottle. She rattles it and the pills knock about inside. The pills sound as if they are made of plastic, too. "They make me feel sick." She puts the bottle back down.

Jakob had come in to collect a kidney-shaped metal basin that she had filled with blood-streaked globs of stuff from her lungs. He looks down at the basin before covering it with a towel. One thing he has learned: blood in the lungs always seems to foretell severe illness. She is quiet now; the tears have stopped. Her eyes are nice—oval-shaped and turned up slightly at the edges, like a cat. He can tell she was once beautiful.

"I'll bring you a clean one." He puts the basin on his cart and turns away. He'll ask one of the nurses to go in with the new one. He quickly wheels the cart around and follows it out of the room.

*

In the storage closet, Jakob pulls Maria down. He pulls hard. They tumble to the floor, her lying on top of him. He can just see the round outline of her eyes in this light, and can't read her expression. Those ragged, lusty breaths that fill the space like cotton—those can't be his. But the sounds fill his ears as he reaches up and unbuttons the front of her dress, pushes his hand in and under her bra. Her breast is large and soft and spills out of her bra and it warms his hand which is cold from washing the basins. The basin of that woman. He pulls Maria's breast out until he can see her nipple—large and dark and tight. He puts his mouth over it and sucks hard. He hears her gasp. His cock, straining up against her body through his trousers, pains him; he reaches between her legs but she pulls back and then moves off him. She is quiet and he can't hear her breath, it is drowned out by his own. She pulls her bra back over her breast and buttons up her dress.

"You wanted me to do that." His voice sounds weak here in the dark of this closet. Suddenly he hates this closet.

He watches her let herself out. When she opens the door, a wedge of white daylight falls on him: bright and accusing. Then the door swings shut and he is alone in the dark.

*

Maria doesn't meet him in the closet the next day and Jakob finds her working behind the desk in the labour room. Three naked and expectant mothers lie on beds in the room in different stages of labour.

Maria looks at Jakob then looks back down at a chart.

"I thought that's what you wanted." He does his best to sound convincing; he tries to convince himself.

"You weren't gentle."

One of the patients lies on her side and watches them. "Daughter, you must be very young if you still expect gentle."

Maria ignores her and stares at Jakob. "You used to be different." She studies his face. "Were you upset about something?" Jakob wills himself not to look away. He shakes his head, not trusting his voice. Something like anger makes his muscles twitch under his skin; he is supposed to be a man.

"I'm sorry." He hates the sulk in his voice. He turns and leaves. On his way out, he hears the patient tell Maria that a man who says sorry is one worth holding on to, gentle or not.

*

Maria did not take the labouring patient's advice. For three days, Jakob went to the closet and let himself in to find it empty. Today he goes all the way in, to the overturned bucket and sits down on it. He looks at the second bucket and then puts his foot on it. His clubbed foot. He has not looked at it for a long time. He lifts his trouser leg and twists his leg this way and that for a good view. It is still ugly.

He knew, deep down, that this sweetness could never last. A girl like Maria. He touches his lips and remembers the way hers moulded under his. The bristle above his upper lip is scant but he shaves nonetheless, with a razor stolen from the surgical suite. His mind runs through an inventory of things he could find in the hospital and bring back for Maria, but she is beyond that, now. And how can he blame her? He can barely understand his own wild swings in temperament. One minute he is calm and patient, the next minute he is feeling like a caged animal. *Aliyense*. Everyone. Ha. Perhaps this is his problem: he is too many people, a whole family of different personalities, of siblings that could have been, all jostling for space in one small body. Ever since that day he watched the boy threaten Dr. Bryce he has felt the anger inside him spring out at all the wrong times. Little things set him off.

This time, it was the woman. Seeing her so ruined. It sickened him and he needed something round and full and healthy and whole. He looks at the thick hairs that are filling in over his forearm and he wonders if this is being a man. Savaging the pure. Ruining beauty.

*

His mother is sleeping when he approaches her tonight. Jakob stands over her cot and studies her in the moonlight and he is taken by her gauntness; even in this light he can see how she is a skeleton under that blanket. But she has the warmest and thickest blanket that he could find. This is one of the first things he brought her when he was new on the job and had access to every cranny of the hospital. It was a donation. Someone in the West didn't want this blanket. Perhaps it was not thick enough or warm enough. He leans over and bunches it up below her right leg so she won't notice her missing foot when she wakes up.

He looks down at the food in his hands: a few pieces of lemon cake—today's dessert at the doctor's lounge.

"Eh, I'll have some of that, Brother." The man in the cot beside Jakob's mother is eyeing the food. Jakob passes him the cake. His mother won't want it, even if she were to wake up. She has no appetite these days. He settles on his pallet beside her bed, lies down and listens to the ward breathing hundreds of breaths. It sounds like ocean waves—all the breaths rise and fall together in some mysterious harmony. He dreams of Maria, and falls asleep.

*

"My mother is dying." Jakob doesn't look at the doctor when he speaks. Instead, he studies the mop strings; the strings are many shades, all grey. He moves the mop to the other side of him and the wet floor shines briefly. For a moment, he can see himself in the floor, looking down the length of the pole. His face is mostly shadow and then it is gone, swallowed up by the disappearing water. He now glances up briefly at the doctor's face, to see his reaction. He has strung together the most convincing words he knows.

"Which one is your mother?" Jakob can tell that the doctor—the big surgeon named Ellison—is annoyed to be stopped like this on his way to his lunch meal.

"She is in the TB ward. She has been there for months. She is shrinking. She is coughing. She is dying." And then he adds: "You took her foot."

The doctor looks at Jakob for a long moment and then says, "Let's go see her."

Soon they both stand over her cot. Her eyes are closed, but Jakob can tell that she is not really sleeping.

Dr. Ellison lifts the blanket over her missing foot and Jakob winces. The stump looks as it always does: wrong. Jakob feels guilty every time he sees it. Dr. Ellison is running his finger along the line where the skin was sewn together; it is now just a dark line in her skin like a clumsily drawn tattoo, surrounded by dark dots where the staples used to pierce the skin. Now Dr. Ellison pokes his thick finger into the end of her leg and his mother moans some awful sound and shifts her leg away. Her eyes are still closed, but squeezed closed now, with a furrowed brow stitched together overtop of them.

"Hm," says Dr. Ellison. Just to be sure, he pokes again, and again his mother cries out in pain. "We'll get an x-ray to confirm, but she may have osteomyelitis. An infection in the bone."

"Again?"

"Still."

"It never went away?"

"Yes."

Jakob feels his heart shift into his belly again, like it did so many months ago. "Even after taking the foot? Even with all the medicine?"

"Has she been taking it?" Dr. Ellison says this mildly, as if he doesn't care what the answer is. As if he wouldn't be surprised to find she'd been throwing it away. Jakob feels it again, under his skin: an irritability, his muscle's own desire to strike. He knows she's been taking her pills. She may be weak, but she is not stupid.

"Yesss." Jakob hears the hiss, coming from between his own teeth. "She takes it every day. All of it. Even though it makes her feel sick. It makes her stop eating." He has seen her push herself up on her stick arms so she can sit and take the pills. She places them in her mouth individually and it takes a painfully long time for her to swallow each one, wincing, complaining in between. But she does it.

He wonders when he last saw her smile. She has a wide, uneven grin with crooked, yellowed teeth. She would crack this grin right before the funny part of a story and Jakob would feel like laughing even though the funny part had not been told. She used to hunt with the men. This was before Jakob, before she became a mother of one, before her family moved to the city. He wonders if it was true or if it was a fable, another of his mother's stories, another joke. Everyone tells a story. He feels strung along, a pawn in others' stories, the butt of others' jokes.

"If the x-ray confirms it, she'll need another operation." Dr. Ellison is saying. Jakob hears it through a thick window of glass, from the other side of where he stands alone in the ward. He knows, suddenly, that his mother will soon die.

Her face is relaxed, now. The pain is gone, or better at least. He had no idea she had pain. She is telling him nothing, now. He feels her loss of trust as a sharp pang deep in his gut where his heart is lodged.

"Will she have something for her pain?"

The doctor nods. The surgery is a fable, too. He knows as well as Jakob does that there is no point. Jakob wishes he had not said those words: my mother is dying; they were composed to get the doctor's attention and now they are no longer a story. He has been proven a truth-teller, not a storyteller. He wishes he was a storyteller like everyone else. Why should he be forced to utter only truths? And Jakob wishes that he had not brought her here, that he had not said yes, okay, that he had not had any anger, that he had been willing to let her die at home.

*

He passes Maria in the halls, soon after his conversation with Dr. Ellison about his mother. When he smells Maria's coconut smell, when he sees the rounded soft swells of her breasts beneath her uniform, he cannot bear it. He wants to pull her to him, to push her away, to pull up her dress and take her there in the hallway, the closet be damned. He wants to ransack the closet, break everything in it. He doesn't want to be near her, he can't stand the sight of her or any other soft, womanly shape. As he marches past her down the hall hating his rolling gait, he can feel her staring after him. She calls out his name once but he doesn't stop. He can't stop.

He ends up in the closet and grasping a stack of metal basins he hurls them to the floor. The noise helps the rage and he eventually sits and lets his breath return to normal. He stares at the mess on the floor.

His foot aches.

Chapter 28

Iris carries the bag of saline in one hand and pushes the metal pole with the other. The bag is warm and heavy. It swings briefly from its pole as she pushes the intravenous line into the tube at the bottom of it—a short piece that dangles like a length of umbilical cord. Fluid makes its way down the tubing and she holds onto the other end of it until saline begins to spill out of it onto the floor. Then she gently attaches the end of the tube to the line taped to Dr. Bryce's arm. The line that leads, ultimately, to his heart. She pats down the hair there, on his arm. The red-gold hairs.

Dr. Bryce shifts in his cot and opens his eyes. Even his lashes contain some of that gold. His eyes are blue. A pale, almost colourless blue.

Dr. Bryce turns his head toward the yellow wall, or perhaps the window—this is where his gaze seems to automatically rest, turning like a compass in the direction of the village, and Alile.

He has been quiet since their return to the hospital. Iris can tell he has been doing a lot of thinking, which worries her. She is beginning to adopt some of her grandfather's strategies: think less, do more.

She watches him watch the window for a moment longer then touches him again on his arm. "I miss her too, you know."

Dr. Bryce finally turns his head toward hers. His skin is a better colour, now. No more yellow. And his beard has been trimmed; he allowed her to do this for him the other day. He looks good, she thinks, and feels a certain pride in this which immediately embarrasses her.

"Tell Ellison I want to do something for these people." He waves his arm out from the cot, gestures around the ward, indicating all the bodies that he lies among. "Make a change." His jaw tightens as he says this. So he has not lost his stubbornness. So his experience has not broken that in him.

"I will." She says, and then before she can walk away, he calls her name.

"What if it's all just belief?"

She looks at him.

"That's a dangerous place to go. As a doctor."

Something else passes between them, unsaid. And then she walks away between the rows of beds.

*

"Hey, boy!"

Jakob hears the call, that high, girlish voice coming from that room. He pushes the cart past the doorway and pretends he doesn't hear. He hears her cough once and then her voice again, slightly weaker, slightly more lonely. "Boy?" He stops the cart, knowing that she knows he has stopped the cart because the wheels squeak. Now he has no choice. He leaves the cart and enters her room, hovering by the doorway.

She is sitting on the bed again, still in her bathrobe. It is as though she has not moved and has spent all the days since then right here in this same place. Nothing has changed. Except everything has changed. His mother is now dying where before she had been sick. He is now alone where before, for brief stolen moments, he'd had Maria. This woman is now expanding where before she was withering. He looks at her again. She smiles. She looks better. Somehow more whole. More full of something—life? Hope? A future, he decides. Somehow, she has been given back her own future.

"How are you feeling, ma'am?" He asks to say something, but already knows the answer.

"Much better." She confirms. "These are working. They are foul, but they work well." She rattles the bottle of pills.

"You look better, ma'am."

She is looking at him in a way that makes him uncomfortable.

"Do you have a woman, boy?" She asks. He notices she chose the word woman, rather than girl. He supposes that Maria would be closer to a woman than a girl. He thinks of her buttocks that strain through her dress, and her breasts and then, aware of his wandering thoughts with the woman watching, feels his face get hot. She laughs.

"So you do."

Jakob shakes his head. "No. I lost her."

The woman laughs harder. "Still a boy and already he has had a woman and lost her." She shakes her head. "Such history in such a little body." She stops laughing. "Such loss." Now she looks so serious that he is worried she will start crying again. "Such loss." She repeats. "What have you lost, boy? Who have you lost?"

Jakob shrugs. What has he lost? Nothing. Everything. He knows what he is about to lose, and now, suddenly, wishes to be alone.

He says: "I have to go. There are patients waiting." He turns and leaves without waiting for her response and as he pushes the cart away he thinks that she is a patient, and she is waiting. She is waiting, too.

*

When he gets to the nursing station, he asks Lila at the desk about that woman.

"Miss Makombe?"

He frowns. "In the private room."

The nurse nods. "That's her."

"She said something about a husband."

Lila makes a face of disapproval. "She was a minister's mistress. He was generous. He gave her a house." She looks at her own hands, ringless. "If he were her husband, she'd be in South Africa now."

"Mmm." He agrees, and then asks: "What medicine is she taking?"

Lila gives him a bored look. It is like all her other looks. But she answers. "The stuff in the locked cupboard. The stuff you have to pay for."

"What locked cupboard?" He has never heard of this.

"They don't tell most patients about it. Unless they have money. But I think they should let everyone have the chance. They should at least let them know." She returns to her work, her boredom wiping over their conversation, ending it.

Jakob wanders away. He wonders if this relates at all to an argument he overheard once between two doctors. It was Dr. Kumwembe and Dr. Bryce. They were arguing about how to treat a patient. One wanted to offer an expensive medicine to the patient. The other argued against as it would bankrupt the family. Jakob left before he could hear the final decision and who won: the patient, the family, or the doctors. It is always the doctors. He left the room feeling like his own soul was the rope being tugged to one side then the other. He wanted to tear himself back from their powerful grip. No one should be allowed to pull on him like that, make him feel that way. Now it is back safe inside him, coiled like a snake. But the knot in the middle is still there and so tight from all the pulling that it won't come undone.

*

"So how did you lose your woman?" Miss Makombe asks, calmly taking her pills out and placing them in the palm of her long, smooth hand. They are a colourful batch of flat, chalky circles and bright, shiny capsules.

Jakob watches her swallow them with the water he has brought, this time without asking. She takes them all at once and he can see them move down her throat, he can tell when they have reached her flat stomach. The medicine, although making her gain weight, has caused her face to thin and her cheekbones to rise like hills growing beneath her large eyes. He doesn't know how much to tell her about Maria. He settles on what little he knows.

"I wasn't gentle."

At this, Miss Makombe releases a peal of laughter. Jakob watches her and wishes he could laugh like that. When the laughter settles and she wipes her eyes, she says, "Oh my goodness. This woman of yours is such a lady."

Miss Makombe reaches out for Jakob's hand and grasps it. Her nails, somehow, are still painted red. "I tell you what," she says. “You can get her back. But . . . ” She raises an elegant finger, “you must be firm. Firm and gentle. This is possible. It is the best way.”

When he is ready to leave her room with her empty water cup, he pauses at the door.

“Would you like me to bring you your medicine tomorrow?”

She raises her eyes. They are bright now, with the medicine. Like Maria’s were when they used to meet in the closet. Shiny and full of secrets. “Yes.” She says. “Please.”

Lila is grateful to be relieved of one duty related to Miss Makombe. “That’s fine. I hate talking to her,” she said when he told her that the patient had asked that he bring in her pills. She showed Jakob which bottles contain Miss Makombe’s pills. Today, he takes the keys from Lila’s hands and goes to the locked cabinet. He finds the pills. He takes them from the bottles as instructed by Lila. He takes two of each and places one in her pill bottle and the second in his pocket. Then he takes the bottle with her medicine into Miss Makombe’s room.

*

Jakob has been rearranging resources inside the hospital. He has been taking them apart and putting them back together in a way that fits better, like a jigsaw puzzle, so the overall picture makes sense. He moves things so they function better. Like food. If it is not being eaten here (there is always excess in the doctors’ lounge) then he moves it there (he finds the hungriest patients). Blankets being kicked off a body already too hot are removed and thrown overtop of one that shivers. And now this: Jakob examines his latest find, a piece of the puzzle that does not fit. A pad of thick paper and a palette of water paints, the little round cakes of paint planted neatly in the white plastic case. Little happy faces of primary colours smile up at him. The paintbrush is small and red with short, fat plastic bristles.

He tries to imagine the people who sent this here, what sort of place they call home. He tries to imagine a hospital where the children inside it are well enough to sit at a desk, or stand at an easel, and paint pictures. The children at The Queen Elizabeth Hospital are all lying down in cots or stretchers or their mother's laps. They are all listless with hunger or illness or something even worse. These children cannot paint, cannot even stay upright long enough to take a glass of water, it must instead be fed into them through a plastic tube.

This is the first time that Jakob has taken a resource and used it himself. But when he saw it, he needed to unpack it. And when he unpacked it and knew no child could use it, he needed to do something with it. The palettes, so neat and tidy in their little compartments were begging to be wet, begging to have a brush dragged through them. So Jakob, with only brief hesitation, took this gift and brought it here.

Here is a rock just the right height for sitting in a field behind the hospital. It is empty in this field, the grass is nearly dead around him and refuse piles are the only inhabitants. Some piles have been burned down to a scrubby assemblage of half-burnt scraps that still release the acrid smell of burning plastic, and others are piles waiting to be ignited. It is ugly here, but it is quiet and empty and no one will see what he is about to do.

Once the paint is unpacked and his cup of water is positioned on the ground, he dips the brush in, smears it in the blue cake and holds it dripping above the paper. He decides to paint what he sees, so he begins with the blue of the sky, and marvels how the colour so easily mimics what is above him. Then he paints the refuse piles around him: tarry black with dirty white and the remnants of colour from things half-burnt. Then he paints the hospital: grey blocks housing red blood and yellow sputum and cloudy spinal fluid and black vomit and the white circles of scared eyes around brown centres, black empty dots in the middle staring back at him. He paints the clear straw fluid that leaks out before a baby arrives and he paints the yellow-white cream that coats the soft brown of newborn skin. Then the thick purple coils of the umbilical cord and the dead white ends of the cord once it is cut. Then the worried relief on the mothers' faces once the babies have arrived and the flat faces of the staff who lean over the old and the sick, their mouths one straight, dark line. The maze of halls and rooms that don't end, and the morgue where the bodies lie stiff and silent and naked and alone. On the last blank page, he paints his mother but he takes some liberty and doesn't paint her as she is in the hospital. She has both her feet and even her womb and he surrounds her with many children and bush animals and all her aunties and uncles and above them blue sky and below them Lake Malawi which he imagines to be expansive and radiant with blue-green waves which would rock her to sleep and above all of that the warm, yellow sun. This is what he wants to paint but by now all the colours have been mixed together and are all the same muddy brown and so he smears the page with this—dirty, almost colourless brown and then he picks up the pad all heavy and wet with paint and hurls it as far as he can. Then he stands, staring at it, the sodden mess. More rubbish.

Chapter 29

Somehow Henry had hoped he would find Juma here. A silly, naïve and romantic notion of coming full circle. Also, he needed Juma's smile and his faith in him, at least when he started back on rounds. Something to give him confidence. Henry was sure that the patients would be even more doubtful and frightened of him when he rose from among them and began to lay hands on them. But the opposite happened. Word had spread among the patients that he had climbed Mulanje Mountain, faced Sapitwa in a fierce battle, and had survived. All true, he supposes. The fact that he survived somehow redeems the foolishness of climbing Sapitwa in the first place. Like a knight returning from battle. Scarred, but stronger. This is where the patients superimpose their own hope on the story. That he returns stronger. As he limps between the beds and leans on IV poles for support, he knows it is all hope. But he will take it: this hope. It is something he has not felt in this place since planting his first step on Malawian soil except, perhaps, from Juma. Now he sees a little of Juma in all these faces that look at him in a certain way. In a way that considers what he might do for them. That it is possible he may do something for them while they are here.

He walks crookedly up to the next bedside where a young woman lies, watching him from under her blanket. Ellison has made his mark by extracting a premature infant from her belly and the wound, although ugly, is now healing well. The infant fights for his life in the neonatal intensive care unit, tiny tubes inserted everywhere: through the mouth and into the lungs, through the nose and into the stomach, through the thin, wrinkled skin into a vein in the leg. This was one of his first cases upon returning to work: resuscitating this infant. There was no paediatrician in house at the time, and he was next in line. And he did it: the infant breathes and eats and wiggles and cries.

Henry places a hand on the woman's shoulder, tells her about her baby although she cannot understand a word. He is her firstborn.

The woman is infected with HIV. No clinical evidence of it, though. No AIDS, yet. She watches him as he talks, studies his face, hair and beard, then looks at his arm reaching down to her shoulder, but he leaves it there as he talks. Then he palpates the abdominal wound, satisfies himself that it is clean, and the dressings are dry.

He pats the woman's shoulder one more time, scribbles some instructions down on her chart, and hobbles over to the next patient.

*

Lunchtime in the cafeteria, he eats alone. Kumwembe has not forgiven him, it seems, but gazes at him across the tables with an analytical look, an expression that indicates he has not made a final decision. He is being watched. For now, Henry waves to Kumwembe who nods. Henry washes his hands in the aluminum basin beside his plate and then picks up a piece of *nsima*. He pushes it through the relish, puts it in his mouth, enjoys the flavour of the relish, the smoothness of the *nsima*. He washes it down with a cool, sweet drink of water.

*

Miss Makombe smiles and pats the bed beside her. It has sheets on it so she doesn't have to sleep on the vinyl mattress. It looks comfortable.

"Sit." She commands, lightly, then smiles up at him. Miss Makombe has a fetching smile, now that there is a robustness to her again. Jakob has not heard her cough for a long time. Her arms are less skinny and her rings don't slip and slide as much on her fingers. When she stands up and paces her room he can see that her bottom is also filling in, becoming two round globes where there had been nothing but pokey bones before. He is amazed at the power of the drugs—simple little packets of dust—he has broken one of them open to see. He is not sure what he had expected to find in the capsules, but he still questions how something so small and easily misplaced could result in such sweeping changes in a body. He has been hoping to find the courage to ask Miss Makombe if there is something else. What else has she done to achieve this? Who else has been helping her? What *sing'anga* has been visiting, flying in like a bat in the night and disappearing before any of them can see him, impregnating her with the seeds of new life, but instead of a baby it is she who is reborn? If only she would share her secret with him, then he could ask the *sing'anga* to visit his mother, because the pills have been doing nothing for her. But what is the price for this twisting of fate? What has she traded in exchange for the return of her youth and beauty? For indeed they are back: her lips and eyes and new curves demand his gaze. He cannot stop it; his gaze keeps going to her, wandering over the secret places under her robe and then he must pull it back, push it down to the neutral territory of the floor.

For such a dramatic change, he would be willing to negotiate. For his mother. He would do it. He wonders what a truly skilled, truly powerful *sing'anga* would demand in exchange for the return of his mother's foot.

Miss Makombe pats the space on the bed beside her again.

He sits down there and feels the mattress puff and then sink under him. She moves a little closer to him, sliding down into the dip he has made in the bed. Her robe now touches his leg. He looks straight ahead, each of his hands placed resolutely on one of his knees. He glances sideways and she is smiling at him still.

"I am leaving tomorrow. Did you know that?"

He didn't know. The nurses didn't tell him. Perhaps they thought he wouldn't care. Perhaps they thought he'd care too much.

"So, I suppose it will be goodbye soon."

He looks over at her. She has fixed those tilted eyes on him and he can see how she seduced the minister. He can see why he bought her rings, and fine clothes, and a house with a garden.

"Do you think I am beautiful?"

Jakob nods. She leans in and their lips touch, press together and then open. As soon as this he is already trading things; the negotiation has already begun. A kiss with this renewed spirit-woman for what? The kiss itself is similar to

Maria's kisses, but different enough. Miss Makombe is more in control, her mouth is stronger, her tongue less hesitant and he feels her tugging on him with her lips and her tongue and he is not sure, not sure he wants to follow, but soon, with her tugging and her warmth and wetness, he forgets that this is a negotiation, that he has to keep his head clear, that he has to watch for whatever dark thing beckons to him from her, inside her.

His mouth still on hers, his breath forcing itself through his nose, he pushes down on his cock that is pressing uncomfortably from between his legs and reaches over and slips his hand under her dressing gown where her breasts have been hidden for so many weeks. He places his hand over one breast and finds it much smaller than Maria's and it is slack and empty. Jakob now remembers her breasts as they were when he first met her: deflated and defeated, the dangling nipples flaccid and useless. Like a witch's; appealing only to the bewitched. He snatches his hand out from her robe and stands up, backs away from her and into his cart. Metal basins clatter behind him. Now he knows that her apparent recovery is magic, just magic, for the sorcerer has only tended to the visible areas and the hidden areas under her dressing gown, still shrivelled like an old woman's, are proof.

A sigh comes out of her, slow and stale like dead air, with his breath on it. "We shouldn't have done that," she says. She looks at him. "You're just a child." This sounds like an accusation. She looks up at the ceiling and her neck is too skinny, as though it won't be able to hold her head, and he can see scales there in the lizard-like triangle of skin underneath her jaw. Tears roll down from the outer corners of her eyes, drop onto the shoulders of her bathrobe which still gapes open where he had his hand.

"I am a man." He says to her lizard neck, to the hole between her collar bones, to the space in her body which he now knows is empty.

From Miss Makombe's room, Jakob goes straight to the locked medicine cabinet; if Miss Makombe is leaving, he won't be able to go there any more. Inside the room of medicine and supplies, he unlocks the cabinet and picks up one of the bottles of pills she has been taking. He pinches out one of the long oval capsules—one half of it white and one half blue. When he squeezes it, it buckles under his fingers and then pops back into shape. He contemplates taking several more—maybe another week or two of supplies. This may be his last chance. His only chance. He settles on taking one more week's worth, and slides seven of the blue and white capsules into his trouser pocket.

"Those are not for you to take."

The voice behind him is male, familiar. In this moment Jakob imagines the future as it will unfold before him and it involves shame, hunger, and then death—first his mother's, then soon after, his own dissatisfying and premature end. He turns around because that is all that he can do and sees Dr. Ellison standing in the doorway looking at him with a grim face.

"What have you been doing with them? Have you been taking them yourself?"

"No."

"Have you been selling them?"

"No."

"Who have you been giving them to?"

"My mother." He stares back at Dr. Ellison. He dares him to question his motives, this man who just took things away from his mother. He just took and took.

But the doctor just heaves a large sigh. "They won't help her. Your mother doesn't have HIV. Those pills treat HIV. You can't cure her with those."

Jakob clenches his hand around the capsules in the bottom of his pocket.

"There's a hundred people in this place you could help with those. But not her. You can't cure her." Dr. Ellison repeats.

Jakob throws the seven blue and white pills at Dr. Ellison. They hit him on his chest and then scatter to the floor.

"Help the other hundred then." He thinks this, but doesn't say it. His throat has closed up and no sound will come out.

Jakob waits for the dismissal. He waits for someone to come, tap him on his shoulder and send him on his way. But it never happens. The rest of the day after his run-in with Dr. Ellison passes uneventfully. And then another day passes. And another. He looks for evidence that it is being discussed in the nurses' faces, or the other doctors'. But the hospital staff go about their days like they usually do: expressionless, voiceless.

He even looks for some judgement on his mother's face, especially when he stops bringing her the extra tablets, as if somehow she would know. But his mother just interacts with him like she has since they entered this place—with her eyes closed.

So it is, he thinks. He strokes her hands. He hides her missing foot under the thick blanket even though she won't be looking for it. He pulls the blanket up over her narrow shoulders and lets her rest.

*

Iris pushes her cart through the ward. The wheels have by some miracle been recently oiled, and it glides silently between the cots. It is stuffed with needles and intravenous line and bags of fluid. Bottles and vials of medication fill the lower shelves. She stops near a woman who looks to be about her mother's age. By the chart she is two years younger. The woman sleeps deeply as though this room is hers alone, and the shutters are pulled, and it is quiet. Iris tries to imagine her mother in her place, lying exactly here in this bed. She would not sleep like this. She would be sitting up, glaring at other patients, glaring at the nurses and avoiding the eyes of the doctors altogether. She would complain about the intravenous that would have to be stuck in her arm, and the food, and the smells, and the shared toilets or worse, the bedpan.

Her mother asked her something recently, about Mapiri. She said: did you feel at home? Her answer had come quickly to mind but Iris had been unable to form a reply, not sure which answer would hurt more. She has already decided that she will allow herself brief visits to see Alile and her grandfather and her grandmother's *kachisi*. She will arrange the trips in wide intervals, allow herself just a little of this strange bliss, in pieces too small to have much effect on her life here in Blantyre, here in the hospital. The aftermath of these indulgences is too disturbing, like a tremor in an earth that should by all rights be stable. Visits to Mapiri encourage too much contemplation, raise too many questions. Questions about her decisions. The choices she has made. What she has and what she lacks. She has come to the conclusion that choice encourages doubt. And doubt encourages regret. And there is too much that still needs to be done here to allow herself any kind of regret. There is no room in her life for this sort of nonsense. Just a look around the ward affirms it.

And, in the silence following her mother's last question while Iris was turning all of this over in her mind her mother spoke again. Her mother said one more thing. *Bring me home.*

Iris pushes the trolley on, not wishing to disrupt the woman's deep sleep. She pauses next by a man who lies on his side, fully awake, caressing his enlarged belly like a woman with child. The doctors are still sorting out whether this belly grew from Carlsberg or malnourishment. Or both. She is to draw blood for this, to check the liver and count the blood cells and the protein floating through his bloated body. What has been discovered by modern medicine through the invention of the microscope and other technologies is what her people have always known. That the answers lie in what ordinarily can't be seen.

To her mother who now has no more questions she said yes. Yes, mama. I will bring you home.

*

"Jakob. I think you'd better come."

The nurse who said this to him was Neva, the one who used to work in the ICU and who would give him such angry stares. But the look in her eyes when she beckoned him was something else, and then it was gone because she looked away, she couldn't meet his gaze. And then he knew.

His mother when he found her was lying as usual on her bed and she looked as thin and frail as she always did. But there was something different about her. It was her eyes. They were open. She was looking for him and when she saw him enter the ward and come toward her, she smiled.

She died later that same night when the hospital was quiet under a moonless sky. Jakob went outside afterwards and he saw nothing when he looked up at the black. It had emptied itself out earlier that evening, all the stars and moons and planets poured into his mother's body where he had caught a glimpse of them shining there before her eyes closed forever.

*

When did Sarah stop coming here, to the forefront of his mind? When did she stop running her nails down his back, secretly, so only he knew why he was shivering? Perhaps she hasn't. Perhaps he can handle it better now, all those memories, all his regret, all her anger. Did she blame him? Odd, now he is not sure. It may have been all him, phantom blame created exclusively out of his guilt.

Henry has nearly picked up the phone many times. That slippery, yellowed plastic. He still knows the numbers; they are etched in his mind like the code for a lock. And then one day he does. He watches his finger punch down each numbered square. He listens to the strange and distant ring, feels the round earpiece hard against his right ear. When the phone is picked up on the other end and he hears Sarah's voice again it is like he just arrived here and they have just said goodbye and Emma, Emma has only just laid down to sleep.

Somehow Sarah knows. She says his name and it is said without anything else. No judgement. Only loss.

"Sarah, I…"

"Are you okay?"

"Yes, yes I'm fine."

"It's good to hear your voice, Henry."

"So much has happened."

"You've been gone a long time."

"It's more than that. More than time passing."

"I'm sure it's difficult there. I can only imagine."

"Can you?" He wonders what she imagines, all the way over there.

"What happened to that boy? Juma."

She remembered.

"I sent him to a healer."

He hears a sound on the other end and at first it sounds like laughter.

"Oh, God. I wish we had those over here. Healers, I mean."

"Me too."

Alile. He thinks, suddenly, of her hands.

"We need to touch more."

Quiet.

"I should have touched her more." He thinks of them in that room with Emma. Always a distance away, on opposite sides of her bed.

She is crying, on the other end. In Toronto. He never intended that. He wanted to make it better and then he recognizes it again: his inept desire to fix everything. Everything can't be fixed. Some things will stay broken.

"I miss Emma so much."

"She's your daughter. You can't stop being a father." As though the answer lay in these truths all along.

"Yes."

"Too bad you had to go where you did to find all this out."

He wipes his eyes and laughs. "God, if only you knew just where I had to go."

"So when are you coming home?"

A pause.

"I already am. For now. That's what I wanted to tell you."

After this, they talk for a long time and when they say goodbye, they agree to talk again.

Sometime soon.

*

It shames Jakob. That his mother's death has released him. But it has; her death made any chance of a deal with Miss Makombe the witch-woman an impossibility. If his mother had improved, Jakob would have wondered what he had paid, and when the *mfiti* would come to collect. Every morning until she died he checked for both his feet and they were always there, the right one no uglier than usual. When he thinks of the kiss, he cannot remove the threat of it, some darkness in her moving into him like a sooty wind. After it, he walked through the days like a thief, sneaking backward looks, waiting to be caught, waiting to be forced to pay. But then his mother opened her eyes and smiled on him. And since then something has lifted from his shoulders and the anger, even the anger, has lessened, buried under the brightness of the cosmos that poured out from his mother in those final hours.

*

Maria said: a baby is another chance. This was when one of them came, wet and bawling, needing to be rubbed into pinkness, rubbed into life.

She said it as she massaged vigorously, moving the towel all over the brand new skin, massaging each limb and each finger until the creature stopped his indignant cries, became quiet and ponderous.

Jakob isn't sure if she said it because she thinks about it every time a new baby arrives (and they come often, many a day, more in the night). Or did she say it because of his mother, and his loss, and the need to console him in some way, by saying little things like a baby is another chance?

Whatever the reason, it did make Jakob feel better because it put into words the thing that keeps him in the labour and delivery room watching it all happen in a flurry around him. Also what he sees in the babies' eyes when they lie curled up on their backs in the incubator, wrinkled arms and legs springing back like rubber bands to the position they held in the womb; they are still tightly folded secrets, not yet ready to blossom. When their petal-limbs have been rubbed until the blood flows freely through them, when they are warm under the sunshine lamp, when the shock and violence of their arrival is forgotten: this is when their eyes peek open just enough for them to experience, for the first time, the brightness of this world's light. And he can feel the wonder as their eyes look with such solemn quiet, still containing all the darkness and boundlessness of the night sky, or the deepest ocean, or the place from where they came. He has whispered things to them. He can tell they are listening, already taking it into their new bodies, their new minds and hearts what all this is, what all this means.

Maria turns around and spots Jakob where he stands beside the incubator in which another recently delivered baby lies blinking, looking right at him.

"Jakob," she says, "can you pass me my stethoscope? It's over there, on the table in the corner."

Yes, anything, he thinks, anything for you.

Maria has one hand on a labouring woman's swollen belly, the other one squeezes the patient's hand. She is saying something to the woman, probably words of encouragement, or reassurance. It is the time of labour when things are not yet frantic, and the mother has moments, in between contractions, to breathe, to listen to things like Maria's soothing voice. Maria has a rounded figure with just the right amount of fat in just the right places. If she were pregnant, her belly would swell out, first to balance her buttocks, then to surpass them, and it would assume the beautiful, asymmetric profile of a mother with child, a baby upside-down inside. His seed, if planted inside her, would flourish, he has no doubt. It would grow and grow and its heart would be so enormous and strong that he would be able to feel it all the way through the tight, thick skin of Maria's belly that she would rub every night with the sweet-smelling coconut oil he would buy for her, special from the market. He would walk miles a day to collect it for her and sometimes she would let him rub it in, rub it on that swollen brown belly and he would run his fingers over it afterwards, still slippery with the oil, and feel her folded navel and imagine the navel of the baby before it is a navel, still tethered to Maria, still serving as a bloodline, a lifeline.

Chapter 30

Across the table in the pub, Ellison peels away the label from a sweaty bottle of Carlsberg. It is green and gold and the paint sticks to his fingers. They have been coming here after work, to Ellison's favourite restaurant. Ellison has been keeping an eye on him. He seeks Henry out wherever he happens to be in the ward at the end of the day and coaxes him out the doors, down the hill. They have a meal, share a drink. Henry has obliged. He feels better in company these days, a side effect of the attendance he always had in the village. He was never left alone.

There is a man watching them from the bar. After a time, the man approaches. He wipes at his shiny forehead and smells of sour, anxious sweat. He manages a smile.

"Hello Doctor." He looks at Ellison. His smile falters.

Ellison looks up, waves lazily. He returns his gaze to his glass of beer. The man waits for a moment, uncertain, then turns and walks away, out of the pub. Ellison glances at Henry.

"His sister's on the ward. Resected a Kaposi's off her leg. No good. It's metastasized. She's done."

Henry watches him for a moment, then speaks.

"Aren't you going to talk to him?"

He swirls his beer, doesn't look up. "Hm?"

"Him. That man. With the sister in hospital. Aren't you going to say something?"

Ellison is casual but attentive. "What could I say. Tell him the truth?"

"What would you do in Sydney."

"Hm?"

"What would you do in Oz. If a dying patient's brother showed up in your pub. What would you do then?"

"What're you going on about, mate? I'd do the same thing."

"No, you wouldn't."

"I'd do the same damn thing. What difference would it make where the hell in the world I am?"

"You tell me."

"Stop speaking in fucking riddles, mate."

Ellison half rises out of his chair. His eyes are vague, but he isn't drunk. He is more irritated than drunk. Henry clenches his thighs, feels his bad leg tighten painfully. He picks up his glass then puts it down again.

"All I'm saying is we owe them something. As their doctors. If we can't save them. We still owe them. They're suffering."

"We're all suffering! The whole world is suffering!" Ellison throws his hands up in the air, spills some beer on the ground then finishes off what remains in one long swallow. "Look, all *I'm* saying is you need to keep your distance. To keep your sanity, you need to keep your distance." He shoves his chair backwards and stands up, strolls over to the bar where a shapely woman leans, chatting with the barkeep. He puts his hand on her waist and she turns to him warily then smiles widely in recognition, touches his arm. He places his order with the barkeep then looks over at Henry. Speaks loudly across the tables. "You don't keep your distance, you're no use to anyone. You should know that better than anyone, Bryce. Am I right?"

Henry downs his glass, places it back on the table carefully. "No."

Ellison leaves the bar. The woman sizes him up as he walks back over to their table.

"You know, Bryce, it goes both ways."

"I'm not sure what you mean."

"It goes both ways. You think they treat us the same?"

Henry stands. "So what does that mean."

"That means you do what you can and then you call it a day. I've called it a day." He points in the direction of the hospital. "That was my day." He plants a thick finger on the table. "This is my night. I owe myself that." He looks at Henry. "You ever think about what you owe yourself, Bryce?"

Henry gets up and limps out of the bar. He hears Ellison calling after him. "Have a drink, share a fuck. You owe yourself at least that. Beneath it all, you're still a man, Bryce. You can't forget that. It's an important detail."

Henry limps all the way home.

*

Henry found the boy. For awhile, he wasn't sure he was real. He could have as easily been a dream, appearing at his bedside at a time when he still drifted between waking and sleeping states involuntarily. But he found him in the TB ward, passing out pieces of some yellow crumbly bread or cake he held wrapped up in a napkin to patients in the ward. Henry tapped him on the shoulder.

"Where is your mother?" He asked him when he turned around.

The boy gazed up at him with large, unfathomable eyes. Henry couldn't place his age. He had features of a child, a teen and an adult, all in one lean body. It was his strong, stubborn jaw and his testy quickness, though, that placed him as an adolescent. Henry put him at seventeen, give or take a couple of years. At Henry's question, the boy turned and pointed at a woman in a bed directly behind him.

"She used to sleep there," said the boy. "That used to be her bed."

The woman in the bed was nursing an infant. The baby was scrabbling for her breast, had not yet achieved a satisfactory latch and the woman winced as the baby's mouth took hold.

"I'm sorry," said Henry to the boy.

"She went in peace," he replied. He licked the crumbs off the napkin stained with oil from the cake and looked at Henry.

"That's good."

"It's okay," said the boy.

"Are you okay?"

"I'm okay," he said. And looked it.

*

Iris is overseeing the wards tonight; she is in the office flipping through a chart but thinking of other things when a man is brought in. When she sees the new patient wrestling with his caregivers, unwilling to lie down, when she sees his wild eyes, red and yellow, she calls in the doctor. This man cannot wait till morning.

Dr. Bryce arrives within the half hour. She had hoped it wouldn't be him. She had hoped for Dr. Kumwembe, or even a surgeon. Anyone but Dr. Bryce. But there he is, looking serious and determined, not yet knowing what is coming.

Together they hold the man down; he has no family with him. A group of strangers found him outside a pub and dragged him in; he fought with them the whole way. "Probably poisoning," they mutter to each other, staring down at him. It is a courtesy they are willing to provide: bringing him in. They'd want the same if they were the target. Once on the stretcher, the man still struggles. He looks around savagely at them all, not really seeing them. The strangers leave, exasperated. They don't turn around when Iris says, "*Zikomo.*" Thank you.

Dr. Bryce and Iris do the usual things: vital signs, obtain IV access. Once they have collected all the basic information, Dr. Bryce steps back from the patient. Iris joins him. They watch him; he has quieted now. He lies on his stretcher and stares up at the ceiling, then turns his head and looks at the empty space above the bodies in the ward. He is completely disoriented; he couldn't state his name, or the place, or the correct date.

"Could be meningitis. Malaria. HIV."

"All three, maybe," adds Iris and she feels him nod beside her.

She collects the blood and hands the tubes over to Dr. Bryce. There is no lab technician in the hospital at this time. He will go to the lab himself. She watches him walk down the hall toward the lab. He still has a limp. He is still injured. She turns away and returns to the ward.

*

Henry walks down the corridor of the hospital. The concrete floor dips and humps in places; it was laid down unevenly and smoothed over by hand. Like a sculpture. It exaggerates his limp. And he feels the pain in his leg, now. It aches each time his muscles clench around his femur. He is grateful that Ellison did not need to take him into the operating theatre. The fractures were well aligned, somehow. He thinks, again, about Alile and her touches, her listening, her handmade medicines. He imagines that under her care the bone fragments shifted, realigned like metal shavings do in response to a magnet. How else can it be explained? Some sort of random miracle?

He walks and passes windows open to the air. The night-creatures are silent outside. He is now aware of silence, of the different types of it, as he moves through the world. Night brings a whole new kind. And a different one here than in the village. When he lies in his bed in his stark apartment he listens to it, feels the absence of sound in his bones. He knows that at some unperceived frequency the silence exists as movement; it resonates, it speaks. Nothing, he has learned, is completely empty.

Henry reaches the lab and enters it. Here, the silence is broken by the quiet whirr of a fan someone left on. He sits down on the stool and wheels himself up to the workbench. He dons gloves and waits for a minute, feels the intermittent breeze on his back as the fan oscillates in the room. His hands are already sweaty under the latex when he picks up a tube of the man's blood and draws out a small amount with a pipette. He drops a single drop of blood on the glass slide, then drops a single drop of oil overtop. He puts the slide under the microscope and leans over, peers through the eyepieces. His eyelashes brush the eyepieces when he blinks. A red blur. After some fiddling with the dials, the man's red cells emerge out of the disorienting fog. There they are: malarial ring forms inhabiting the cells. Multiples within a cell. Everywhere. He has to search hard to find a normal red blood cell. There is one: a single plump and rosy cell amid the parasitic invasion. Henry pushes himself away from the table and continues to sit on the stool, waits for the brief passing of fanned air across his back, suffers the heat in between. Sweat is gathering under his shirt and his hands are soaked under the gloves. He peels them off and leaves them, inside out, on the counter beside the microscope.

Malaria falciparum, no doubt. The worst kind. It goes to the blood, the liver, the brain. It brings a high risk of death, particularly when treated late.

There is a small refrigerator humming quietly behind him. Inside are vials of blood, stored for running additional tests, or repeat tests. One of them, he knows, is marked: "Dr HB." He is afraid of that vial of blood, of what it might show. Or worse, what it might not show. In this vial he would have to confront the frightening strength of his body, or the frightening strength of his mind. And he is not ready for that. He will probably never be ready for that.

He thinks of the man on the ward, how brutalized he was by this illness. How his eyes looked: not human anymore, all red and yellow like a beast. He stands up and fans out his shirt, allowing some cool air between the cotton and his skin. He will do for this man what was done for him. Here is a chance to turn another life around, to clean up the mess.

*

The man died at sunrise.

Iris and Dr. Bryce did what they could. They gave him fluid, antimalarials, antibiotics, all the usual resuscitative measures. At 5:55 AM, Dr. Bryce looked at his watch. "Time of death," he muttered, although they do not record such things in the medical notes. He wrote it down in his notes anyway: Time of Death: 5:55 AM. Iris saw Dr. Bryce's face: too blank. His eyes were too fixed. He went about his morning tasks too stiffly, he moved like he was wooden. At 6:30, before the morning staff were due to arrive, Iris approached Dr. Bryce where he stood staring at a bedside chart. "Shall we get some breakfast?" she asked. And he followed.

*

Now they sit across from each other in the canteen, sipping tea. She looks down into her cup, swirls the tea around inside.

"Why did I recover?" He asks this while looking away, across the canteen at the empty tables and empty chairs. "I was as far gone as he was. Why did I respond? Why was I the lucky one?"

Iris looks at him and struggles to contain her annoyance. Why should she have to explain something so obvious? Why, again, must she be the adult in a room full of children?

"What do you know about luck? You've been making your own your whole life." She tries not to sound too snappy, too impatient. She breathes and continues. "Good substrate. You have it. The strength, the ability to do whatever you want." She waves a hand around. "Be a doctor. Travel to Malawi. Save lives. Be healthy. All these things."

He starts to respond: "We had the same illness, received the same medication … " Iris shakes her head and cuts him off.

"If you want to talk about luck, then yours started in the womb." She thinks about the patient they tried to save. "His bad luck started at the same time. Bad substrate. Bad substrate means you can't make luck. It is outside of you. You take what you get." She looks down at her tea again. She tries to take a sip but her throat is too tight to manage it. She struggles to contain this, whatever is rising up inside her. But she cannot contain it; it overflows and the tears appear. She holds her fingers against her eyes and swallows the feeling down. Her throat is still so tight.

"Let's not talk about luck." She finally manages.

Henry looks at her. Nods.

"Let's talk about strength. And love. You have both. You've had both all your life. That's what got you through."

Henry looks out the window.

They both look out there. Through the window, Iris can see a few sparse and stunted yellow grasses, trampled into the red dirt. Above this, laundry dries on a line. Behind the billowing sheets and fluttering gloves is the white-blue radiance of the sky.

"Emma had those things. Strength and love."

Iris breathes before she speaks. "Your child."

He looks at her. "Yes."

"Then she had all anyone could have asked for."

His gaze has moved back to the window.

"And you. You also have knowledge," Iris continues. "You know what you are capable of. I hope you do. And you don't believe that you will fail, do you?"

Henry turns back to look at her, right in her eyes, which is something he rarely does. And she shares his gaze boldly, does not look away.

"No." He smiles. "No, I don't believe that."

He reaches over now, and puts his big, warm hand over her small cold one and even then, she does not look away.

*

After breakfast, they part ways. Iris leaves for home and Henry walks the corridors back to the medical ward. He notes the point at which he passes from grey to yellow, and how he feels in doing so. No different, he admits to himself. He trails his fingers along the yellow wall, though, like he has seen children do. It feels good: the smooth, clean paint under his hands.

He makes his rounds on his youngest patient first. The woman with the newborn. The baby has made it out of the intensive care unit and he sleeps, swaddled tightly in cloth, in the woman's arms. Henry leans over and studies the infant's face. Still too young to be out of the womb. His face is small and puckered, wizened like an old man's. All the tubes are out, now. The baby is ready to take milk. Henry has already explained to the woman that breast milk is not allowed, to reduce the risk of the child contracting HIV. Here is something he can do: protect this child by preventing the infection in the first place. Together, he and the mother will keep this child healthy.

The baby shifts and frees a tightly bundled fist before his face reddens and he releases a hearty squall. The woman clucks, nestles him close to her breast and he quiets again, chin up, fist loosened, face like a Buddha. The woman turns her own face up to Henry. Her gaze is steady, almost defiant. This is her son. Strong and healthy. Already a survivor.

"Doctor, please." She points at Henry, then points to her swaddled son. "Name."

Henry watches the newborn sleep. His tiny brow pinches in tight, then smoothes out. Eyebrows lift, then settle.

Already rudimentary emotions are crossing his face, marring his natural state of bliss. But they are transient as clouds across a clear blue sky.

"I don't—" He starts to say, then thinks of the young man in the village, the game of bao they played. Ba-wo. El-eye-as. But Elias is one of our names, he thinks. Biblical. The infant shifts, his brow flickers, another cloud drifting across his consciousness. There is the hint of a smile on the child's face.

Juma.

He says it with certainty.

The woman smiles and Juma sleeps.

Henry weaves between beds. Elias. Bao. Alile.

He feels a pang of something that if he didn't know any better could be grief.

If he were to hitch a ride on the back of a pickup all the way to Mlele. If he were to walk down the hidden path all the way to where the huts begin, scattered in the flat red earth strategically, people standing around them like seeds in a game of bao. Would he feel like that—like he has walked into a game he does not see or understand? Would Alile stand at the threshold of her hut obeying unsaid rules? He gained entry by default. By being ill. This was the only way in and health forced him out. And now?

He is foolish to want to believe more than he can. He is only capable of so much of the stuff.

Belief.

And yet.

He tucks down beside his next patient who has a place on the floor. The man, knowing what is coming, obligingly sits up, leans forward and lifts the back of his shirt. Even before Henry can place his stethoscope on his back, the man is taking large, exaggerated breaths, as if to prove his fitness. Henry presses the diaphragm of the stethoscope onto his skin, between ribs, and listens. The air moves as it should, the exhale is long and soft like a sigh. Henry lets the stethoscope drop to his chest, pats the man on his shoulder.

"All clear."

Iris pushes the heavy hospital door open and steps into the warmth of the morning sun. She joins the crowd of commuters but she is moving against the flow; most are going in toward the city and she is walking out toward home. She takes a tangerine from an offered tray and hands over a few *kwacha* to the vendor. She begins to peel the fruit and walks on the path beside the road, away from the hospital. The path takes her through a cluster of magnolia trees that are just green now, their blooms spent months ago. A mottling of bright sun and cool shade moves across her skin as she passes beneath the trees. She continues to peel the tangerine and breathes in the sharp citrus fragrance, feels the oiliness of the peel on her fingertips. Saliva bursts into her mouth in anticipation of the first piece of the fruit. This is the world revealed to her after a night shift. Everything is clearer, brighter, more striking and noteworthy.

She continues along the path and out from the cover of the trees. In this wide open space, the sun can press its warmth down on her shoulders. She unpins her hat and pulls it off, crumples it in her hand and now the sun warms her head, a breeze flutters across her bare neck. She sees up ahead the familiar cluster of bougainvillaea bushes, their papery blooms vivid pink against the blue sky. Thin but generously adorned branches cascade over the wall, bow and bend to its shape, to the wind, to her passing hand which pulls them forward with her before they fall back, dropping into place behind her as she moves on. She tilts her face up, feels not the warmth of the sun pressing down but the cool weightlessness of the sky above and the space, all the space it offers her. Today, Iris can't help but feel the open expanse of the sky as she moves up the hill and closer to it. She rarely looks there. She rarely looks up at the sky. The colour of it is like a clean pool of water and she thinks about it like that. That she is returning to water. This is why her movements are so fluid and effortless. This is why she feels lighter.

Acknowledgements

I owe an enormous amount of thanks to so many incredible people for their vital contributions to this collaborative project. This book would never have taken flight without them.

To John Metcalf whose insight, wit and passion made the editing process a revelation.

To Dan Wells, Tara Murphy, Kate Hargreaves and Chris Andrechek for their enthusiasm, diverse talents, intelligence and professionalism in bringing this book into the world in the best possible way.

To Annabel Lyon for her mentorship, and her support of and belief in this project, and to Larissa Kostoff, Elle Wild and Zazie Todd for giving so generously of their time and advice.

To Matthew Engelke for sharing his expertise on religion and traditional spiritual practices in the region, and to Elizabeth Hull for allowing me access to her research.

To the students and faculty at the University of British Columbia Optional Residency MFA program for their thoughtful feedback and for creating such a nurturing environment in which to share early pages.

To *Descant*, *Prairie Fire* and their fellow literary publications who, against all the odds, continue to support and encourage emerging Canadian writers.

To the works of Rabindranath Tagore, Rumi, Malidoma Patrice Somé and Brian Morris which provided unique insights, perspectives and inspiration. I have excerpted from the collected works of Rumi for the section headings.

To the wonderful families, and especially the children, of Nkudzi Bay for opening their hearts and homes to me.

To Linda, Lisa and Edna for their unfailing support and encouragement.

To my amazing family: Peter and Donna, Tom and Richard, for being there with love, for cheering on each small success, and for being my very earliest readers.

And always to Eric for his love, support and time to allow this book to be born, and for never doubting its successful gestation, and to Amber and Aidan who have been an inspiration just by being their beautiful selves and loving me back.

About the Author

Lucie Wilk grew up in Toronto and completed her medical training in Vancouver. Her short fiction has been nominated for the McClelland & Stewart *Journey Prize Anthology*, longlisted for a CBC Canada Writes literary prize, and has appeared in *Descant*, *Prairie Fire* and *Shortfire Press*. She is working toward an MFA in Creative Writing at the University of British Columbia. She practices medicine and lives with her husband and two children in London, UK.